Indulging His Desire

Kings of Hawthorn Series

A.M. McCoy

COPYRIGHT

Copyright © 2022 by A.M. McCoy

Contents

To all the dirty little voyeurs who like to watch at first. And to all the brave souls who love to put the show on for others to begin with.

This one is for you.

Chapter 1 – Dexter

S o bloody tired.

The elevator opened, and I walked out in a trance to my front door, sliding the key in and opening it on autopilot.

I needed to fucking sleep.

I walked through my dark apartment, avoiding the edges of the furniture I had never used, and made my way to my bedroom. Pulling my tie off and shedding my jacket until I stood at the end of my bed and stared down at it longingly as I unbuttoned my shirt and toed off my shoes.

Maverick and Cora, my best friends, had come back to work a few weeks ago after their three-month long hiatus and I was finally getting my life back to normal since their absence. For the first time in months, I was home from work before eleven pm, though not by much.

To be honest, I wasn't home late tonight because of work as usual. I was home late because Reid, my other best friend, had decided that we all needed to go out and *let loose*.

Fucking Reid and his need to party. Sure, I had given in and gone along with the group, enjoying myself, but now I felt empty and slightly drunk.

Two things I hated being at the same time because it left me with idle time on my hands to think and no filters to stop myself from wallowing in the self-pity that accompanied that free time.

I tore my shirt off my arms and tossed it across the room in frustration as I felt that darkness trying to descend over me and drag me under for the rest of the night.

A flash of light outside of my dark window caught my eye and dragged my attention from my problems. As I looked across the courtyard to the bright light in the apartment across from me. The architects designed the building in a square shape, with a courtyard in the center, resulting in only two large apartments on each floor. Both residences occupied two sides of the square building and faced each other, and the apartment across from mine had been empty for the last few months. Apparently, I had a new neighbor. I looked out of my bedroom windows and directly into my neighbor's bedroom, which was lit up with the shades open. I looked through the other wall of windows into the living space of the apartment and sure enough, almost every light was on out there too, and not a single blind was closed.

The bedroom was sparse, with boxes lining one wall and a large king-sized bed against the other wall facing the windows. The door to the bathroom was wide open and as I let myself pry into the privacy of my new neighbor. After a while, a flash of tanned skin walked past the opening. I didn't tell my feet to move, but before I knew it, I was walking forward to get a better look into the private space on display for me.

The bathroom was full of steam and as I waited for another glimpse, I could almost feel the humidity against my skin, like I was in the room myself.

Fucking tequila shots that Cora had insisted I drink for her were messing with my head.

The tanned skin moved inside of the bathroom again and I glimpsed bright-colored tattoos down one arm as they walked past the doorway again.

"Slow down," I muttered under my breath as I watched. I couldn't explain why I was staring like a full-on creep into my neighbor's windows, shrouded in darkness, hiding from them. And I also couldn't explain why I was getting angry that they were moving too fast for my muddled brain to make heads or tails of what I was seeing other than it was skin.

A lot of fucking skin.

Something stirred inside of my chest as I rested my hands on the sill of my window and leaned forward to look through the haze in my brain and the steam in the bathroom, aching to see more.

I bit my lip and focused on the doorway, intent on catching a better glimpse the next time, when suddenly they walked straight through the doorway and into the bedroom. My lip popped from my teeth as the skin I'd hungered to see more of came into view, unobstructed by anything but a white fluffy towel that hung low on the hips of the man that walked out of the bathroom.

Disappointment should have been the next thing I felt, knowing that my new neighbor, who had no issues walking around half naked, was a man and not a woman. But the disappointment never came. I was too busy tracking his movements around his bedroom to feel anything other than... fascination.

He was probably in his early thirties, though it was hard to tell. He had dark brown hair that hung to his shoulders, and I ached to know if it was as soft as it looked because it looked like silk.

"What the fuck, Dex?" I muttered again at the ridiculousness of this moment, but I still leaned closer to the window instead of walking away like the logical part of my brain was telling me to do.

Too bad the tequila was making logical Dexter quiet tonight.

Tattoos covered not only his right arm but his left arm and part of his chest as well. They were brightly colored and flashy, drawing my eyes to them as they danced over his ripped body as he moved.

Ripped.

Like, spent every day at the gym ripped.

I was no shlep, but as I thought of my own six-pack, I felt envy when looking at his cut abdominal muscles that led to the deep v above the tie in his towel. He ran his hand through his dark hair, flipping it over one side of his head before gathering it up into a bun and tying it off with a hair tie. He stood with his profile facing me and his hands dropped to his towel.

Look away.

Look away, Dexter.

I knew what was going to come next, but I couldn't tear my eyes away from the display in front of me.

His large hands gripped the towel and pulled the two ends apart, dropping the fabric to the ground as he stepped forward and opened a drawer in his dresser.

My eyes fell right below his waist and didn't move. It wasn't like it was the first time I'd seen another guy's dick; I played sports in school and went to the gym regularly. And then there had been those few times years ago that Maverick and I had taken home the same girl to fool around with together.

But this was different.

This wasn't one of those side-eyed appraisals of your bro's package when he was changing to see if he was as big as he acted like he was.

This was... carnal.

Hungry.

Needy.

From my vantage point, it was hard to tell exactly how big he was because he hung heavily between his muscled thighs where he stood.

I sucked in a deep breath as he grabbed a pair of black briefs from the drawer and stepped into them, pulling them up his long-tanned legs. Before he pulled them up over his hips, he reached down and wrapped his hand around his dick, stroking it quickly.

Once.

Twice.

I groaned when he did it a third time.

His head hung down with his chin against his chest as he watched his hand slide over his dick the same as I did as he widened his stance and twisted his hand over the head of himself before stroking the length again.

"Shit." I groaned, knowing exactly what he was feeling as he jacked himself off. My cock stirred in my slacks, lengthening until I was rock hard as I watched him pleasure himself and I ached to stroke myself in time with him. But I couldn't do that.

I was straight and that would be...

No. I couldn't do that.

But I could at least still watch him as he jacked off.

That didn't make me gay.

He shook his head, smiling to himself before pulling his briefs up and over his now hard cock. He shook his head again and walked out of his bedroom and into the living room, turning off lights as he went. When he turned towards the windows in the living room, his piercing green eyes met mine and I stumbled backward into the shadows as my heart leaped in my chest. Holy fuck.

I'd just been caught.

He stepped forward, looking deeper into my windows from his own with a scowl on his face but I knew he couldn't find me again in the dark. He backed up into the darkness of his apartment with a perplexed look on his face.

I watched him with my heart racing and my skin on fire as he walked back into this bedroom and stood next to his bed with only one light left on and I ached for him to leave it on.

I wasn't ready to end this little voyeur episode of mine.

But he was. He clicked off the lamp and with the moonlight shining in his still wide-open windows, I could just make out his shadow as he climbed into bed and then he was completely out of sight as I stood in disbelief.

I stood in my window for quite a while before it dawned on me that with his lights off, he could probably see right into my window now that the moonlight was glowing down on me.

"Fuck." I cursed.

How long had I stood there staring into his window after he crawled into bed?

Five minutes?

Ten?

Did he see me when he turned in the living room or was he unsure of what he saw looking back at him through the night?

"Fuck." I said again and forced myself to pull my drapes shut, blocking out the world as I tried to comprehend what had just happened.

Did I just get hard looking at a naked man?

Fucking tequila.

Chapter 2 – Dexter

"**D**o you feel as shitty as you look? Or are you just getting nearer to death as we speak?" Maverick asked me as he walked into my office.

I glared in his direction and tried to ignore him. Honestly, I was afraid if I opened my mouth and answered him I'd throw up.

Again.

So I just looked back at my computer screen hoping he'd leave.

"I told you to leave him alone." Cora, Maverick's wife, said as she followed him into my office. She looked bright-eyed, and bushy-tailed in a warm yellow dress, and I hated her for it when I felt so hungover and miserable.

But then my eyes fell to her pregnant belly, and all was forgiven. She was carrying my niece and there was nothing she could do to upset me, and she knew it.

"I've earned this harassment right here," Mav said with a glint in his eye. Fucking guy could drink me under the table, and he knew it, yet I let him do it anyway.

"Bull." Cora scoffed and pushed Maverick's back towards the doorway to my office, trying to get him to leave. "You're pissed and wanted to make him suffer for it. And I told you to leave him alone."

I looked back up from my computer, intrigued. But as they said, curiosity killed the cat, because it was only then that I noticed the anger in Maverick's stance, even if he was trying to pretend he was calm.

"What are we making Dexter suffer for now?" Reid added as he walked in behind them, and I groaned.

"Doesn't anyone work around here anymore?" I snapped as my three closest friends stood in my office like there weren't a million other things they needed to be doing.

The CEO, CFO, and VP of Jones Holding all stood in my office on a Thursday morning, yet somehow, I, the lowly lawyer of the group, was the only one concerned with productivity.

Go figure.

"Reid, how nice of you to join us." Maverick sneered. "Your skull is next on my list to crush in for your role in helping my wife obtain a prenup before our wedding without telling me," Mav said, glancing over his shoulder at our other friend where he froze a few feet inside.

"Shit," Reid said, blanching as he stepped back towards the door. "Uh- I have a- thing." He stammered and ran back the way he came.

"Coward!" I called out after him as Maverick stared me down with an annoyed Cora at his elbow.

"I'm sorry." She grimaced. "It came up and… well he didn't take the news well."

"Clearly." I deadpanned and stood up, buttoning my suit jacket. "Go on and leave him to it then. I'd hate for you to get blood splattered on your pretty dress so early in the morning." I said to her and nodded towards the door that Reid had just escaped through.

I knew this day was coming. And to be honest, I was surprised Maverick had walked into my office with any semblance of calmness inside of him. I had always figured he would have been knocking down walls like the Kool-Aid man when he found out.

"Oh stop it, Chase," Cora ordered and stepped between us. "Neither of you is throwing fists." She said pointing her finger at her husband's chest. "We talked about this Mav. It was important to me."

"Then you should have talked to me about it." He snapped. "Instead of, once again, running to Dexter."

Ah, so this was from a much bigger problem than just the non-legally binding piece of paper Cora had signed to prove a point before she married Maverick and suddenly gained a portfolio worth billions overnight.

"Cora it's fine," I said, nodding towards the door again. "Let him have this."

"No." She sighed. "We're not doing this, again."

When Maverick had let his insecurities get the best of him and left Cora after her family tried to have her killed, again, as payback against him, I'd overstepped some boundaries to support her in his absence.

I'd taken her to her very first ultrasound to see their baby when it was clear that Mav wasn't going to, and then I'd kicked his ass into gear, forcing him to overcome his fears and beg and grovel for her forgiveness.

And he'd never quite forgiven me for it, even if he was appreciative of it at the same time.

So our friendship hung in this weird limbo space now.

Maverick eyed her and then looked at me before sighing and throwing his hands out to his sides. "What good is being the boss if I can't make my employees miserable?" He grumped in typical Maverick fashion and then walked out towards the hallway. He was almost through the doorway before he turned and looked at me again. "We will finish this conversation, Dexter Chase."

"Wouldn't dream of getting out of it bud," I said with a nod and a tight smile pulled at his lips even as he tried to hide it.

"Of course not." He said and walked out.

Our friendship would be fine. That there was the proof we'd both been looking for.

With my office now down two of the original unwelcomed guests, I stood looking at Cora for a beat before falling into my desk chair and sighing.

"Rough morning?" She asked as she walked forward and sat down in a chair across from me.

"Hmm." I mused and pointed my finger at her, "I was supposed to be the designated sober friend, remember? I claimed it the morning of your wedding. Then you go and get..." I threw my fingers towards her belly and scoffed. "And now I'm stuck being the schlep that has to keep up with the two of them when we both know I don't stand a chance."

She smiled sweetly as she idly ran her hands over her stomach. "It's not as though I have a choice in the matter now, do I?"

"Pft." I scoffed again and leaned back in my chair. "How are you feeling?" I asked genuinely.

"I'm perfect." She smiled and I could tell she meant it. She was past the rough beginning of her pregnancy, and not quite to the part where she was miserable again.

"The honeymoon phase of pregnancy." I mused as memories flooded my brain. Hope, my ex-wife had never really had a phase of pregnancy that she didn't find things to complain about during, but I'd been such a lovesick fool at the time I had been enamored with it all, nonetheless.

"Hey," Cora said softly from where she sat watching me closely as I rolled my wedding ring over my finger like I always did when I was lost in thought about that time in my life.

I snapped out of my trip down memory lane and cleared my throat, trying to turn the attention back to her. There was something about Cora's calm and sensitive nature that always made me open up to her in ways I'd never even done with Maverick or Reid. And she did it without me even realizing I was opening up to her. It was unnerving.

"How's the auction coming along?" I asked her and her eyes squinted, letting me know she didn't miss the way I shifted the conversation back to her.

"It's going fine." She sighed and then sat up in her seat higher, "Actually, now that I think of it, I need your help with something." She said and I shook my head quickly, cutting her off.

"No."

She stuttered and scowled at my interruption. "You haven't even heard what I need yet."

"Doesn't matter, the answer is no. Maverick is literally on a blood trail currently, after me for helping you." I said, shaking my head again and refusing to look at her because if she wanted me to help her with something, I'd fold in a minute flat if she gave me her puppy dog eyes.

I was a sucker for her puppy dog eyes. And once again, she fucking knew it.

"Dex, it's a bachelor auction for a good cause!" She tried, leaning forward on my desk. "And I need bachelors!"

"Ask Reid." I cut her off again.

"I already did. But I need more than one."

"Then I'll find you some others. But I'm not doing it." I said firmly.

"Dex."

"Cora."

"Ugh." She huffed. "We'll table this argument for a later date. But we will continue it." She said in her best head bitch in charge voice, and I couldn't help the smirk that pulled my lips back at her attempt at authority over me.

It was endearing, really. Like when a cute puppy tries to boss around a big dog.

"Whatever you say, Mrs. Jones." I joked and she rolled her eyes at me. "Now respectfully, get the hell out of my office so I can get back to work," I ordered lightheartedly.

She stood up and smoothed her skirt back down. "Fine, but only because I have a meeting in a few minutes." She winked at me before pointing her finger at me and scowling again. "Hey, you never texted Mav to tell him you made it home safely last night. Did you get distracted and forget about us?" She asked before walking out and calling over her shoulder. "Don't let it happen again Dexter, or I'll call the police to do a welfare check on you next time." She walked out of my office and down the hall to her own, but I was lost in my head again.

I nearly swallowed my tongue as memories of last night flooded my senses. When I'd woken up this morning, bits and pieces had assaulted my hung-over brain as I tried to make sense of it all. But it wasn't until I was riding the elevator up to my office that I finally remembered all of it.

And the part I'd tried to forget was how after I'd watched my new neighbor streak around his apartment like a creep, I'd been unable to settle down to go to sleep myself. I'd been swinging a full mast post for the better part of an hour before I'd given in and jacked off, the whole time telling myself that it didn't mean anything. That it didn't mean anything that I was thinking about toned muscle and inked skin as I stroked myself. Or that it didn't make me gay if I imagined what his large, calloused hand would feel like wrapped around me. Or worse yet, what it would feel like to fuck him and hear his moans of pleasure as I gave it to him.

I was drunk.

That was it.

Nothing else.

But I had pushed the memory from my brain until this morning and on the ride up, I'd remembered exactly what I'd thought about as I exploded in my hand in the center of my bed like a teenage boy.

Him.

"Fuck me running."

Chapter 3 – Kyson

"Ky! Oh my God! This looks amazing!" My client swooned, looking over the display I'd laid out on the bed for her to choose from for tonight's event.

Being a celebrity stylist had its perks. And being in the bedroom of one of America's sweethearts, choosing the gown she'd walk the red carpet in at her movie premiere was one of the best of them.

Not all of my clients were nice or sweet, some were raging bitches or giant douche bags. But Samantha was sweet as can be and I jumped at the opportunity to dress her anytime she called.

"I'm glad you love it." I said, lifting the white silvery gown up and draping it over my arm. "It will pair with your red lips and dark eyes perfectly to go with the look of the movie."

She squealed and clapped her hands together excitedly. "I'm so happy you were available for tonight Ky; I couldn't have walked this event without you being the one to make sure I look my best." She said genuinely.

I scoffed and rolled my eyes. "You are the star darling; I just find the clothes to pair with your perfection for the world to fawn over."

She giggled again as her assistant called time to dress and we were off in a flurry of hurriedness, getting her dressed and out the door to the premiere. When all was said and done, I sat back and took a deep breath in the silence of the empty hotel room. Another starlet dressed and ready to face the world, and a job well done.

I gathered my bags and left the swanky hotel to go home for the night. I loved events that kept me in New York because there was just something about sleeping in my own bed that left me grounded and calm. Too many nights traveling in a row made me anxious and jumpy.

And even though I had a new posh apartment, my bed was the same and it had the same effect.

To be honest, my new apartment was phenomenal, which for New York City, was a blessing. I'd lived in some less than stellar places as I perfected my craft and made a name for myself, but I was finally feeling secure in saying, I'd made it.

And I had a beautiful new home to prove it. Last night had been my first full night in my new place, and after spending the entire day moving in, I'd been bone weary by time I crawled into bed.

So I wanted to go home and actually enjoy my space for a bit tonight before I crashed.

I just had to wait for the slow as hell elevator to return to the lobby of my new building. I heard the front doorman greet another tenant behind me and listened to their banter shamelessly.

"Evening Mr. Chase." The doorman said.

"Saint." The mystery tenant replied with a deep rumbly voice that sent shivers up my spine. "How was the game yesterday?"

"Aw man, it was phenomenal. The kids had the time of their life. Thanks for setting me up with your guy for those perks Mr. Chase. They haven't stopped talking about it all. They got a bat signed by Frankie Swanson and everything!" The doorman replied enthusiastically.

"Good." The man replied. "I'm glad they enjoyed themselves. Every kid should get to Yankee Stadium at some point in their life. It's a rite of passage."

"Absolutely. Thanks again, you have a great night Sir."

"You too, Saint. See you around." I listened as the man's shoes tapped across the marble floor towards the elevator bay behind me as the door opened and I walked in, pushing the button for the tenth floor.

I looked up as the man neared and let my eyes rove over his sharp blue suit and polished shoes. He was the type of man that designers and stylists like me dreamed of dressing. He had dark blond hair that laid perfectly in waves on the top of his head and crystal blue eyes.

Crystal blue eyes that widened a fraction when he looked at me as he stepped into the elevator. His jaw was covered with a fresh five o clock shadow and his tie was loosened a bit around his neck, showcasing a day of hard work behind him.

I nodded to him as he stood next to me with one hand in his pants pockets and the other wrapped around his briefcase handle. I tried but failed to look away quickly because he was just that damned good to look at.

There was an air of mystery about him that intrigued me as the doors to the elevators closed us into the small space.

"Uh, what floor?" I asked him, clearing my throat, and hoping that I didn't sound as stupid as I thought I did out loud.

His blue eyes held mine as I looked up at him for a fraction of a second longer than polite society would deem appropriate before he looked down at the panel in front of me and nodded to the lit-up buttons.

"Ten as well." His deep voice rumbled, once again spreading shivers up my spine like I was a naïve schoolboy again.

"Neighbor then?" I asked with a raised eyebrow, and he smirked slightly, showing off a dimple in his cheek. Was this the man I'd seen in the window last night from across the courtyard? I'd thought I'd been imagining things, or that there was a ghost lurking in the dark apartment on my floor because I hadn't been sure of what I'd seen. But I had sworn I'd seen a man looking at me.

Which meant he had seen me naked moments before that.

But would this man, this broad, strong backed, immaculately dressed businessman have been lurking and peeping at me strutting my shit naked through my apartment last night?

"I guess so." He said, dragging my internal dialogue to a stop.

He was an inch or two taller than I was but that mystery about him made him feel larger than life, while I was trapped in the small space with him. I cleared my throat again and turned to face him, shifting my bags to my other hand.

"Kyson Hart." I held my hand out to him and he looked down at it briefly before grasping it in a strong dominant handshake.

"Dexter Chase."

"Nice to meet you." I hating how... breathy it sounded as we stood staring at each other, for once again, longer than appropriate. He was the first to drop eye contact, followed by pulling his hand from mine, and I felt disappointment at the loss.

The elevator door opened, and we were on our floor.

We both stepped out, me going right and him going left to our respective doors in the main hallway. When I slid my key into my lock I hesitated, feeling like something else needed to be said to the mystery man named Dexter Chase that left me feeling... unsteady.

He turned after unlocking his own door and looked at me, almost like he wanted to say something too. But he just stared for a moment and then nodded.

"Have a good night." He said before disappearing inside of his dark apartment and locking his door behind him.

"Yeah, you as well." I said to the now empty hallway as I pushed my door open and went inside.

As soon as it was closed behind me I sagged into it and rested my head against the surface as I took a deep breath trying to wrap my head around what it was that had affected me so deeply about that man.

Being a gay man in New York City, I found myself attracted to many men that I interacted with day to day, but there was something different about tonight.

About Dexter himself.

I pushed up off the door and forced myself to shake it off as I put my things away and tried to relax. My eyes kept moving to the windows of his apartment across the courtyard, but they remained dark, and I didn't see any proof of life inside.

Had I not seen him go inside, I would have thought no one was home.

I could see a few feet into the windows thanks to the glow of the city lights around us, so I knew his blinds were open but still, I didn't see him inside.

Part of me wanted to close my curtains knowing I was on display to him thanks to the way our windows lined up, but the daredevil in me left them open. Chances are the view wasn't that clear from this far away.

I took off my jacket and kicked my shoes off, going in search of some food when my phone rang, nearly making me jump out of my skin.

I looked at the caller ID and saw my sister's name and picked it up with a smile.

"Hey Lo."

"Oh my god! Did you see Samantha Swift walk the red carpet? She looked phenomenal!" She gushed on excitedly in my ear. "Oh my God Ky, you did so good!"

I leaned on my kitchen counter and felt the excitement ooze into my own body as she pratted on.

"I just got home; I'll look for the photos later." I said. "You know she makes it easy on me."

"Dreamboat pretty Kyson." She gushed, using the term our grandmother had used often when we grew up.

"I know Lo." I said and something caught my eye from Dexter's windows but by time I looked over, it was gone.

Darkness stared back at me mockingly.

"Are you there?" My sister asked and I realized I'd missed what she said.

"Yeah," I said, shaking my head to break the hold my new neighbor seemed to have on me. "Sorry I was... distracted."

"By what?" She asked with a hint of speculation in her voice. She was my twin, and she knew me better than anyone else, so of course she would hone in on the tone in my voice.

"Uh." I said, once again looking out my window hoping to see something but got met with nothing. "Doesn't matter. How was your day?" She was a sports medicine doctor for an NHL team in the middle of America and she had a player that had been driving her nuts lately. And usually when she called me this time of night, she wanted to bitch about him, which was fine with me. Because it distracted me from the fact that I didn't have a man in my life currently and hadn't for way too long. So I listened to her stories of obvious sexual tension, though she claimed it was egotistical alpha asshole-itis that was all on him and I lived vicariously.

"Spill it." She demanded and I could almost see her sitting up in the center of her bed, now fully alert.

I chuckled at her, "Fine, but I need wine first." I said and walked over to the small fridge I'd stocked before I worried about a morsel of food being placed in the main fridge yesterday and pulled out a red I favored.

"Ooh, this is going to be good isn't it?" She hummed excitedly.

"Hmm. Good or pathetic, I'm not sure." I deadpanned and grabbed a glass from the cabinet. The second thing I unpacked when I moved in yesterday.

I had priorities after all.

And wine after a day spent with celebrities was high on that list.

"Yes! Tell me everything."

I tsked at her dramatically and put my phone on speaker as I worked on pulling the wax covering off the top of the bottle.

"I... met my new neighbor." I said pathetically, unsure what more to say about it because I didn't know why I was so affected by it.

"And..." She droned on, waiting for the rest of it.

"And..." I huffed. "I don't know. He's..." I stopped again. "God, how did he send me so sideways in less than five minutes?" I asked hypothetically.

"Start at the beginning." She sounded confused and I laughed at my predicament.

"His voice alone sent me into overdrive, before I even saw his face." I admitted. "He came into the lobby downstairs after me and we rode the elevator together. And Lo, my God." I nearly fanned myself as I stood there with my hands flat on the counter staring, once again out my windows towards his.

"He was that good looking?" She gushed.

"Like Adonis himself had a love child with a tall, dark, and handsome stranger. The man oozed dominance and mystery and authority that made me want to drop to my knees and say things like *yes sir*, and *please daddy*."

She snorted into the phone and giggled. "Tell me you gave him your number or said something witty to leave him wanting more."

I scoffed. "I hardly was able to say my name when I introduced myself, let alone say something witty. I think I said *um* more than once. And now I'm lost in thought, staring pathetically across the way to his dark apartment waiting for a glance of him as he walks by his windows. Like why is his apartment dark when I know he's home?"

"No!" She gasped dramatically. "You're never at a loss for words around men! What is so different about him?"

"Hell if I know, he's definitely straight." I joked and then cursed. "That's it." I started pacing, taking my phone with me as I walked to the utensil drawer for my corkscrew. "He's got to be straight and now my body is short circuiting because it knows I'll never get a chance with him."

"Well certainly not if you said *um*, when you introduced yourself."

"Shut it." I chided her and searched for my corkscrew, not finding it. "Where the fuck are you, you devious little prick." I muttered.

"Um, currently some hotel in Michigan." My sister replied. "Or Missouri. Montana? It's not Massachusetts" She quipped. "Shit, I've lost my ability to differentiate my M states anymore."

I chuckled at her through my frustration briefly before the longing for wine outweighed my humor and I hunted once again anew.

"What are you looking for?" She asked, listening to me continue to curse and rummage.

"My corkscrew." I slammed the third drawer shut as I looked around my apartment like I was going to tell from the blank labels on the cardboard around me which box it was in. "Why didn't you make me label my boxes?"

"Ha!" She jeered loudly, "I told you that you were going to regret leaving them blank!"

"Screw you."

She gasped, "Wait!" She yelled into my ear. "Go ask Mr. Hot and Mysterious if you can borrow his!"

I froze in place and looked back towards his place again. "What? No."

"Yes!" She rushed on. "It's perfect! You can see what his apartment looks like, which we know tells so much about a person and then you can redeem yourself! Make small talk, borrow his corkscrew, let him fold you into a pretzel in the center of his bed. The possibilities are endless!"

I snorted at her and shook my head. "You're depraved."

"I'm horny. And lonely. No point in both of us being miserable Ky, go knock on his door!"

I shuddered. "Okay, first of all… ew." I said. "And second of all, a pretzel? Really?"

"Well I guess you only get to be a pretzel if he salts you at the end."

"Lo!" She fell into a fit of giggles and I shook my head. "You've been hanging out with those sweaty meat heads too long; they're rubbing off on you."

"If only they were rubbing me off." She panted.

"Lauren Louise!" I snapped cringing. Sex talk wasn't new for us, the joys of rooting for the same team all of our lives, but this was a whole new level of brazen for her. Normally it was me being the scandalous one.

She laughed again, "I'm sorry, I'm done!" I doubted it. "But really, go and knock on his door! It's perfect!"

"I don't know."

"Stop it, I know you're staring at a bottle of wine longingly right now. Don't even try to deny it, just go. Don't think about it. Just do it."

The longer I stood there contemplating it, the more I felt drawn to his doorway.

"Fuck it." I said and sighed, "What can it hurt?"

"Yes!" She screeched in my ear. "Call me the second you get back to your apartment."

"No. I'll call you tomorrow." I said firmly, drawing boundaries.

"What? You can't make me wait that long to find out if you got salted—"

I hung the phone up and shuddered. Those professional athletes were getting the best of her locked away in the Midwest without delicate company around to entertain her.

I tossed my phone down on the counter and grabbed my bottle of wine and slid my feet back in my boots, forcing myself to keep moving so I didn't back out. I looked down at my outfit from the day and while it had been fresher looking twelve hours ago when I put it on, the white cotton v neck tee, black slim fit slacks and motorcycle boots were going to have to do.

I walked out into the hallway and around the corner to his door and paused holding my bottle of wine, full of uncertainty.

He was probably straight.

The sexy as hell alpha ones were always straight.

"What am I doing?" I whispered as I stood outside his door. I shook it off and tried to ignore the fact that for the first time since my young adult days, I was nervous to interact with a man. "Just do it." I whispered and slammed my knuckles down on his door, far harder than I'd intended and grimaced.

I stood there awkwardly, waiting to hear something from inside, but was met with only silence.

What if he had left again?

More silence.

What if he just didn't want to deal with me?

Fuck.

I knocked again, hoping that perhaps he had just not heard the first one, but was met again with nothing from the inside of his place.

Shit balls.

I stepped backwards, feeling the rush of blood to my face in embarrassment at being ignored and turned back towards my own place with my head falling in defeat.

I was just rounding the corner when his door opened, and I turned around so quickly the world spun, but I froze.

Because the sharp dressed man from earlier stood before me in a pair of black joggers that hung dangerously low on his narrow hips and... nothing else.

Well that's not entirely true. He wore water.

Rivulets of water dripped down his washboard abs and thick corded arms as he held the door open and leaned his elbow against the doorframe.

"Kyson?"

"Uh—" I stammered and tried to shake it off as I walked back towards him. "I was hoping I could bother you for a screw." I said and his eyebrows rose to his wet hair line in surprise as my words replayed in my head. "Fuck." I said, my own eyebrows snapping up to my hairline.

"A... what?" He asked leaning up off the door, watching me intently.

I shook my head rapidly, kicking my awkward ass the whole time. "I meant a corkscrew." I said holding up my bottle of wine. "Not a screw, or a fuck." He just continued to stare at me, but something shifted behind his gaze before he blinked it away and stood taller. I rushed on. "I can't seem to find mine in the sea of boxes and I'm in desperate need of a drink. Care to help put me out of my blatant misery?"

He gave me the same one-sided grin from the elevator earlier and his dimple drew my attention to his mouth, and I found myself captivated by the sculpted lips that relaxed back into

an expressionless position before I snapped my eyes back up to his.

"Come in." He said, stepping backwards into the dark apartment behind him and holding the door open for me.

I walked forward on auto pilot, hardly able to believe that it had worked and that he was inviting me in, but any thoughts I'd been able to form quickly dissipated the second I walked past him because his fresh out of the shower scent filled my senses and rendered me useless. He let the door shut behind him and he reached over to flick on a light switch next to me, bathing his apartment in warm low light before he walked around me and held his hand out.

"The bottle Kyson." He said firmly and I quickly handed it to him, hating the way his warm fingers brushing over mine sent my heartbeat skyrocketing even higher. He looked down at the label and smirked. "Caymus Cabernet." He said looking back at me. "Good choice." He nodded towards the kitchen that mirrored my own, "Follow me."

"Thanks." I walked in after him and looked around his space quickly instead of at the muscles of his back that rolled as he walked. It was then that I noticed the clear as day view into my own apartment across the courtyard.

Holy fuck, my entire kitchen and living room were on display for this man like a stage in a theater.

And something inside of me told me he watched me last night as I moved in and got comfortable in my new space.

Chapter 4 – Dexter

H e was here.

In my kitchen.

Act cool Dex.

The man I'd watched last night had been in the elevator when I got home tonight, and I'd been forced to ride up with him, trapped in close proximity. I'd nearly groaned out loud when I caught his cologne on the air around him, and I couldn't understand why my body was reacting like a horny teenage boy.

I had always appreciated the male body before, but I had never thought that I would be attracted to it.

But my body's reaction to this man... Kyson... was visceral.

I opened the bottle easily as he watched me, letting his eyes travel over my hands and arms appreciatively before looking away and pretending to look around my space. As I handed him the bottle of wine, I stood in his personal space like a challenge, and I felt something burning inside of me I hadn't felt in so fucking long. I was addicted.

His hands brushed against mine as he took it, and I knew he felt the tension in the air as well. His jaw tightened, and the muscles beneath his ear twitched under the pressure. Every time he locked his eyes on to mine, his pupils dilated. He had his hair pulled up into a bun on top of his head, but I wanted to see it down, brushing across the wide expanse of his shoulders.

Earlier in the elevator, he wore a black leather jacket, and he held a couple of bags hiding most of him from me, but now he stood in my kitchen in a white v-neck tee and tight pants, giving my eyes the free rein they ached for.

He wore a couple of leather bracelets around his left wrist and a gold cross around his neck that laid against the smooth skin right below his collar bones. We were nearly the same height with me barefoot and him in his black boots and I enjoyed having his piercing green eyes even with mine when he stared.

And boy, did he stare.

At my face.

At my hands.

At my bare chest.

At my stomach.

I hadn't planned to be in this state of undress around him, but I also hadn't planned on him surprising me seconds after I got out of the shower, either.

When I first got home, I'd stood in my dark kitchen and watched him meander around his apartment on the phone for a few minutes before forcing myself to walk away and take a shower. And then I'd opened my front door to find him walking away, with his tanned skin flushed with a blush.

And he'd asked me to screw.

And fuck.

Or at least that's what he had stumbled through on his way to ask me for a corkscrew. And instead of just retrieving one and lending it to him, I'd invited him inside and opened his wine for him.

And now we found ourselves lost, staring at each other as electricity crackled around us, with a bottle of wine aerating between us.

"Thanks." He said, nodding to the wine in his hands.

"You said that already." I chided, enjoying the way the flush crawled up his neck again as he looked away with a shy smile on his face.

"Right. Sorry."

"Don't apologize," I said firmly and his eyes snapped back to mine like the authority in my voice resonated with him.

I knew next to nothing about this man, short of what he looked like naked and that he had great taste in wine. But if I had to take a guess, I'd say he was usually more submissive to his partner in a relationship.

Not a full sub, he had too much backbone to comply completely, but he definitely fell in line behind someone else.

And I couldn't help but wonder if that someone was usually a man or not.

"Were you..." He started, and a blush raised to his cheeks as I waited patiently. "Were you here last night?" He asked, looking around my home.

I paused, feeling my heart rate kick up at his question.

He'd seen me.

I could have played it two different ways, but only one would be the right way.

"I was," I said finally.

"Alone?" He asked hesitantly.

"Like most nights." I finished and his lips parted in surprise, but he said nothing else, instead, he stared back down at the bottle of wine in his hands.

"Well..." He said hesitantly before he took a deep breath. "I guess I should get back to my unpacking, so this doesn't happen again." He smiled and his bright white teeth glowed perfectly against his dark features.

I should have agreed. I should have let it be at that.

But I was high on his presence and clearly out of my mind, so I did the opposite.

"I didn't mind," I said coolly, tilting my head and smirking back at him as his lips parted. "What else are neighbors for?"

"Hmm." He hummed, before blinking out of his trance and taking a step back. "Right. Well, if you ever need a cup of sugar or anything else, you know where I am." He said, nodding his head towards the windows looking into his lit-up apartment, and smiled again.

I leaned back on the countertop and put my hands on the cool surface on each side of my hips as I crossed one ankle over the other, trying desperately to remain calm and unaffected.

Also praying my cock wasn't as hard as it felt because if it was, there was no way it wasn't tenting my sweatpants obnoxiously.

He walked backward a few steps before turning and heading to the door, so I called after him. "I know exactly where to find you. And I look forward to doing so, Kyson."

He let his eyes travel from my eyes down to my bare feet and back before shaking himself out of whatever held him up. "Me too, Dexter." He said, with a bit of temptation in his voice and a wicked gleam to his eye.

After he walked out of my place, I turned the lights back off and stood in the dark, watching his front door as he walked back through it.

His eyes instantly went to my windows as he searched each one for me before a devilishly handsome smile crossed his lips.

I thought for sure he'd walk over to the glass and pull the shades shut, knowing exactly how clear of a view I had of his apartment since seeing it firsthand.

Instead, he simply walked over to his empty glass, filled it with the aromatic wine I'd opened for him, and took a long pull off the glass as he looked back over into my windows.

Blood rushed through my body at the cat-and-mouse game we'd started briefly, and it roared to a full inferno inside of me as he took his shirt off over his head and moved towards his bedroom, turning off his lights as he went.

He knew I was more than likely watching.

Yet he was stripping.

For me.

Heaven help me.

I walked into my bedroom and stood at the end of my bed and watched him as he took another sip of his wine, setting the glass down on his dresser. I walked closer to the window, unable to resist as he drew me in, and rested my fists on the sill, leaning forward and staring out through the night.

He kicked off his boots, then paused front of the chest of drawers, exactly like he did last night in his towel, giving me his side profile. His hands dropped to his waist, and he undid the buckle of his pants, opening them up, before pushing them down his muscled thighs and tossing them onto the floor.

His ink mesmerized me like an ancient language written across his skin that I ached to decipher.

He picked up his glass and took another drink, leaving the rim against his lower lip as he swallowed like he was contemplating something.

"Do it," I whispered, reaching down, and palming my erection through the cotton of my sweats. What the fuck had gotten into me the last two days?

Was I really stroking myself, watching Kyson strip? Knowing he knew I was watching? Did he think I was gay?

Did I care?

He smiled to himself against the glass and set it down on the dresser again before turning towards the windows and looking from one window to the next, looking for me. I knew the second he found me in the darkness. I could feel his piercing green eyes on me as he hooked his thumbs into the waistband of his black briefs and pushed them down his legs.

I felt my body's reaction, like a branding iron kissing my skin. My cock ached and I couldn't seem to keep my hand off of it through my pants. I didn't know if he could see me clearly, or if he could tell what I was doing below the sill of the window, but I didn't care.

I didn't care if this man knew he was driving me crazy with lust or not.

For the first time in years, I was going to embrace life instead of shying away from it.

Kyson stood facing the window, completely nude, but unlike last night, his cock was already hard when he wrapped his fist around it. His eyes fluttered closed as he stroked his impressive length and I ached to be standing right in front of him, instead of in a whole other apartment. But it would have to do because I couldn't tear my eyes away from him for a second if I wanted to.

"Yes." I hissed as I slid my hand down under the elastic of my waistband and fisted my cock, stroking myself in time with his movements. He bit his lip as he opened his eyes and watched me jack off.

He reached up and undid the elastic in his hair, letting it fall to his shoulders like I'd beckoned to see earlier, and I groaned. He dropped his chin to his chest as his dark locks fell over his face. His hips pumped against his fist and his ab muscles flexed with each movement.

Why was this incredibly masculine man so fucking sexy?

In a pretty way?

And why the fuck did it turn me on?

His eyes opened as he lifted his head back up to look at me again, and I could tell he was close. Which was good, because I was right there too.

The taboo of this situation had me on edge the second I wrapped my hand around myself. I stroked my cock with deep, tight pulls, shoving my pants to my knees because the restrictive material hindered me from the pleasure I craved.

He slid his free hand up his chest and into his hair, brushing it back out of his face and fisting it around his locks as his hips started jerking wildly.

"That's it," I whispered. "Come for me."

He threw his head back and started coming the second the words fell from my lips, like he could hear what I was saying. I watched in rapture as his come coated the pile of clothes on the floor in front of him, with his lips parted and a flush of red coloring his chest and neck.

His eyes opened lazily, and he walked closer to the window, staring at me through the glass with his chest heaving erratically.

And I was done.

My orgasm ripped out of me like my soul leaving my body for the afterlife. I laid one hand on the window and roared through it as I coated the glass with my come while he watched.

"Fuck." I grunted, stroking myself long after the physical release had ended, enjoying the way the aftershocks coursed through my system, and the whole time I kept my eyes locked on his glowing green ones.

Kyson smirked at me with his devilish smile and then drew his curtains closed, shutting me out almost in a challenging way.

He had looked ravenous as he watched me jack off, and it was oddly emboldening. Yet, after the tingles of release subsided and faded, I found myself consumed by darkness and emptiness.

Welcome back old friends, I was afraid you'd gone and deserted me finally.

Chapter 5 – Kyson

My alarm was blaring on my end table as I slapped wildly at it to silence it. Fucking twat.

I rolled over and buried my head under my pillow trying to figure out why it was going off if it was still dark ass thirty out, and then I remembered.

I shut my curtains last night.

After, I jacked off while watching Dexter Chase jack off.

Holy fuck.

My hot as sin neighbor had driven me wild the entire time I was in his apartment last night, and when I walked back into my space and saw the faint shadow of him looking at me through his window, I'd jumped into the crazy pool headfirst.

"Oh, God." I groaned into my pillow, remembering how good he had looked shirtless with the light dusting of dark hair across his chest and abs with that happy fucking trail running down into his sweatpants.

I usually found myself attracted to more feminine men, preferring the hairless and lean type. I had never found overly masculine men attractive before, but Dexter was absolutely delicious.

The entire time I'd been near him, I felt the chemistry between us, even though we never discussed its presence. But he had said things like he hadn't minded the intrusion and that he was looking forward to the next time, so I'd brazenly leaped.

As soon as I looked out of his windows and into mine, I realized he probably could see me walking around my apartment naked the night before after my shower, and the idea had struck me to test the theory out when I got back.

My phone started screaming at me again and I groaned, reaching for it and slamming my hand down on it again in the dark, but it wasn't my alarm again.

Because suddenly my sister's voice rang out into the air.

"Ky? Hello?"

"Fuck." I grunted and grabbed the phone, bringing it onto the bed next to me. "What do you want?"

She screeched out loud. "What do I want?" She asked exasperatedly, "I want the fucking details of your encounter with Mr. Sexy!"

I rolled over on my back, trying to figure out what to tell my twin sister because I hardly understood any of it myself. "Uh, well." I started and then got diarrhea of the mouth and bared my soul to her. "He answered his door, fresh out of the shower and shirtless, and invited me in while he opened the bottle for me. We made small talk full of chemistry and longing and I nearly jumped him right then and there, but went back to my place. Which turns out, that you can see directly into my apartment from his when I leave my lights on and curtains open and I got the impression that he liked that. So I came home, high on testosterone and horniness, and jacked off in the middle of my bedroom while he watched from his."

"Oh, my god!" She gasped, screeching in my ear again. "You did not! You slut!" She gushed and then giggled. "Oh, my god!"

"I know." I groaned.

"What did he do?" She hurried on excitedly. She was eating it up like cat nip, much to my mortification.

"He... jacked off too."

"What?" She squealed. "You saw his dick?"

"No, I didn't actually see it. He was too close to the window." I said, hating how disappointed me.

"But he saw yours?"

"Uh, yeah. I wasn't hiding anything."

"Oh, my god." She said again and sighed, "Why is that so... hot?" She asked.

I snorted at her. "Thinking of your brother jacking off is hot?"

"No! Ew! Don't put it in that context. I meant the mutual mastur-bation mixed with a little exhibitionism. That's hot."

I thought back on it. "Yeah, it fucking was."

"Well, now what? Are you guys like hooking up?"

"Pfft. I don't even have the man's phone number, Lo. So I don't have an answer for you there."

"Damn." She said and then fell quiet for a moment.

"Yeah," I replied and stared at my ceiling until the anxiety about what I did tried to make me feel ashamed of it, and I wasn't about to let that happen. "I have to get up and get going. I have meetings later and I need to work off some of this... energy."

She snorted. "Work it off, how exactly?" I knew what she was implying, but I doubted a morning romp with my sexy neighbor was on the agenda.

"I'm going to start with a run around the city and go from there." I deadpanned.

"Fine. But I want a status update tonight. I'll be back at my apart-ment, so I'll have wine. We can video chat and have a wine date."

"Sounds good sis, talk to you later," I said and then hung up. I pulled myself out of my bed and forced myself to leave my curtains shut as I got dressed in a pair of running shorts and sneakers, forgoing a shirt thanks to the late summer humidity, and threw my hair up in a bun.

I took a protein shot and grabbed my earbuds as I walked out of my apartment door. My step faltered as I rounded the corner and spotted Dexter standing and waiting for the elevator, once again looking like a sharp-dressed businessman in a charcoal gray suit.

He turned when he heard me, and his eyes dropped to my naked chest before snapping back up to my eyes. His jaw was smooth where last night there had been stubble, and I caught the scent of his after-shave on the air around him as I got near to him. And God, he smelled divine.

"Morning," I said, unable to form another coherent thought as I felt a blush crawling up my neck. I was thirty years old and hadn't blushed around anyone in years, yet the man somehow made me turn crimson with a simple look.

Awesome.

Dexter raised his eyebrow at me and let his eyes travel back down to my chest and stomach, and then nodded. "Good morning."

I stood next to him awkwardly as I fiddled with my earbuds case, trying to decide how to proceed here.

"You shut your curtains last night and didn't open them this morning." He said finally, turning his body to look at me. My lips parted in surprise that he was going to talk about what happened, but quickly shook it off. I knew it wouldn't take long for the elevator to show up and I wanted to figure out this man as much as I could in the time I had.

"I just rolled out of bed, to be completely honest," I blurted. "I'll open them up again when I get back." Fuck if I knew why I felt like I needed to do that for him, but I did.

He watched me closely for a beat and then dropped his eyes to the floor between us. "I like when you leave them open." He breathed, like it was some big declaration, which I guess in a way because I was a stranger, it was.

So I wanted to give him a piece of my vulnerability back. "I enjoyed knowing you were watching." I held his surprised stare as he took an almost unnoticeable step closer.

"I don't understand this." He said finally, and it sounded like it pained him to vocalize it.

"The voyeur in you?" I asked with a smile.

"My attraction to you." He said instantly. I could see the uncertainty and almost fear in his eyes and things clicked and my smile faded a bit.

"I'm not your type normally?"

He smirked a bit and nodded his head. "You could say that."

"You're not gay," I whispered, almost to myself as the elevator doors opened, revealing a blessedly empty car. "And clearly, I am." I walked in, trying to wrap my head around that bit of information as he walked in after me.

He answered truthfully, "I've never been attracted to a man before, no." Everything else aside, the openness and vulnerability between us, two strangers who shared something intimate, was... refreshing.

Even if I didn't understand it.

"But you're attracted to me?" I asked as I leaned back against one side of the elevator.

His eyes once again traveled down my body, and he tilted his head to the side. "Painfully so." The fire burned in his eyes and my veins as we stood there, only a few feet of space separating us. "And I don't understand why." Neither of us moved to hit the button to take us to the lobby, so we sat suspended in the car.

"Do you need to understand it? You could just trust your gut and go with it."

"Go with it?" He asked, taking another one of those almost unnoticeable steps forward towards me. I wasn't sure if he realized what he was doing or not, but he was closing the distance between us, and I ached to touch him. But I didn't want to spook him, either. "And do what, exactly?"

I raised my eyebrows at him and stood up to my full height, which brought us so close all I had to do was take one more step and my chest would touch his. His hand tightened around the handle of his briefcase, and his jaw muscles twitched. "At this point? I'd indulge you in just about anything you asked from me." I said in a breathy voice so full of need that it would have been embarrassing if I wasn't sure he was right there with me in the same boat.

"Kyson." He said in that deep gravelly voice that echoed with a hint of authority and got me drunk. His eyes fell to my lips, and I licked them, knowing what effect it would have on him yet doing it, anyway.

Dexter had made me feel more desired in the last twelve hours than I had felt in months by several other people. This visceral and consuming need that burned between us was raw and instinctual, I didn't doubt it or worry about its authenticity as I did with other people.

"Maybe you can't wrap your head around what it means to be attracted to a man; to me. And until you figure out if it's something more than morbid curiosity, you can't really find your footing."

"What are you trying to say, Kyson?" He asked, with more bite to his voice. He wanted me to spell it out for him because he was so unsure of his own headspace, he wanted me to make sense of it for him.

"Kiss me. And then tell me what you feel after that." His eyes fell to my lips again, and I took that last step forward until we were inches apart. "See if you're just hyping it all up in your head or not."

He looked torn, his nostrils flared, and his pupils dilated as his eyes searched my face before his resolve snapped. He dropped his briefcase as he brought one hand up behind the back of my neck and pulled me in against him. His lips crashed against mine aggressively, and I moaned in surprise as I melted into him. His lips were warm and surprisingly soft as they tentatively moved against mine, exploring and searching.

I let him set the pace, knowing deep inside that this was the first time he'd ever kissed a man, and I was more than willing to be his test dummy. Normally, the idea of being some gay experiment for a straight man would have sent me into a tailspin, but not with Dexter. I could feel how this wasn't some sort of side-show fun for him. It was authentic.

He opened his lips and cautiously ran his tongue against my bottom lip, coaxing me to open to him, and I did so willingly.

It was hands down the best kiss I'd ever had before, and I was struggling to stay reserved and let him control it when I wanted nothing more than to jump him right on the spot. The second his tongue fully pressed into my mouth, I lost the battle. I slid both hands over his stomach and pulled the button open on his suit jacket to feel the body heat radiating off his tight abdomen under his expensive shirt. He groaned and tilted his head, deepening the kiss, pushing me back into the wall of the elevator, and pressing himself into me from head to toe.

I bit down on his bottom lip and sucked it into my mouth, drawing another groan from his chest that vibrated against my own. I hooked my fingers behind the leather of his belt and rocked my hips forward, letting him feel how hard he made me and, in turn, felt his own erection against me.

And Oh. My. God.

He was packing, and I moaned into him again before breaking off the kiss and pushing him backward. I took a deep breath and stared up into his blue eyes as his chest heaved up and down, just like mine. I brought my fingers up to my lips and felt the tingle he left there against the swollen flesh. "Holy fuck." I whispered, sagging back into the wall again.

His jaw clenched, and he took another step back. "Sorry." He apologized, looking down at the floor as he ran a hand through his hair. The elevator groaned and started descending, called to another floor beneath us and he quickly adjusted his erection in his tight slacks as he looked down at mine out of the corner of his eye.

"What are you apologizing for?" I asked, suddenly feeling bad for pushing him away.

"It was... too much. I was too much. I'm sorry." He said, not willing to meet my gaze.

I chuckled at him disbelievingly and shook my head. My laugh drew his eyes back to me as I grabbed my cock through the fabric of my shorts and squeezed myself boldly before tucking it into the waistband of my briefs to hide it as the elevator neared the lobby floor. His nostrils flared again, "Dexter, I assure you, that wasn't too much for me to handle. It was just going to get indecent in here if we kept it up." I said nodding to the ticker above the door showing our arrival to the lobby seconds before the door opened and let the rest of the world into our secluded bubble, "And aside from my apparent flare for exhibitionism with you, I'm not interested in putting on a show for a lobby full of strangers."

He relaxed a bit and grabbed his briefcase off the floor and stepped out into the lobby with me following behind him. The clerks were busy assisting a delivery man at the front door, and I followed Dexter through the side entrance to the tenant parking lot before he stopped and turned around.

"So," I said, standing awkwardly as he walked to a sleek, expensive car and unlocked his door, tossing his briefcase in before turning back to me. All the sexual bravado from turning the large alpha man in front of me into a ball of unrequited need a minute ago faded in the bright early morning sunshine as I tried to figure out what came next in this very uncharted territory for us.

"That was a very unexpected start to my morning." He said with a small smile on his lips that were still slightly red from our kiss.

"Really? I thought you kissed strangers in elevators all the time, you seemed like a natural." I joked, and he rolled his eyes at me as he scratched his chin.

"I have to get to work." He said, checking his watch. "And... process all of that."

I nodded and kicked a stone with my sneaker; I hated how it was making me feel, not knowing his thoughts about the kiss. Aside from his physical reaction to it, I wanted to know what his mental reaction was. "Got it," I said, taking a step back and turning to walk away, feeling slightly... dejected. Maybe being an experiment for him was going to send me into a tailspin after all.

"Hey!" He called out, "Wait." I looked back at him, where he stood with a scowl on his face and his hands in his pants pockets. "I'm not trying to... offend you." He said.

I nodded and gave him what I hoped was a sincere smile. "No problem," I said and turned away again.

"Kyson." He called out after me with the bite of authority he'd shown a few times now and goosebumps covered my bare arms as I faced him again. This time though he was walking over to me with determination on his face, which made my feet stay still even though I wanted nothing more than to get away from the straight man who was about to say that kissing me had cured his curiosity while it left me awestruck. "Don't walk away from me like that." He said firmly, holding my stare until I nodded.

"I was just trying to give you the space you need. To process it."

"If I didn't have a meeting in twenty minutes, I'd be dragging you back upstairs to finish what we started." He said, and I shivered at the intensity in his demeanor.

"Oh," I said, feeling stupid butterflies in my stomach.

This fucking man.

"Let's just... agree to come back to it. Tonight perhaps?" He asked, letting the authority in his tone fall away to hope.

"I have an event tonight; I won't be home until late," I said, leaving the ball in his court.

"Okay, how about I give you my number and you can text me when you're free, then?" He said, and I nodded.

"That works," I added his number to my phone and then pocketed it again as another tenant came out of the door to walk to her car, eyeing us just standing there. "Good morning," I said to her with a smile, and she let her eyes roam over the both of us with an appreciative sparkle as she sashayed to her car.

I smirked after her, and Dexter just shook his head and rolled his eyes again. "I'll see you later, Kyson." He said, backing up to his car and opening the door again even though he looked like he was less than enthusiastic about leaving.

"Have a good day, Dexter," I said and winked at him before turning and jogging away. When I was a block away and set my pace for my run, I finally took a deep breath and let the gravity of this morning's events replay in my head.

I kissed Dexter Chase; my obnoxiously sexy, straight, next-door neighbor who had a flair for voyeurism and a newfound attraction to me.

What the actual fuck?

Chapter 6 – Dexter

I sat at my desk, staring out the window unseeing. I ran my thumb back and forth over my bottom lip.

I could still taste Kyson's mouth on me hours later.

Kiss me. And then tell me what you feel after that.

He told me to kiss him and find out if my attraction to him was solely in my mind. And I fucking did.

And it was... soul-crushing.

Because it was the best kiss I'd ever had. Yet I still had no clear sign about what it was that drew me in so strongly to him. On my drive to work, I looked at every male I came across, trying to see if I felt anything towards any of them as instantaneous as I did the first time I saw Kyson in his apartment. But I didn't feel even a glimmer of arousal looking at any of the hundreds of men I passed on the streets.

Leaving me even more confused than before.

And hornier.

Because hot fucking damn, Kyson could kiss. The way he moaned the second I'd pulled him against me had electrified me. And when he had slid his hands under my jacket, against my stomach and under my belt, my cock had grown so hard I was afraid I was going to explode in my pants against him.

I wasn't lying when I'd told him I was seconds away from dragging him back up to our floor to finish what we started. I had wanted him and was acting fully on what my body was telling me, ignoring the confusion in my head.

"Hey, so about this bachelor auction," Cora said, stepping into my office and shutting the door behind her as I groaned at the interruption. "Whoa." She said, stopping short when she got close to my desk. "Are you sick?"

I scowled at her, "No."

"Are you sure?" She asked again, tilting her head to the side.

"Yes, I'm sure. Why?"

She sat down opposite me in her favorite chair and put her feet up on the other one. "Because you look... rumpled." She said with a scrunched nose. "What's going on?"

I scoffed at her and brushed it off. "Nothing. And we're not talking about the auction." I said, hoping she actually would talk about the auction instead of my disheveled and distracted appearance. I'd been running my hands through my hair in frustration all day and had ditched my jacket and tie hours ago, leaving me looking wrecked.

"Wait. Hold on. Go back." She said, not missing a beat. "You were staring off into space when I walked in here, which you never do. There isn't a second in your day that you aren't productive unless, of course, I'm around. But you were already distracted before I walked in. And you look rumpled." Her eyes scanned over my body before they widened, and she dropped her feet off the chair and smacked her hand on my desk. "And you aren't wearing your wedding ring!" She accused.

Panic filled my system as I looked down at my bare finger for a minute, and I should have known she was going to pick up on it in the first five seconds. Because she was that detail-oriented.

I hadn't put it back on after my shower last night because Kyson had interrupted me. And then, after our little window peep show, it felt *wrong* to put it back on. So for the first time since my wedding day almost six years ago, I tucked the golden band back into its box and put it in my drawer.

And it had felt... therapeutic.

But now I had to come up with some story to hide the real reason I wasn't wearing it.

"Dexter Chase!" Cora snapped her fingers in front of my face. "What is going on with you? You're worrying me."

I scoffed at her again and stood up, running my hands through my hair again. "Nothing Cora. I just didn't put it on today."

"Don't you dare lie to me." She implored, gentling her voice. "Talk to me." I looked over at her and felt the words on the tip of my tongue, but bit them back.

I was so not ready to tell anyone about Kyson and my sudden sexual identity crisis.

She huffed and crossed her arms over her chest, and leaned back in the chair again. "I'm not leaving until you tell me what's going on with you, Dex."

"What do you care, Cora?" I snapped, a little more aggressively than I had intended, and she flinched a bit. Which, of course, left me feeling like a steaming pile of dog shit. "I'm sorry." Sighing, I ran my hand over my face. "I didn't mean to yell."

"Sit down." She said, pushing the chair next to her out and pointing at it. "Now, Dex." I stared at her before folding myself down into the chair as instructed. "Talk to me, please. You're obviously upset about something. Let me help."

"You can't help me with this, Cora," I said gently and leaned back in the chair, covering my face with my hands.

"What is it?"

I sighed again. "I—" I stopped, struggling with all the doubt in my mind.

"Dex." She warned.

"I met someone." I bit out, hating how that left so many more questions open to her inquisitive brain.

Her eyes rounded and her eyebrows rose to her hairline as her mouth opened and closed like a fish out of the water as she tried to process it. If I wasn't so worked up into a ball of nerves, I might have laughed at the image.

"Dex, that's great." She finally said, leaning forward and putting her hand on my arm as I rolled my eyes. "It *is* great Dexter Chase." She said firmly. "Why wouldn't it be?"

"Because I can't—" I said and stood back up, pacing back and forth. "It's not someone I can be with."

"Why not? What does that mean? Who is it?" She asked, watching me closely.

I was losing my grip on my sanity the more I talked. Years of numbness were fading and leaving me raw and on edge. "It doesn't matter, it will never work," I said, hating the way it made me feel to say that out loud. I could feel the self-loathing pile of dog shit feeling clawing its way back up my throat. "I just need to get past that and accept that I'm so fucked up in the head, I'll be alone forever," I said and grabbed a cup full of pens off my desk and threw them against the wall by the conference room door where it shattered into a bunch of pieces, sending pens and porcelain raining down. "Fuck!" I roared and paced again with my fists on my hips as I fought emotions I hadn't allowed myself to feel in years.

Anger.

Pity.

Hate.

Bitterness.

I'd numbed myself to it all when I had nearly drowned in it one night and I'd forced myself to ignore it all since then. But now that I had something so close to being within reach that made me feel... alive, the darkness was seeping back in.

My office door ripped open, and Maverick stormed in with Reid hot on his heels, both looking alarmed at the crash and yelling that had come from inside.

"Cora," Mav said, pulling her to her feet and placing himself between us. "What's going on, Dex."

I laughed humorlessly and turned on him. "Yeah, sure. Like I'd ever fucking hurt her." I accused. "Fuck you. Get out of my office." I snapped. Growing more irate by the second.

Cora pulled Maverick back and stepped in. "Mav, I'm fine. It was just a cup."

"Dex, you need to calm down, man," Reid said, holding his hands out at me like I was a cornered animal. And I couldn't help but notice how ridiculous it all was. I was finally allowing myself to feel something, and it was all anger and bitterness.

"Shut up Reid. Get out." I said, pointing my finger at Maverick and Cora. "Everyone needs to just get the fuck out."

"Not until you tell us what the fuck is going on." Maverick snapped back, pushing Cora back behind him and towards Reid, who still stood near the door. Like at any second, I was going to detonate, and Cora was going to be in the line of fire.

"Get out!" I roared at him. And I could feel the blood rush through my body, sending me into fight-or-flight mode as I clawed at the top button of my shirt.

"Guys, get out. We were just fine before you stormed in here." Cora ordered, brushing Reid's hands off her arm where he was trying to drag her out.

"Dex slamming shit off the wall isn't fine, Cora." Maverick bit out, never taking his eyes off of me. "Tell me what's going on."

"Fuck off. I mean it, Mav. Get out of my office right now. I'm not doing this with you." I yelled.

"Doing what?" He yelled back. "What's going on?"

I shook my head and stormed over to my desk, grabbing stuff. I slid my jacket over my shoulders and pocketed my phone. "Nothing."

"Bullshit man." He said, stepping into my path as I tried rounding the desk.

"Maverick! Leave him alone!" Cora begged.

"You're not leaving Dex. Not like this. Calm down and then we can talk about it." Mav said, trying but failing to sound reasonable. He was the least reasonable person in the room.

"I don't want to talk about it. I'm done. Get out of my way."

"Done with what, Dex?" He asked, his eyes squinting as he watched me. "What happened?"

"Hope happened!" I bellowed, shocking myself and everyone else in the room. "My wife fucking happened. She took my son and fucked me up."

His features softened as he dropped his hands, finally getting some understanding. "Dex—" He started, but I brushed him off, shoving him aside and walking around him.

"I need a break," I said, walking out of my office past a sad-looking Cora and straight into an open elevator.

"Dex, don't walk out like this man," Maverick called from my office. "Don't give her that power over you anymore." He said as he walked to the elevators.

I laughed again, shaking my head. "Too late for that."

I paced my apartment, hating how it was only early evening and I just wanted the day to fucking end already. I also hated how every time I looked over at Kyson's apartment, empty rooms met my gaze, constantly reminding me I was truly alone in this world.

I had walked out of work after my explosion on my friends right after lunch and hadn't gone back. Instead, I walked through the city for hours, working out the frustrations in my head with my muscles, and by the time I got home, I was tired and calm, almost numb again.

Numb was comfortable for me because it was exactly what I'd felt every day for years now. At least until I met Cora and allowed her to gradually worm her way into my heart like an endearing, bothersome little sister. She was impossible not to care for with her stubborn determination and giant heart, always thinking the best of everyone else. I hadn't realized it until today, but when my friendship with her started, my numbness faded.

And then I'd met Kyson, and it had melted off, leaving me raw and exposed to everything for the first time. Today in my office, after a life-changing elevator kiss, I'd let those emotions I was feeling for the first time erupt into doubt and anger, and I'd blown up on the only three people in the world that cared for me.

I hated how I left it with them; I hated that I'd scared Cora and shoved Maverick. I hated it all. And I hated the thought of facing everyone on Monday morning after leaving everything unresolved.

I looked out the window again towards Kyson's and groaned. It was going to be a long fucking weekend.

Sitting in the chair in my living room as the light outside faded in the sky and left shadows dancing around my apartment, I contemplated going back to the office to work because I knew everyone else would have left for the weekend by now. Suddenly, a loud knock on my door interrupted my plan.

My head whipped towards Kyson's apartment, looking to see if I'd missed him coming home, but his place was still empty and lifeless.

I walked to the door and threw it open, hating the excitement that had built in my chest and deflated slightly when I looked at the bubbly blonde with a baby belly standing on my doorstep.

"Cora," I said.

"Ouch." She hissed, looking at me accusingly. "You could have at least tried to hide the disappointment on your face when you saw it was me."

I pursed my lips at her and leaned on my doorframe. "What are you doing here?" I asked, but before she could answer, the elevator dinged behind her and Saint, the doorman, stepped off carrying what looked like twenty different bags of takeout food.

"Evening Mr. Chase." Saint said, "These were all just delivered for you." He held up the heavy bags awkwardly as I glared at Cora.

She smiled brightly at the man and then at me. "Mmh, yummy. I'm starving." She walked past me into my dark apartment, flipping the switch and turning on the overhead lights as she went.

I rolled my eyes and took the obscenely filled bags from Saint and thanked him before slamming my door shut and setting the bags down on my kitchen counter.

Cora stood in my living room looking around, wearing a pair of comfy pregnancy shorts and an oversized tee with an annoyingly adorable smile on her face. "Nice place, Dex."

"What are you doing here?" I asked her again, crossing my arms over my chest and eyed her with what I hoped was contempt.

But I'd be lying if I said I didn't welcome her sunshiny disposition, even if I wanted to bitch about it at the same point.

"Remember that time you showed up at my apartment unwelcomed and unwanted, and you took me out for lunch and then came back and watched bad reality television with me for hours and had a million bags of takeout delivered to make sure I actually ate?" She asked and then shrugged her shoulders. "It's my turn to repay the annoying favor."

"I don't need to eat Cora, I'm not a malnourished pregnant lady." I rebuked.

She rolled her eyes. "I know that, Dex. But you're hurting and I want to be here for you."

"I'm not hurting Cora." I sighed. "I'm just-" pausing, "Frustrated."

"Well, lucky for you, I'm a superb listener and an even better problem solver, with absolutely no plans for the entire weekend." She wiggled her eyebrows at me, and I snorted.

"Lucky me indeed." I deadpanned. She started taking containers of food out of the bags and opening them up, laying them out on the counter and my stomach growled loudly. "So, when is Maverick going to come crashing through my door after realizing that you're missing?" I asked her as she scooped a large helping of fried rice onto a plate.

"He knows I'm here, so he won't be crashing through the door at all." She said calmly.

I paused. "He let you come here?" I asked, surprised. After my aggression today, I didn't think he'd let her come near me again.

She huffed. "He was going to come here himself to check on you, but I asked that he give me a chance to help you through your problems first. Because we both know he would not be much help to you in this situation."

"In my pathetic love life, you mean?" I asked, grabbing a container of food and diving in, unable to resist the delicious smells wafting at me any longer. She smiled when she saw me eating, but bit her cheek to hide it.

"My husband is the most romantic man I've ever met before, believe it or not. But he forgets his gentle side with everyone but me sometimes. And I think right now, what you need most is gentle."

I paused, with a bite halfway to my mouth, but she moved on, distracting me, and walked over to my couch before sitting down cross-legged with her plate resting on her belly. "Ta-da!" She said, letting go of it and balancing it on her stomach. "Look, mom, no hands."

"You're ridiculous." I mocked her but smiled nonetheless as I sat down on the other end of the couch.

We ate in silence, enjoying the unhealthy takeout food until we'd both filled ourselves to the brim, and then she turned on my hardly ever-used television to some trashy reality show we'd watched at her apartment a few months ago and she leaned back, putting her dainty little feet in my lap like she was ready to stay the entire weekend if necessary.

I sighed and lifted them, putting a pillow under her heels, and lounged back on the couch, resigned to suffering her company for the foreseeable future. Hours later, I found myself staring out the window into Kyson's apartment again, daydreaming when the words left my lips.

"He's a man."

I hadn't meant to say them out loud. But as soon as they were out in the universe, I felt lighter somehow.

I knew Cora was a safe place for this conversation, but what I worried about most was what Maverick would think when she told him. That had been one of my biggest hang-ups so far.

What would my two very heterosexual best friends think about my new revelation?

"The person you've met and started falling for is a man?" Cora asked gently from next to me and I nodded, unable to meet her eyes. She muted the television.

"My neighbor actually," I said, nodding across the space between our apartments and she followed my gaze and looked into his empty dark home.

"And what exactly troubles you the most about that?"

I thought about that question for a moment before answering. "I'm not attracted to other men. I never have been. But then I met him, and something just *clicked* inside of me."

"Does he know you're into him?"

I laughed lightly. "Yeah," I said, finally looking over at her. "It's hard for me to hide it when I'm around him."

She grinned and sat up, pulling her feet from my lap as she eyed me excitedly. "Does he know you've never... been with a man before?"

My smile fell slightly, "He knows."

"What's wrong with that?" She asked.

I sighed and struggled to articulate what I was feeling. "I told him my interest in him confused me, because I was straight. And he challenged me to indulge myself in my desire to see if it was just curiosity or not. But I think I made him feel used or cheap or something."

Her eyebrows rose to her hair, and her eyes widened. "And... did you? Indulge yourself?"

I groaned and sank further into the couch, replaying every second in the elevator over and over in my head. "I kissed him."

She squeaked and scooted closer. "And? Was it what you were hoping for?"

I shook my head and stared at the ceiling. "It was... so much more, Cora."

"Dex!" She gushed, "You see what this means don't you?" She grabbed my hand and held it tight between both of hers.

I shook my head, not following what was so crystal clear to her.

"It means that his gender and your sexuality have absolutely no bearing here; the titles society has placed on us are irrelevant. Because when you meet someone and it clicks like you said it did, and you feel those emotions so deeply inside of you from mere touches; that means the connection goes deeper than physical limitations can ever come close to understanding Dexter. That's what *soulmates* are made from."

I watched her speak and let her words wash over me as she conveyed to me what I couldn't understand before now. "Is that what it feels like with Maverick?" I asked her.

Her eyes misted over, and her nose turned red as she gripped my hand tightly with hers and I could feel the emotion behind the words as she spoke. "From the very second I met him at five years old. That's why it didn't matter that our relationship wasn't physical or romantic at first, we were just kids, but something so much more powerful than ourselves drew us together. And it's what has helped us defy everything since."

"And you think that's what this could be for me?" I asked, trying not to get my hopes up, but at the same moment, hearing what she said gave me some footing to stand on plausibly.

"I think it could be." She said, wiping at her eyes. "But only if you let it be."

I chewed on my lip and laid my head back against the couch cushion again as I thought it all over. My phone lit up on my lap and I picked it up, opening a message from an unsaved number.

Hey Dex, it's Ky. I hope it's not too late, I just didn't want the day to end without reaching out. I hope you found clarity today in your mind, or at least a little peace.

I smiled down at my phone as my finger hovered over my keypad for a moment as I contemplated what to say back.

"Is that him?" Cora asked from her end of the couch as she leaned back into the cushions with a silly, sunny smile on her face.

"Yeah," I said and showed her the message.

She swooned and smiled sappily at me as I typed out my reply.

Believe it or not, I have. And I have a question for you.

Cora didn't even bother trying to pretend like she wasn't reading over my shoulder and slid right over to rest her head on my shoulder as we waited for Kyson's response.

What could that be?

I typed out my reply without hesitation and hit send before I could think better of it. "Well, here goes fucking nothing," I said and Cora squealed from next to me and hugged me tightly.

"I'm so excited for you, Dex."

Chapter 7 – Kyson

Would you like to go out to dinner with me?

It was almost midnight, and I was riding home in a taxi after a long ass day, and I wanted nothing more than to go home and drown myself in a bottle of wine and find out what Dexter was doing. I had texted him earlier, and he told me he had a question for me.

I had been so nervous as to what he could want from me after his indecision this morning.

I had *not* planned for him to ask me out to dinner, and therefore I chickened out and left him on read, for at first an hour, and then two as I sat staring at my phone wondering if there was some angle he was coming at this from that I was missing but I couldn't produce one.

If he wanted to take a man out on a date, how would that negatively impact me?

It wouldn't. Well, it wouldn't, other than it would just make me fall deeper into the abyss of longing and connection that had formed between us.

My taxi pulled up outside of my apartment and I pocketed my phone, grabbed my bags, and walked in the front door as I contemplated how to answer him.

When I got off the elevator on my floor, my hands itched to knock on Dexter's door, but I forced my feet to carry me and my baggage to my place and walked in.

I flicked the lights on as I walked in and carried my bags into my spare bedroom, and then stood in my desolate kitchen. I instantly searched for some sort of life in Dexter's apartment and my eyes were drawn to the massive windows looking out into the night.

His curtains were open but his lights were off, so I couldn't see if he was asleep or not. I shrugged off my jacket and kicked my boots off as I held my phone in my hand and typed out a response before I could chicken out any longer.

As in a date? Or another part of your experiment?

I hated the way the word experiment rubbed me wrong, considering it had been my idea to push him to do just that. I just didn't expect it to make me feel so *cheap* afterward.

And I guess that was because the kiss was... life-changing. I'd muddled it over on my run and then during every spare minute I had all day, and the conclusion was the same at the end of every internal dialogue.

Kissing Dexter felt like something so raw and animalistic that it had left me shaken.

I walked into my room and then the bathroom, turning on the hot water in the shower as my phone buzzed in my hand. I quickly popped my head back out of the bathroom to look in his windows for some light showing where he was, but it was pitch black.

My phone buzzed again, and it was then I realized he hadn't texted me back, but that he was calling me. I swallowed and answered it, bringing it to my ear as my eyes kept searching.

"Are you hiding from me?" I asked in place of a greeting.

His voice rumbled in his chest as he chuckled lightly. "The view is better when my windows are dark."

I smiled and put the phone on speaker, setting it down on my dresser as I reached over my head and pulled my black tank top off, and threw it into the hamper.

I heard the intake of breath over the line and smirked to myself.

"Well, are you enjoying the view?" I asked him, dropping my hands to my belt buckle, and raising my eyebrow in challenge.

"Immensely." He growled and goose bumps covered my body. "Take the belt off." He ordered.

A wicked smile crossed my lips, and I gently pulled it out of my loops and set it on my dresser.

"Now what?"

"Take your hair down." He paused. "Slowly." His voice was quiet, but the authority in it was undeniable. I reached up and pulled the tie from my hair and shook it out, running my hand through it until it lay in a mess around my face. I could hear him breathing deeper and my cock twitched in my jeans.

"Was that to your liking?" I asked brazenly.

"You know it was." He said honestly. "Now your jeans and socks."

I pushed my jeans down and then my socks, adding them to the hamper, and stood in the middle of my bedroom in my tight black boxer briefs and leather bracelets, awaiting his next command.

"You're so incredibly sexy." His voice was hoarse and needy, and it was intoxicating.

"What do you like most about me physically?" I asked, hooking my thumbs into the waistband of my boxers and standing tall. "What drew you in the first time?"

He groaned again and sighed. "Your tattoos caught my attention first. The bright colors against your tan skin remind me of a pirate treasure map from my childhood." I smiled at his honesty. "And then I saw your long hair, and I ached to tangle my fingers in it." He chuckled softly. "Are you weirded out yet?"

"I'm hard Dex." I offered instantly. "You make me feel *seen.*"

"How is it possible that anyone in the world could overlook you, Kyson? You're breathtaking."

Now it was my turn to groan. "Let me see you," I said, scanning his dark apartment again. "You don't have to strip if you're not comfortable, since we both know voyeurism is more your thing, but let me see you while you watch."

There was silence on the other end of the line and then I heard rustling around seconds before a floor lamp clicked on in his bedroom and I saw him for the first time since walking away from him this morning at his car. He was sitting in a leather armchair in the corner opposite of his bed, facing the wall of windows like it was his own personal big-screen television.

And I was the show.

"There you are," I whispered.

This time when he chuckled, I could see the breathtaking smile on his face, and I desperately wanted to go to him. But at the same moment, I knew this space between us could be good to keep the pace slow while he adjusted to this change in him.

Well... slow-ish.

"Take them off." He said confidently, and I smirked back at him as I slowly pushed my underwear down to my ankles and kicked them off. He sucked in a quick breath when my hard cock sprung free and bobbed between my thighs. "Why is that so hot?" He asked himself and I shook my head.

My fingers ached to wrap themselves around my cock and stroke in search of relief, but he didn't tell me to, so I held off.

I loved the way he took control, even if this was so far out of his comfort zone.

"Tell me what you want me to do now," I said, desperate for more. The steam of my shower warmed up the surrounding room, and I knew I should go turn it off and stop wasting water, but my feet froze in place.

Dexter stood up out of his chair with ease like a lion and slowly walked forward until he stood a few feet back from the window. He wore a black tee and red athletic shorts that were tented in the front around his obvious erection.

Then, I remembered that I still hadn't seen his cock, even though I had felt it this morning.

He opened his mouth to say something, but my phone vibrated across the dresser, cutting him off as a call came in. I looked down and saw my sister's name on the screen and rolled my eyes, declining it.

When I looked back out the window, Dexter stood frozen stiff with an intense look on his face. "Someone important?" He asked.

I scoffed. "No one." I swallowed down the giant lump in my throat. "No one is more important than this right now." I fisted my hands at my sides as my cock jerked and a drip of pre-come leaked from the end.

"Are you sure?" He asked, and I hung my head back and closed my eyes in agony.

"Positive." I groaned, to which he chuckled. My phone vibrated again, and Lo's face lit it up with a video chat call and I nearly threw my phone across the room in frustration. "Fucking hell," I muttered.

Dexter stepped back towards his chair and even from this far away, I could see the storm brewing in his eyes. "I'll let you go."

"Don't!" I rushed out. "It's just my sister." Explaining myself felt like the right thing to do. "She said she was going to call tonight, and I forgot about it. But it's fine."

"Talk to your sister Kyson." He said firmly.

"Are you kidding?" I snapped in exasperation. "You're going to leave me like this?" I said and fisted my cock, stroking it like I'd wanted to since I heard his voice on the phone.

He chuckled and then turned the light off, bathing his apartment in darkness and disappearing once again. "Do something for me, Kyson."

"Anything." I panted. "Whatever you want."

"Go take the shower that you started when you got home. But when you run your hands over your body to wash..." He said and paused as I stood there with my mouth hanging open in agony. "Imagine they're mine."

"Dex." I moaned as my hand continued to stroke myself. "This is torture."

"Hmm." He hummed. "You never answered me about that date." He said. "Now that is torture."

The date.

Fuck.

"I forgot..." I stammered, shaking my head and fighting for focus. "Yes. Yes, I'd love to go out with you."

"Really?" He asked, sounding a bit surprised.

"Really. I'm free tomorrow if you are." I said, hopefully.

"Tomorrow then." He said, and I could hear the smile in his voice. "Go make yourself come while you think of me, Kyson. And I'll see you tomorrow." And then he hung up.

Bastard.

I stood at my kitchen island mixing up an omelet the next morning when my phone vibrated on the counter and Dexter's name lit up.

Good morning.

I smiled down at my phone like a lovesick puppy and replied.

Good morning. Shall I change your name in my phone to the ghost? You somehow hide from me, even in the daylight.

When I woke up this morning to the bright sunshine, I instantly looked over at Dex's apartment but found it empty already. And I felt disappointed but not surprised.

I came to work early; I needed to finish some things that I neglected yesterday.

I poured my omelet into the sizzling pan and replied.

What do you do for work?

His reply came instantly.

I'm a corporate lawyer.

I envisioned him sitting at a desk in some skyscraper suing people and making some company the big bucks with his serious demeanor and scowling face.

That fits you surprisingly well. Are you texting me to cancel our date?

I teased him, but I couldn't help the pang of fear inside of me that he was going to do just that.

Absolutely not, I was actually texting you to find out if you were available at seven.

I flipped my omelet, so I didn't reply instantly, I wanted to not look as desperate for this man as I was.

Seven sounds perfect. Do I get to know where we are going?

Can I surprise you?

I suppose so.

Thank you, then I'll pick you up at seven.

See you then.

I took a deep breath and let the nerves wash off of my body and tried to not count how many hours were between now and seven pm.

I worked for most of the day, answering emails and doing my social media rounds. And then in the afternoon I organized all of my client's outfits for the week and took pictures of them all for my portfolio.

Thankfully, before I knew it, it was almost seven, and I started getting ready. I'd closed my blinds earlier in the day, deciding to be cheeky and tease Dexter, and was slightly disappointed when he didn't text me to tell me to open them.

I was just pulling on my pants when he knocked on my front door, coming to pick me up for our date. I looked down at my watch and saw it was seven on the dot.

And I was late.

I was wearing only a pair of dark blue jeans and my leather necklace and contemplated making him wait while I put my shirt on, but then got the wicked idea to answer the door how I was.

I walked barefoot to my front door and opened it, revealing one of the sexiest men I'd ever seen before.

"Dex." I moaned as my eyes took in the whole package standing before me. He had on a short sleeve white button-up that was fitted and tight around his biceps and chest, paired with a pair of black designer jeans that hugged his thighs perfectly. His dark blonde hair was impeccably styled, and I couldn't resist the bit of stubble on his jaw. "You look incredible."

When I let my eyes go back to his bright blue ones, they were traveling down my body, taking in all the skin I left on display for him, pausing briefly where my jeans were still unbuttoned, and my white Calvin Klein briefs were showing. "Not even comparable to you right now." He said, shaking his head and taking a deep breath.

I smiled, feeling those nerves get the best of me again, and stepped backward. "I'm just getting dressed, come on in for a second." He stepped into my apartment, and I shut the door behind him. I walked around him and saw the way his eyes traveled over to the racks of designer clothes I'd worked on all day by the windows. He looked over at me and raised an eyebrow, and I grinned. "I'm not a cross-dresser, I swear." I held my hands up.

"Just a connoisseur of couture gowns?" He asked with a smirk.

"I'm a stylist, most of my clients are celebrities and I have a few events next week to dress them for," I said, and he nodded, relaxing a bit. "Stay here and I'll be right back."

I walked back into my closet and grabbed the black v-neck tee shirt I was planning on wearing and slid it on. I buttoned up my pants and slid a pair of shoes on, and then grabbed a hair tie off the dresser in my room and tied my hair back.

When I walked back out to the living room, Dexter was leaning up against the island waiting for me and I struggled to keep my tongue in my mouth. He was so devastatingly handsome. "Are you okay?" He asked me, looking mischievous.

The bastard knew what he did to me.

"Can I be honest for a second? Without you laughing at me or holding it over my head for the rest of forever?" I said as I grabbed my wallet and phone off the counter.

"Hmm." He mused, "I mean there are no guarantees in life, but I'll give it my best shot." He laughed and then put his hand on my arm, stilling me as I went to walk around him to turn the lights off. "I'm kidding. Talk to me."

I stopped right in front of him, and he pulled me in until I had no choice but to put my hands on his stomach to keep myself from falling against him completely. Which believe me, I was willing to fall, but I was trying to be cautious.

"I'm—" I paused, biting my lip. "I've never gone out on a first date with someone that I've already kissed. Or stripped for. And I'm finding it hard to keep things... PG." I sighed and closed my eyes as embarrassment flooded my face and rushed on. "I know this is new for you and I'm trying to be patient and respect your pace and not scare you off with my eagerness when all I want to do is kiss you again. It's just new for me too, is all."

He put his hand on my hip and one around the back of my neck, tilting my head back down until I looked at him again. "You want to kiss me again?" He asked, and the trace of a cocky smile pulled his lips, even as he tried to hide it.

I cocked my head to the side and glared. "I said no laughing."

"Oh believe me Ky, I'm not laughing at you. I'm trying... and apparently failing, to keep the shit-eating grin off my face from the overwhelming satisfaction I'm getting knowing you want me still."

I scoffed. "Did you think I'd suddenly stop wanting you?" I asked, and a flash of vulnerability crossed his face before he steeled it. "You're the one who left me hard and wanting last night."

"And I was nanoseconds away from coming over here right before that Kyson." He admitted and I paused.

"Really?"

"Really." He answered effortlessly. "This may be our first date, but our... relationship has had a less than conventional start to it. There's no reason to let society standards hold you back from something that you want with me."

"What are you saying?" I asked, making sure he was on the same page as me.

"I'm saying." He paused, running his thumb over the bottom of my jaw, and dropping his gaze to my lips. "That if you want to kiss me, just kiss me. Don't hold back."

I didn't hesitate; I leaned forward and his hand tightened around the side of my neck as my lips pressed against his. Instantly, I tilted my head and deepened it, using my body to press his into the counter and he reciprocated by standing up and spreading his legs further to give me space to get closer. I slid my hands around his abdomen, clutching at his shirt as his fingers slid into my hair, loosening the bun, and grabbing a handful. "God yes." I panted as his hand slid down to my ass and pulled my hips flush against his.

"You're quickly becoming a drug for me." He murmured as I dropped my lips from his to the skin of his jaw and then further until I was sucking on his neck "Fuck, Ky." He groaned and his Adam's apple bobbed as his head tilted back to give me better access. I kissed back up his neck and sucked the lobe of his ear between my lips and grazed it with my teeth before stepping back and dropping my lips and my hands from his body.

"Sorry." I chuckled, taking a deep breath to calm myself down, but Dexter had other thoughts. He pushed me backward until my back pressed into the fridge behind me and he pressed his body flush against mine, coaxing my lips open again with his persuasive tongue. I moaned into him as he pushed his thigh between my legs and rocked his hips, grinding against me. "Yes." I hissed, laying my head back against the fridge as he dived in against my neck and trailed kisses down to the open v of my shirt collar.

"I've never been so overwhelmed with need like this before." He mused, kissing his way back up my neck. "What are you doing to me?"

"I don't have a clue, but I feel it, too." I panted. "If you still want to go out tonight, then you need to stop. Because if you don't, I'm taking you to bed and showing you exactly what you've been missing your whole life."

He chuckled and rested his forehead against my shoulder briefly as I ran my fingers up the back of his scalp. "You're right." He backed up and put space between us as he reached down and adjusted himself.

My eyes dropped and lingered on the giant bulge in his pants, and I licked my lips at the mere thought of it. "Careful Kyson. I'm hanging on by a thread here." He warned, watching me eye fuck him.

I smirked at him and leaned up off the fridge, adjusting myself as well, and then filled my pockets with my things and opened the front door. "Let's go, Romeo, you promised me dinner first," I said with false bravado as I waited for him to pass.

"First huh?" He asked with a wink as he walked by.

"Dessert usually comes second." I mused as he choked and then laughed. When we got into the elevator, he watched me closely and smirked again. "What?" I asked.

He shook his head and looked up at the ticker. "Just thinking that this elevator will forever make me hard, thanks to you." I snorted at him but bit my tongue as the doors opened and exposed us to the bustling lobby. When we got out to his car, he walked over to the passenger side and opened the door for me with a chivalrous wink. "I hope this is okay?" He said after a beat as uncertainty crossed his face.

I paused before sinking into the seat. "What? Opening the door for me?" He nodded, and I saw that familiar vulnerability in his eyes.

"I don't want to offend you by making you feel inferior or make you think I feel more manly than you, I just... that's how I've always done it. But I've never been in a relationship with a man before and I don't know what's acceptable." He said and then sighed. "I don't want to mess this up with some stupid misunderstanding on my part, is all."

I stood back up out of the car and looked him square in the eye. "You're doing just fine, Dexter." I leaned into him, and he instinctively put his hands on my waist. "It's fair to say that I'm typically known to be more of a leaner in a relationship." His eyebrows dropped over his eyes in confusion, and I chuckled at him and tried again. "I'm naturally submissive. I lean on the man I'm with to lead the way and take more of that dominant position by default. I don't feel feminine or inferior to my partner when they do things like open the door or make menial decisions without consulting me. It makes me feel... *cared* for, I suppose." I tried to define what had always just been natural to me.

"I may not know much about same-sex relationships," He started, reaching up to tuck a loose strand of hair behind my ear, "But from our interactions so far, I've picked up that you are more submissive, and it calls to me in a primal way."

"Primal?" I asked, hearing the desire in my voice as the word warmed me from the inside out. "Like cavemen and alphas?"

He nodded and grinned, showing off the sexy dimples on his cheeks. "Like cavemen and alphas."

"God, that's sexy." I panted and laid my forehead on his chest as he chuckled and wrapped his arms around my shoulders.

"Mr. Chase." Someone called from the door to the lobby. Dexter's body tensed before he dropped his arms from me and stepped back. Instantly, I hated how he put distance between us, as if we were caught doing something bad.

"Yeah Saint, what is it?" He asked the night doorman, who was watching us with a shocked expression on his face.

"Uh—" Saint started and stopped, shaking his head to refocus as we waited. "I just wanted to remind you that your apartment is scheduled for painting next week. We'll be up Monday morning to drape everything, and you'll be allowed back in by Thursday."

"Right," Dexter said, nodding his head and clearing his throat. "Thanks."

Saint looked between us again with uncertainty before smiling at me and then nodding back to Dex. "Have a good night, Mr. Chase." He turned back to me. "Mr. Hart."

I smiled at him and waved as he ducked back into the building and Dex took a deep breath, looking at me out of the corner of his eye, but I stayed quiet as he worked it all out in his head. I was sure he knew his guilty reaction wasn't exactly my favorite, but it wasn't precisely unexpected either, if I thought about it. This was all new to him, it was going to take some adjusting on both of our parts if we wanted to give this a shot. "Ready?" He asked, stepping forward and pressing a gentle soothing kiss to my lips before leading me back into his car once again.

"Ready," I said, watching his long legs take him around the hood of his car.

Ready or not, Dexter Chase was throwing himself into the real world headfirst as a possibly bisexual man.

Hope he was ready for it because the world was cruel on a good day.

Chapter 8 – Dexter

I pulled up out front of Absinthe, the restaurant I was taking Kyson to, and turned the car off before looking over at his face as he looked up at the restaurant in front of us. "Oh, my. I've heard incredible things about this place," he whispered as he let his eyes wander over the brick and ivy of the exterior. "I've also heard that the wait list is *years long*, how did you manage this?"

Winking at him, "I know some people." I got out of the car, handing the keys to the valet, and then walked around and opened Kyson's door as he got out. He looked down at his jeans and tee and then paled. "I'm underdressed." He said in panic, and then looked down at my outfit. "You're underdressed too, but at least you have a collar."

I chuckled at him and took his hand, pulling him with me towards the quaint front door. "This place may be booked for the next few years already, but they pride themselves on a casual, authentic experience. Neither of us needs a coat and tie to enjoy this evening, I promise you."

He glared at me questioningly, but I just tightened my hand around his and pulled him along through the front door. The maître d' looked up from his podium as we walked in and smiled brightly, "Ah, Mr. Chase! I nearly fell over in shock when I saw your name on the list tonight. It's been so long since you've graced us with your presence." He said and shook my hand warmly. I'd been a patron of the restaurant for years and had built a relationship with the older man through that time.

"I know Caz, I apologize for staying away so long." I held my hand out to Kyson as he stepped forward, pulling Caz's attention to him, and I regretted it as soon as his eyes strayed up and down Kyson's fit body. Nearly forgetting that Caz flirted with anyone, regardless of their sex, and I didn't like the attention he was suddenly giving Ky. "My date Kyson and I are hoping for a memorable evening Caz, I hope you can ensure that." The man's eyes rounded as he looked between us while I pulled Kyson in against my side possessively.

"Oh, of course." He said, quickly grabbing the menus and turning to lead us through the quiet restaurant to the table I always requested. It sat in the back corner with both chairs next to each other, facing out over the entire space. "Here you two go, your waiter will be right with you. Enjoy." Caz said and respectfully dipped out.

"Was that a part of the caveman or the alpha just now?" Kyson asked with mischief in his eyes, taking his seat as I sat down next to him. I groaned in response and laid my napkin down on my lap, avoiding the question. Kyson just laughed good-heartedly at me and shook his head. "Well, whatever it was, I liked it." He said and started reading the menu.

I watched him as he was busy and felt myself relax into the dimly lit romantic atmosphere.

I could do this.

I had a few minor freakouts today thinking about taking Kyson out tonight, letting the fear of being discovered as... different shake my resolve.

I guess I had to accept the fact that I was now considered bi-sexual. I knew realistically that my attraction to Kyson wasn't some sort of fetish thing, and that I was, in fact, bi, I just had never allowed myself to explore that before.

Even yesterday on my way to work, I attempted to find another man I was attracted to and was unsuccessful, not because I lacked interest in men, but because Kyson captivates me like no one else.

I just wasn't ready to scream it from the rooftops yet.

Even if I knew that Cora had gone right home and told Maverick what was going on with me. And that didn't upset me, I expected her to, given that he was her husband, and they didn't keep secrets. But I hadn't seen him since my blow up at work yesterday morning and until I did and got an indication of how he took the news, I was worried he was going to treat me differently.

"You okay?" Kyson asked, setting his menu down and leaning in closer. "You look lost in thought."

I smiled at him and took a sip of my water, "Yeah, I guess I was."

"Care to share what about?" He asked gently, and that was something I was learning to appreciate about him. He never seemed judgmental or forceful in anything towards me, instead he always seemed to take a calm and levelheaded approach. And it soothed me and left me with the decision to open up or not, which always left me wanting to.

"You." I answered truthfully. "And me." I said and smirked, embarrassedly. "And everything that's happened the last few days and how it's left me... reeling."

Before he could respond, our waiter showed up to take our drink order. Ky quickly looked back down at the wine menu and then looked over at me with uncertainty in his eyes. "Uh, a red wine, please. House is fine." He said, setting down his menu.

I shook my head at the waiter and took the menu, scanning it quickly. "We'll take a bottle of your best Cab. The Heasman perhaps."

I said, and the waiter nodded, hurrying from the table to grab the bottle.

"You don't have to woo me." Kyson said softly, "I work with celebrities all the time, but I never ache to indulge in the best things life offers because of it. I'm fine with a house wine."

"I know, I can tell you don't pay any mind to things like that." I said and laid my hand on top of his on the table. "And believe me, it's refreshing. But I like to *indulge* from time to time and this is a special occasion, so I figured we could splurge a bit."

His green eyes warmed, and he smiled at me, and I wanted nothing more than to lean across the space and taste his smile, but the waiter returned with our bottle and two glasses. We watched him pour the aromatic beverage and then sat back in our seats when we were alone again as I lifted my glass to Ky.

"To first dates." I said as he lifted his glass and clanked it against mine.

"To indulging on first dates." He said suggestively, and I bit back a groan and took a drink of the wine.

"So tell me more about being a stylist." I said, setting down my glass.

He raised his eyebrows, setting his own glass down. "What do you want to know?"

"Well, how did you get into it? It can't be easy to get access to celebrities' lives like that."

"No." He chuckled. "It's hard as hell, actually." He leaned forward on his elbows. "I've always been into fashion. Not exactly wearing it," He laughed and flicked his hands over his relaxed jeans and shirt combo, "But I loved designing pieces together to create masterpieces for other people. I took every course available in high school and then moved to New York at eighteen with my little three-ring binder full of photos and sketches and worked my way up first as a personal shopper and then as a designer for a boutique in charge of all the items they carried, and I met a couple of high-end clients through that and slowly worked my way into their closets as a personal stylist for events. Sometimes I buy the entire closet's worth of clothes for clients looking to update their wardrobe, sometimes it's just dressing them one event at a time."

"You love what you do, don't you?" I asked at the genuine smile on his face as he described his work.

He sighed and leaned back, his smile deepening. "One hundred percent." He answered easily, "Don't get me wrong," He said quickly, holding his hand up. "Some clients are easier to work with than others." He laughed. "But I love every second."

"That's incredible. Knowing what you want to do for the rest of your life and actually getting to do it doesn't happen all the time. You're one of the lucky ones."

"What about you, did you always want to be a lawyer?" He asked, and I laughed lightly.

"Actually no, my parents always wanted me to go to law school and eventually I just folded into it I guess."

"Ever think about doing something else?"

"Years ago, yeah, but now," I shrugged. "I actually like what I do. I work with my best friends and I'm actually really damn good at my job. So that helps." I laughed again. "It just wasn't what I imagined doing as a kid."

"What did you want to be when you were growing up?" He asked.

"An architect." I answered fondly, remembering the drawings I used to do of buildings that I dreamed of designing someday. "I wanted to build skyscrapers, actually. But now I sit on the top floor of one of the best and I really have no complaints about it either."

"Well, at least you have found your peace with it. Are your parents proud of your decision to be a lawyer?" He asked, taking another sip of his wine.

I felt the smile fall off of my face and his eyes widened in surprise. "They passed my freshman year in high school, actually." I said, and his eyes saddened. "I think they'd be proud. Of my career choice anyway, the rest of the decisions I've made in life," I paused and shrugged my shoulders. "Probably not."

He relaxed a bit and squinted his eyes at me, "Are you trying to tell me that the poised and confident Mr. Dexter Chase had a rebellious streak?"

I laughed again and shook my head. "Not necessarily rebellious, but I lost my way for a while in law school."

"Meaning what?"

I shrugged my shoulders and shook my head, embarrassed. "I uh- partied. Hard. For a few years, and hated the person I'd become and then went off and turned that self-loathing into desperation for vali- dation. And then I met a woman so full of red flags NASA themselves could see it from space, but I fell for her anyway, searching for that happiness I craved."

He grimaced, "I'm guessing you didn't find it with her?"

I shook my head, surprised that I was telling him any of this at all, considering I never spoke of Hope or our marriage anymore. Unless, of course, I was screaming it into Maverick's face in the middle of my office.

Geesh.

"No, she was the exact opposite of happiness."

"I'm sorry." Kyson said empathetically, as he slid his hand onto my knee under the table and traced shapes and doodles into the fabric of my pants absentmindedly. "If it makes you feel any better, I think we've all probably gone down a path like that at some point in our lives."

"Meaning you have as well?" I asked.

He groaned and rolled his eyes. "My sister and I call it my boy band phase." He said and shuddered before laughing. "I dated a guy soon after I moved here, and he was this wannabe rock star who had already worked his way sexually through the east coast, but I was..." He paused and got a faraway look in his eye, "young and enamored with the appeal of it all more than I was interested in him specifically. He was bi, and he told me he wasn't able to commit himself to me because he would always feel unfulfilled if he didn't have sex with women and men equally." He rolled his eyes again, flicking his hand out. "Stupid little teenage me was ready and willing to lap up any scraps he would give me because I ached to feel wanted at that point in my life. I was so stupid." He said again and I could see how he tried to brush it all off like a done and over moment, but I knew he carried that around on his heart still.

"Hey." I said, sliding my fingers through his where they still rested on my knee and held his hand. "I get it. And I don't think you were stupid to want to be desired. That's basic human nature. I think he was a douche canoe for not seeing what he had right in front of him and wasting away what time he had with you."

The skin around his eyes crinkled as he smiled at me warmly, looking lost in thought still. "Can I kiss you?" He asked, looking around the crowded room before looking back at me.

I fucking loved that he asked, knowing this was new to me. But every time I looked at him like I was now, everything else faded into the background and I felt secure in displaying how I felt for him. I leaned forward, not answering his question, but slid my hand around the back of his neck and pulled him to me and laid my lips against his. I kept it light, considering we were in the center of a romantic restaurant and not a rave, but it was just as seductive as all of our other kisses, because it was with Kyson and the rest didn't matter. "Always." I answered him finally before pulling back and enjoying the way his cheeks flushed as he drank the rest of his glass of wine before smiling at me. "So, how did things end with him?"

He groaned. "He got famous, believe it or not, and tried to keep me as a New York City groupie when he came back around, but I cut ties and never looked back."

"Good for you." I said proudly.

"How did things end with the woman who wasn't good enough for you?" He asked, and I felt the shiver of anxiety ripple through my body as I tried to figure out how to answer him. But thankfully, our waiter showed up seconds later with our plates and we lost ourselves in the meal in front of us. And to say I didn't welcome the distraction to avoid the topic of my ex-wife would be a lie.

I drove us through the dark city in comfortable silence, with my hand resting on his thigh under his own hand. We'd spent the entire evening talking and getting to know each other, but I steered the conversation towards him and his life as often as I could. He told me about his sister and her job working in the NHL, and his doting parents who lived down in Florida but visited a couple of times a year, and I felt lacking compared to his happy family life.

He, of course, didn't make me feel that way in the least, but I literally had no one in my life aside from Mav, Cora, and Reid.

Well, and now hopefully Kyson.

I pulled into our parking lot and turned the car off, but neither of us made any moves to get out. My fingers traced back and forth over his muscular thigh and his fingers did the same to the top of my hand. The touches were so innocent compared to what else we'd done, but they still left me feeling high as a kite, and I wasn't in a hurry to give that up.

"So." Ky said, turning to look at me with a smile teasing his lips.

"So." I replied. "Where do we go from here?" I admit, I was looking to him for some guidance. Back in the day, it was rare for me to leave a date without having sex with a woman because I rarely dated anyone who wasn't an obvious, sure deal back at that stage in my life. But it had literally been six years since I dated, and almost four years since I'd had sex.

Something that I felt I needed to divulge to Kyson.

"Before you answer that." I interrupted him as he started talking. "There's something I want to get off my chest." I said as he leaned back against the door with trepidation in his eyes. "That woman that we talked about earlier," I started, letting my eyes fall to the gearshift between us. "She did a number on me. And I'm embarrassed to say that I haven't been with anyone physically since, because I haven't allowed myself to feel worthy long enough to be."

"How long ago was that?" He asked gently.

I sighed, "Almost four years."

He sucked in a quick breath and I inwardly cringed, waiting for him to say he wasn't interested in being my drought breaker or something. But what I wasn't expecting was for him to lean across the center console and slide both hands around the back of my neck, tilting my head up to look at him. "It's been four years since you were last touched like this?" He whispered, only an inch away from my lips.

"Yes." I replied and gave into my desire, leaning in against his touch, hungry for that comfort it promised.

"God, Dex." He groaned and leaned in, sealing his lips over mine, coaxing them open and teasing my tongue with his. "Stay with me tonight. Let me give you the world." He said, and I fell headfirst into the allure of comfort and intimacy.

"If you're sure you want to get into this with me." I said, pulling back to look at him. "This isn't casual for me, Kyson. I wanted you to understand that first, I don't do one-night stands or casual hookups anymore."

He groaned and kissed me again. "I don't want to be just a hookup for you, Dex. I want to be more. So don't worry about scaring me off."

I kissed him deeper, letting our touch express everything I didn't have words for. "Let's go. Before I take you right here in the front seat." I growled, forcing myself to pull back and get out of my car.

By the time I got around the hood, he was shutting his door and meeting me with a quick pace as I opened the lobby door and followed him to the elevator. The second the doors were closed behind us in the empty car, he pushed me against the wall and kissed me again, pressing his body against mine from head to toe. "I don't think I've ever wanted someone as badly as I want you." He hissed, kissing down my neck and sliding the top few buttons open on my shirt.

"Same." I grunted, grabbing the elastic from his hair and tugging it free. "Fucking same." I threaded my fingers into his long brown hair and slid them through, savoring the silky feel against my skin. "I've imagined fisting you hair in my hand so many times the last few days." I admitted as he kissed his way down my chest as he opened more buttons. I would have been worried about someone knowing exactly what we were doing in the elevator if we weren't the only two that lived on our floor.

"Well, lucky for you, I'm really into having my hair pulled." He said cheekily before stepping back and walking backwards out of the elevator that had stopped without my notice. Challenge blazed in his eyes as I stalked forward down the hall towards his apartment door. I felt like a hunter as I chased him, feeling a spur of electricity jolt through my body when he turned and ran for his door, sliding the key in the slot as I pressed my body against his back. I pushed his hair aside and latched my lips onto his neck, nipping the skin as he moaned and pressed back against me before throwing the door open and pulling me inside. His apartment was dark, but we didn't bother with the lights.

We both knew the layout like the back of our hands, for several reasons. He kicked his boots off, and I followed suit before he pulled me down the hallway towards his bedroom.

When we got inside, I kissed him again as my hands grabbed the bottom of his shirt and pulled it up over his head, breaking the kiss only long enough to toss it to the side. I brought my hands down flat on his abs; they twitched under the contact, and I groaned at how right it felt to touch him like this. He unbuttoned the last few buttons of my shirt and pulled it free, pushing it down my arms before leaning in and kissing his way across my chest, sucking on one nipple briefly before moving to the other.

"Fuck." I grunted, threading his hair through my fingers again and using it as a handle. "Do you have any hard limits?" I asked, gasping as his fingers pushed their way behind my belt and into the waistband of my briefs. My brain was short circuiting from his touch, but I wanted to do this right. "Kyson, slow down." I panted, and he pulled back to look up at me, with such longing in his eyes I hated saying anything at all. But I couldn't screw this up. His blinds were open, letting the moonlight cast a magical glow over his body, and I wanted to explore every inch of him.

He chuckled and ran his hands through his hair, taking a step back. "Sorry." He looked down at my body and shook his head. "Your body is so fucking sexy Dexter, I just got carried away." He took another step back and sat down on the edge of his bed, taking a deep breath. "Degradation." He finally said. "I don't like to be degraded. But that's it. I'm a bottom, though I have topped before, and I like to be fucked hard and rough or slow and passionately." He shook his head. "I'm not complicated."

"This is all very complicated for me." I said honestly but didn't feel the anxiety trying to overtake me like I'd assumed it would when faced with having sex with a man for the first time. "I've done anal before, but I don't know what to do to make it feel good for you as a man. At all."

He stood up off the bed and walked back to me where I still stood, unmoving by the door. "Why don't we start with just exploring each other, so we can learn what each of us like at the same time?" He asked, leaning in and gently kissing me. "You don't have to have experience with a man to be an excellent lover, Dex. Just be giving and honest. That's all I need from you."

"Giving and honest." I repeated, letting my head fall back as he teased his way back down my neck. His whiskers were incredibly stimulating, leaving a trail of shivers everywhere that he kissed. "I can do that."

"Good." He said and pulled me towards the bed and then pushed me down to sit on the edge with a hungry look in his eyes. He slowly sank to his knees between my legs and kept his eyes locked on mine as he undid my belt and the snap of my pants. "Let's start with letting me finally see your cock." He said greedily. "I've seen the movement of your arm as you've jacked off, and I've seen the bulge in your pants. I've even felt it rub against me, but I haven't seen it." He said.

As he tugged on the waistband of my pants and boxer briefs, I raised my hips to aid him in removing them. I watched him fixating on my groin as my cock was exposed. He pulled my pants off the rest of the way and then slid my socks off, all the time never letting his eyes leave my erection.

It twitched under his watchful stare, and the tip leaked pre-cum as he slid his palms flat up my thighs towards it. "Holy fucking shit, Dex." He whispered, tearing his eyes away from it and up to look at me. "You're going to ruin me for any other man."

"Can you take me?" I asked, suddenly unsure. I knew I was hung, but I'd never had much trouble getting it inside of a woman if I gave enough attention to foreplay for her.

He smirked at me. "I can. But you'll be the biggest for me and it'll take some time to get ready for you."

"Show me how." I said easily. I suddenly ached to please him and touch him.

"After I taste you." He said, sliding forward between my thighs and reaching up to run his thumb over my bottom lip. "Can I suck your cock, Dexter?"

I growled deep in my chest and bit the pad of his thumb before sucking it into my mouth and letting it go with a pop. My hands fisted the blanket under my hips as I fought to keep them still. "Only if you teach me how to return the favor." I answered honestly and his eyes fluttered closed as he bit his bottom lip.

"How the fuck did I get so lucky with you?" He mused, but he didn't wait for my reply, instead he leaned forward and ran his tongue up the underside of my cock where it stood hard between us. "Mmh." He moaned, swirling his tongue around the head of it, tasting me.

"Ky." I groaned, letting my head fall back briefly before tilting it back down; I didn't want to miss watching a second of this.

He looked up at me as he wrapped his lips around the tip and slowly worked them down the shaft, twirling his tongue around me on the way back up and then repeating it until the head of my cock was pressing down the back of his throat. My fists tightened and my thighs bunched around his chest as he relaxed his jaw and pushed more of my cock down his throat.

Blinding pleasure crashed over me as he hummed and twisted his head back and forth, twirling his throat around my cock until his lips kissed the base of me. He pulled back up off of me, gasping for breath with a sinful smirk before doing it again.

"You're a fucking god, Kyson." I panted, feeling drops of sweat beading up between my shoulder blades as I tried to control my restraint to keep from blowing my load already. I wanted to savor this, but he was fucking talented.

He pulled up off of me again and wrapped his fist around my slick shaft, sliding it up and down as he licked his lips. They were swollen and puffy from sucking me off, and I ached to kiss them. "I want you to fuck my mouth." He said, flicking his tongue out over the slit in the end of my cock, making my hips jerk madly. "Grab a handful of my hair and take the pleasure you've been suffering without over these last four years, Dexter."

"I can't." I said quickly, shaking my head. "I'm already so on edge, I don't want to lose control and hurt you."

He smiled wickedly and leaned back, pulling me to stand in front of him. "I'm on my knees for you, Dexter. I want you to lose control." He slid one hand under my cock to tease my balls, massaging them and pulling on them as I moaned. "I want to make you feel better than you've ever felt before, baby. I'm not some delicate flower that you need to be gentle with. I can take it."

I stared down at him as he leaned forward and licked up the underside of my shaft again before sitting back and sticking his tongue out flat, raising his eyebrow in challenge. My brain misfired, and I stepped forward, fisting my cock and slapping it against his tongue before thrusting forward and into his hot, waiting mouth. I growled as he relaxed his throat and let me press my cock all the way down it in one thrust.

My hands moved of their own accord as I slid them through his hair, holding his head how I wanted him, and pulled out before thrusting back in all the way again. He hummed and moaned there on his knees as I used his mouth to pleasure myself and it was the biggest fucking turn on ever.

For him to be so selfless and requesting for me to find pleasure in his body without giving him any in return was something I'd never experienced before. Thrusting powerfully into his throat as he dug his fingernails into the backs of my thighs, holding on as I lost control. "I'm so close." I gasped, unable to hold off a second longer than my orgasm ripped its way through my body. "Kyson." I groaned as the first burst of come shot out of the end of my cock and down the tight confines of his throat as I kept thrusting. He hummed appreciatively as he swallowed with each thrust, constricting his throat muscles around my cock even tighter, and I catapulted into the longest orgasm of my life.

My hips slowed but kept lazily thrusting my cock down his throat as he played with my balls again. I finally forced myself to pull free of his sexy as hell mouth and he licked my cock clean before licking his lips and smiling up at me as I fell back onto his bed in shock.

He chuckled at me, proud of himself, and laid down next to me while I gathered my wits. "I've been doing it with the wrong sex my whole fucking life." I mused, and he smirked, gloating.

"Nah baby, man or woman, doesn't matter. It's me you've been missing in life." He said confidently, and I rolled over towards him, covering his body with mine.

"I don't think I've ever heard anything more correct before." I said before leaning down and kissing him passionately, pushing my tongue into his mouth and moaning when I tasted myself on his tongue. "I want to do that for you, though I know that I won't even compare to your skill level."

"You could blow air on my cock right now and I'd come all over your face, Dexter." He said, laughing as I smiled down at him.

"Show me." I said, sliding off his body and tracing my fingers down over his abs to the button on his jeans. I undid them and he lifted his hips to help me pull them and his briefs down his legs. He scooted up the bed and laid on his back with his arm under his head, staring down his sexy cut body at me. "You're so sexy." I whispered before kneeling between his spread thighs, face to face with his cock.

He was thinner than me, but nearly as long and I knew that someday I was going to take him in my ass, and it was no doubt going to be life changing. My cock twitched at the thought, but I forced myself to focus on his pleasure and pushed my own to the back burner for a moment.

"All men are similar, Dex." He said, sliding his hand through my hair before trailing his fingers down the side of my face. "Just do what you like done to you, and I'll enjoy every fucking second. I promise."

"Okay." I said, turning my head and kissing his palm before wrapping my hand around him, reveling in the way it felt to hold someone else's cock. I leaned forward and kissed the very tip of it and smirked when his hips jerked and he twitched in my hand. A drop of pre-cum leaked from the slit, and I tentatively licked it up with my tongue. I was expecting something repulsive to flood my tastebuds, but it wasn't unpleasant at all. Salty, but not anything I couldn't manage.

I spit on the head of him and slid my fist up and down his length before sucking on the head of his cock as my fist kept working up and down. "Just like that." He hissed and thrust his hips up. I pushed my head down as far as I could go, feeling him push against the back of my throat before I gagged in a very unsexy way and then pulled back off. "I don't need it deep, just suck the head hard." He instructed, pulling my bottom lip down before throwing his head back onto the bed as I sucked hard, like he said. "Fuck!" He grunted and his body tensed. I rolled his smooth balls between my fingers as I gave him the attention he asked for and he gasped. "I'm going to come. Pull off if you don't want it in your mouth."

I forced myself to keep my lips wrapped around his cock and not over think it as he roared and started filling my mouth with come. I tried to swallow it down as fast as it came, but lost some out around his cock as he went limp under me, gasping for breath. Running my tongue up his cock like I was licking a melting ice cream cone, I cleaned him up like he had done for me as he continued to twitch and jerk in my hand.

He slid his hand around the back of my head and pulled me up the bed to lay next to him as he rolled over to kiss me. Our legs tangled together, and our hands explored each other lazily as we both enjoyed our post orgasm bliss. I noticed his eyes getting heavy as he slid in closer to me and took that as a good sign to pause and relax.

"Are you sure that was your first time?" He asked sleepily.

"Hmm. First of many, I think." I replied.

"God, I'm a lucky son of a bitch." He joked and then yawned. "Just need a minute to come back down to earth."

I laid my head down on a pillow that smelled like him and relaxed as he snuggled deeper into my chest, feeling the most at ease that I'd felt in years.

Maybe Cora was right about that soulmates stuff after all.

Because I would never find anyone that could compare to Kyson now that I'd had a taste of him.

Chapter 9 – Kyson

I hadn't meant to fall asleep after the life-changing blow job Dexter had given me. But sometime later I woke up, tangled up with him in my bed, and felt fucking giddy about it. Despite being nearly the same height, I adored how his larger build made him loom over me when we cuddled like this. He laid on his side and had both arms wrapped around me where I lay with my head against his chest. I looked up at his face as he slept and realized he looked relaxed, something he didn't seem to be often. Even after I sucked him off, he was eager to return the favor and hadn't rested for long.

But even though his face looked relaxed, his cock was... anything but. He was hard against my stomach, and I desperately wanted to play more with his delicious body. I leaned forward and kissed his chest, teasing the skin with my tongue and before long his body was stirring against mine. His hands tightened around my waist and his erection twitched between us, causing my own to harden against his leg.

"Kyson." He breathed out seductively with his eyes still closed as a whisper of a smile pulled his full lips back.

"I need you," I whispered into the moonlight, not even caring how desperate I sounded at the moment. His eyes opened, and he looked down at me and the blue around his pupils shrunk as desire burned bright in them.

"I'm right here." He said, stretching and thrusting his cock against my stomach and groaning. "Hard and ready." He added.

"I need to go prep," I said, feeling shivers of excitement chasing away the sleep as I thought about how good it was going to feel to take him inside of me for the first time.

"What do you mean?" He asked.

"I need to... loosen myself up to take you." I cringed at the awkwardness of having to explain it.

"I know what prep means, Ky. But what I don't understand is why you have to go somewhere to do it." His arms tightened around my body as he rolled us over until I was on my back and he was lying on top of me. My legs spread wide to accommodate his body and his cock nestled right against mine, drawing moans from the both of us.

"I usually just do it in the bathroom before sex," I answered truthfully.

"I don't want you locking yourself away to prep your body to take me. I want every part of this." He said, sliding his hand down my back and over my ass before squeezing it. "I thought it was a part of foreplay, something that I could help you with."

I groaned as his fingers inched closer to my ass because I realized something then; I'd never been in a relationship with a guy who cared much about my comfort during sex. It had always been up to me to make sure I was ready for it. And now this brand new bi-sexual man was laying in my bed wanting to pleasure me and be a part of my comfort and I didn't know what to do with that.

"No one has helped me before, to be honest," I said quickly and his hands stilled.

"None of your past boyfriends have played with your ass outside of shoving their cocks into it?" He asked indignantly, and I shook my head. "Jesus fuck." He cursed. "Roll over." He said and leaned back on his knees before flipping me over onto my stomach. "What do you use?"

I looked over my shoulder at him and had to take a deep breath to focus because he kneeled behind me, straddling one of my legs with his cock hard and angry looking swinging between his thighs as he stared down at me. He was so sexy and dominant, and I nearly melted under his stare.

"Kyson." He growled, "Stop eye fucking me and tell me what you use to loosen yourself up so I can get it and get you ready." He said authoritatively before reaching down to stroke his cock. "Because I'm fucking dying to bury myself in your tight ass, and I want to make sure you feel nothing but ecstasy when I do it."

"Uh-" I paused and then shook myself free of the mental images he was conjuring up in my dirty brain. "Lube and my fingers." I nodded my head to the bedside table, and he leaned over me to grab the bottle and the towel I kept in there for the mess. "How are you so confident right now?" I asked him, confused.

He leaned down and laid sweet gentle kisses on my shoulder and then down my spine until he kneeled behind me again. "I might be fucking a man for the first time in my life, but I already told you I've done anal before. I know what goes into it beforehand."

"Mmh." I hummed, unable to form a coherent sentence as he opened the cap and poured some lube onto his fingers. He grabbed a pillow and lifted my hips to put it under me, arching my back and popping my ass up into the air. Fucking man knew what he was doing.

"Reach back and spread yourself open for me." He commanded, and I did as I was told, opening myself up to his gaze seconds before he dripped more lube directly onto my tight entrance. I hissed, and he chuckled. "Sorry. I'll warm it up next time, but I'm far too eager right now."

I groaned in response as he stroked one of his thick fingers against my hole, massaging the ring of muscles. "Dex." I moaned. The touch was so light it was torture. "Put it in, please baby," I begged.

He chuckled again, and I felt his cock twitch against my leg as he slowly pushed his finger inside of me, twirling it around and then deepening it until his other knuckles pressed against me. "Fuck you're tight." He groaned, slowly sliding his finger back out until only the tip was in and dripping more lube on me. "You're going to strangle my cock."

"Dexter," I warned in frustration. "I'm going to come all over your pillow if you keep talking to me like that."

"My pillow huh?" He asked as he pressed a second finger against my opening and added it to the first. His free hand grabbed onto my ass cheek over my hand where I was holding my cheeks open and he squeezed like he was trying to restrain himself.

"That feels so good." I moaned, dropping my face into the blankets and biting them as he started fingering me with both thick digits.

"That's not even half the girth of my cock." He growled, leaning forward, and biting my shoulder as he started scissoring his fingers inside of me. I moaned and writhed under his large body as he edged me closer to an orgasm I knew was going to wreck me. "Where is your prostate?"

I choked on my tongue, coughing uncomfortably, considering he was still fingering me. "Why?"

"I thought it was a pleasure point, like a g-spot." He said, suddenly sounding unsure.

"It is-" I stuttered, "But you don't have to-"

"Kyson." He growled, cutting me off. "Stop shying away from pleasure."

I groaned, feeling thankful that it was dark and my face was buried in the blankets because I was sure my face had turned as red as a tomato. Dexter's free hand came up and grabbed a fistful of my hair and pulled my head back until I was nearly looking at the ceiling. I groaned as painful pleasure tingled down my spine. This man knew how to grab a handful of hair.

"Tell me. Now."

"Forward." I gasped, moaning as he added another finger into me. "We call it a p-spot. Point your fingers forward towards my cock."

He twisted his wrist and on the next penetration, his fingers rubbed directly up against that heavenly spot deep inside of me and my toes curled. He twirled his fingers around, scissoring them again, and recognizing the difference in the texture of that one spot, he chuckled, kissing my spine right above my ass. "There it is." He cooed.

"Fuck." I panted, arching my hips further to take more of him. "Yes. Oh god."

"You like that, don't you?" He purred seductively as he started thrusting his fingers in faster and deeper. "Am I making you feel good?"

"Better than I've ever felt before." I gasped, and he pulled my hair again, tilting my head back. "I'm so close, I need you, Dexter," I begged. "Please fuck me."

"Are you ready for me?" He asked through clenched teeth, and I could tell he was struggling to control his own need.

"Yes!" I almost screamed. "Please. Give me your cock."

He bit down on my shoulder again as he let go of my hair, letting my head sag back down into the blankets as he eased his fingers out of me. "I'm going to fuck you so good, Ky." He moaned into my ear before reaching over me and grabbing a condom from the table.

"Please." I moaned, letting go of my cheeks and looking over my shoulder at him. He rolled the condom on his thick cock and his eyes fluttered closed for a moment before he grabbed the bottle of lube and poured it on generously.

"How do you want it?" He asked, pausing as he rubbed the lube onto his cock and then wiped his hand on the towel.

"Just like this." I panted, shaking my hips back and forth to entice him to fuck me already.

"I can't reach your cock if you're flat on your stomach." He said in a disturbed voice, like it pained him to hesitate any longer.

"I don't need you to touch it, Dex! I'm going to come from the pleasure of you inside of me alone." I said frustratedly. "Please, just fuck me!"

He straddled my legs and pushed my cheeks apart before slapping the head of his cock against my hole. "If you insist." He growled as he pushed the thick, bulbous head in past the first ring of muscles.

"Jesus Christ." I groaned at the swift burn that accompanied it and gripped the blankets in my fists. "Holy fuck."

"You're telling me." He bit out between clenched teeth as he pulled the head of his cock back out of my ass and then pushed it back in. "You have no idea how sexy you look taking my cock like this, Kyson." He moaned. "I've never been so aroused in my life."

"Fuck me," I begged again, as I lifted my hips and pushed back on his erection, causing us both to groan.

He flattened his hand against the small of my back and lifted himself into almost a push-up position and then pistoned forward, burying his cock balls deep inside of me. He hissed and then gave me everything I begged for.

His hips slammed into me, and pleasure and pain mingled, drawing me into the headspace somewhere between awake and out of it as I pushed back into him with each thrust.

He leaned forward and wrapped his hand around my throat, tilting my head back to kiss me as he groaned words of praise and affirmation with each thrust.

"You feel so good."

Thrust.

"Take it."

Thrust.

"You're heaven wrapped around my cock."

"I'm so close." I panted. "You're fucking me so good, Dex."

"Me too." He hissed, and then he stilled. "Up." He commanded, wrapping his hands around my hips as he pulled me up onto my knees. I protested the change, but seconds later his feverish hand wrapped around my cock, fisting it tightly as he started thrusting again, and I was lost.

Utterly fucking lost to it all.

He laid himself against my back and bit my ear before sucking it into his mouth. "Come for me Kyson. I want to feel you lose your mind because of me."

"I-" I gasped and arched my back even further as my orgasm crashed over me. "I'm coming," I grunted, seconds before my dick exploded all over the towel he had managed to lay down under me without me noticing.

"Yes." He hissed. "I'm right there with you." His hips slammed forward one last time, and I felt his cock jerk inside of me as he filled the condom. I let him ride me through his orgasm as he brutally fucked me just how I'd begged him to until he stilled and fought to get air into his lungs.

I tossed the towel to the floor and fell forward on the bed, and he let me go, dragging his cock from my body. My ass felt deliciously used, and I was fucking satisfied so deeply, I didn't think I'd ever come down from it.

I was distantly aware of Dex cleaning up and then felt him wiping me clean before settling on the bed next to me. I rolled onto my side and snuggled in against his chest with a smile I couldn't get to fall from my face.

He kissed my forehead and wrapped his arms around me, pulling me even closer. "Did I do okay for my first time?" He asked, and I snorted and bit his peck beneath my cheek at the ridiculousness of that question. But I also wanted to reassure him at the same time.

"I've never felt so treasured in my entire life, Dexter Chase," I said with a sigh. "But the more important question is, did you enjoy yourself?"

"Hmm." He hummed like he was contemplating his answer and I groaned, drawing a chuckle from his chest under my head. "Yes, I did Kyson. I'm anxiously awaiting the moment I can do that to you again."

"Hmm." Now it was my time to hum because I was trying to not sound so eager, but we both knew I was more than willing for round three.

"Go to sleep." He said, once again kissing my forehead. "I don't plan on leaving this bedroom for quite a while, and you'll need your rest."

Hot damn.

Chapter 10 – Dexter

I didn't make good on my promise not to leave his bedroom, because at seven am Sunday morning, my phone started ringing off the hook about some emergency crisis that Mav needed me at work for. I'd almost told him to fuck off, but figured given how I left things Friday, I was lucky he was calling me at all and not finding a new lawyer for his company.

So I frustratedly got out of Kyson's bed, leaving the sleepy and rumpled-looking sex god laying there, and went to my apartment to shower and then went into work. Kyson had been understanding, but it still chapped my ass a bit to leave him after what we shared.

The further I got away from our apartments and closer to work, the more anxious I got, and the ache inside of me to go back home was rising.

But I forced myself to park in the garage and go into the office as though nothing was amiss. When I got off the elevator, Maverick, Reid, and Cora were all standing in Mav's office waiting for me.

"I didn't realize this was an all-hands-on-deck type of problem," I said, standing in the doorway with my hand in my pocket. When Maverick had called me this morning, he had told me that the terms of a merger with a tech company out of California had changed drastically and that he was on the verge of walking away from the deal if they didn't shape up. So he needed me to come in to deal with the new contracts, combing over them with a fine-tooth comb to make sure they weren't trying to get one over on him. But that didn't tell me why Reid and Cora were here on a Sunday morning.

I looked over at Cora and she smiled at me, but it didn't quite meet her eyes as she sat on the couch with her feet up. Then I turned my attention to Mav and Reid, who simply sat staring at me like I was some sort of mystery to them.

Tendrils of dread climbed up my spine as unease settled over me.

They knew.

"I'm not a sideshow." I bit out, "If you can't get your heads out of your asses and treat me the same way you did last week, then say so now, and I'll quit."

Cora sighed and stood up, holding her hands on her swollen belly over her purple sun dress. "Dexter." She warned, walking over to Maverick's side, and he pushed himself back in his chair to make room for her as she sat in his lap. He still said nothing, though.

Which was very un-Maverick-like.

"You think we care that you're gay?" Reid asked, sounding offended. "Do we not get a little more credit than that? After years of friendship?"

He sounded wounded, which was not normal for the charismatic social butterfly.

"I'm not gay." I huffed out and then rubbed my hand over my face. "If it's not because of that, then why are you staring at me silently? I've never known either of you to bite your tongues a day in your life, so why start now?"

"Because we're offended," Maverick said sternly, his eyebrows dropping over his eyes in anger. "Why did you think you couldn't tell us that Friday?" He asked, "Have we not been there for you and supported you through everything in the past?"

I sighed and tossed my case down in a chair and walked over to the desk, taking my usual seat next to Reid, across from Mav.

"I didn't tell Cora in place of you guys," I said, trying to make sense of everything for them. "I told Cora because she was at the right place at the right time, as I fucking figured it out."

"That you're gay?" Reid asked again.

"That I'm bi-sexual. Or that I felt attracted to a man for the first time," I snapped and then groaned. "It was... pretty unnerving and I'm figuring this out as I go." I finished.

"How did last night go?" Cora asked gently, and I looked at Mav and then Reid in question before she just rolled her eyes. "I told Mav, and he told Reid." She huffed. "The date though, how did it go?"

I leaned back in my chair and took a deep breath, trying to work up the nerve to have this conversation with the three most important people in my life. "It went great."

Cora smiled brightly and leaned into Mav's chest more with happy doe eyes. "So now what?"

"I don't know." Shrugging my shoulders, "I would have had time to figure it out more this morning, but someone woke me up and dragged me to work when I planned on staying in bed all day." I said dryly.

Maverick finally showed some emotion besides hurt as he rolled his eyes. "I've never known you to sleep in on a weekend, Dex. Even when you were married."

I laughed lightly and raised my eyebrows at him. "Yeah, well, I'm getting old."

"Or you have a bed mate finally worth staying in bed for," Reid said with a wink.

Leave it to Reid to take it there.

"So, who is this mystery man? And when do we get to meet him?" Maverick asked, tightening his arms around Cora's belly.

"Ooh!" She said excitedly, sitting up straighter on his lap. "Bring him as a date to the auction on Saturday!"

"Wait a second!" Reid jumped up. "You don't get out of being auctioned off like a head of cattle just because you're shacking up with someone now!" He said, pointing a finger at me sternly. "If I have to parade myself around up on that stage, so do you, fucker."

I laughed and leaned back in my chair. "I never was a part of the auction to begin with," I said, and Cora scoffed but said nothing. "And I don't think I'm going to bring him around the likes of you three soon, or else he'll run for the hills for sure."

"Hey!" Mav recoiled. "We're civilized and well-mannered individuals." He tried to stay stern, but his grin split wide open before he finished the sentence, and he lowered his face into Cora's neck to hide it.

"Cora is well mannered and civilized, but you two, not so much." I deadpanned before clearing my throat and taking a more serious note. "But back to Friday." I started, but Reid just stood up and walked over to the bar alongside the room, interrupting me.

"Don't worry about it man, it's not like we haven't put you through enough the last few months, I guess you earned a bit of retribution." He said, as he started rifling through the liquor bottles on the cart. "Hey, why are you bone dry over here?" He asked, turning with two empty crystal decanters in his hands.

"Because you have a drinking problem, and I'm no longer going to be the dealer you use to feed it," Maverick said sternly, and the air in the room changed around us.

"I don't have a drinking problem." Reid snapped, returning the bottles to where they were and turning back to us with fire in his eyes.

"It's not even eight am on a Sunday morning, Reid. That's a problem." I said, nodding to the empty glass still in his hand. His brown eyes darkened as he looked from me to Mav and then to the door.

"Whatever." Rid snapped. "You three have a merry ol' Sunday at Hawthorn tower then. I'm not needed for the merger; the numbers haven't changed. So I'll be seeing my way out."

"I'm implementing some new rules, Reid." Maverick bit out, rising to his feet and depositing Cora in his chair. "Sobriety checks every morning and strict no alcohol rules here inside of Hawthorn." He said, staring down at our best friend. I felt myself looking between the two of them, waiting for one of them to throw punches, simply because that was the kind of friendship they always had.

"This is bullshit Mav, I only started drinking the hard stuff because you served it around the clock to swindle all of your clients."

"You're not my client Reid!" Mav snapped, "You're my fucking CFO and I need you to be clear-headed and on the fucking ball when you're here. And for too long, I've turned a blind eye to it all in the name of friendship and because I was just as fucked up as you were. But no more. We need to be better."

"We?" Reid scoffed, moving towards the door and shaking his head. "You two have it all figured out, huh?" He demanded, looking at Maverick. "You've got your perfect blonde bombshell of a trophy wife carrying your baby, ready to continue on the Jones family line for generations to come." He turned to me. "And you've had some shelf awareness life-changing moment and suddenly you're bi-sexual and happy after a week of knowing someone. Even after four years of pathetic self-induced celibacy because some chick hurt your feelings." He said with a snide grimace.

I stood up so fast from my chair that it toppled over behind me. "She didn't hurt my feelings, Reid, and you fucking know that; don't you dare diminish my pain because you're hurting now too." I roared, pointing my finger at him, and his face whitened. "How could you even fucking say that when you were the one that shoved your fingers down my throat to make me throw up after finding me unconscious with an entire bottle of pills in my stomach?" I snapped and hated how the memory assaulted me after numbing it out for so long. "She stole what I thought was my only reason to live when she stole my son. You're pissed and hurt and embarrassed and I get that, but don't you dare throw me down in the fucking dirt just so you'll have someone to wallow with down there." I turned and righted the chair I'd been sitting in and then stalked over to grab my briefcase. Taking a deep breath, I walked out. "I'll be in my office when you need me."

I fought to keep my heart rate level and my temper down for hours after that conversation, but even the boring and monotonous legal contracts I was reviewing didn't dull me down like usual. Maverick had sent Cora home and had spent the rest of the day in my office with me, silently taking up space near me and communicating when needed. It was nearing the early evening before he finally spoke about anything other than our jobs.

"Why did I never know about the pills?" He asked softly, with no anger or dominance in his voice. I looked up at him across my desk and dropped my pen, leaning back in my seat and mulling it over in my head before I opened my mouth.

"Because I was ashamed at how close to death, I'd been when Reid found me," I answered truthfully. "And I made him swear to never tell you about it." I shrugged my shoulders and tapped my fingers against the desk in nervous energy. "He promised to keep it from you if I made good on my promise to fall down the straight and narrow after that, but he said if he ever got any inclination that I was headed towards that slippery slope again, he'd blow me in and call in the cavalry."

"You could have told me. I could have helped you, Dexter." He said.

I nodded my head, "I know. But I'd learned my lesson already by that point and I chose to numb everything in my life rather than live with the pain any longer."

"And now?" He asked, threading his fingers back and forth in front of him.

I sighed and rubbed my palm over my whiskers. "And now I'm slowly thawing out, which is allowing me to feel good things again, like joy and excitement."

"And the bad things?"

I nodded. "Also coming back in, but I'm finding that time has eased a lot of it."

He turned and looked out the window on the side of my office and nodded, lost in thought. "Do you ever think of him?" He asked, turning back to me. "Sammy?"

Just hearing my son's name again after so long of avoiding the fact that he still existed reignited that burning pain in my chest that had been festering since he was taken from me.

I looked deep into his blue eyes and forced myself to admit the truth. "Every single day."

He shook his head like the answer pained him. "Dex." He sighed. "I wish I could fix that for you, take that pain away for you somehow."

I shook my head and took a deep breath. "I know, man. But you didn't cause it, so you can't take it away." I sighed. "I don't think it'll ever stop hurting to think of him, but I know that when I try to envision who he is today, I feel joy, however small, in knowing that he's probably still the happiest kid in the world. Hope had her pitfalls and faults, we know that, but she was never a bad mom to him, and that's the only thing that gives me any peace in this."

He nodded and then swallowed. "I'm terrified of becoming a dad. To be honest with you."

I watched him for a moment, trying to remember the last time he was openly vulnerable with me like this. "Why?"

"Because I'm going to fuck it up." He said instantly, "At some point, I'm going to hurt Cora or our baby and that will destroy me."

"You're not the same guy you were before Mav, you've grown so much, even in the last few months."

"I left her, Dex." He said exasperatedly. "I walked away from my wife days after finding out she was pregnant. What kind of fucking idiot does that?"

"The kind of idiot who genuinely thought he was doing what was best for her all along," I said, leaning forward on my desk and looking him straight in the eye. "Mav, regardless of my personal agreement, your decision to remove yourself from her life was driven by a genuine belief in her safety."

"But she wasn't, was she?" He asked and shook his head. "She was so sick while I was hiding away from her, she needed me, and I failed her. What if I do that to her or our daughter?"

"You won't," I said confidently as he protested, but I held my hand up, silencing him. "You won't Maverick. Because from the very first time you see that little girl, the first time you hear her angry wail, or feel her soft skin against your chest, you'll be hooked. It's indescribable until you've experienced it firsthand, Mav, but it's life-changing to meet your own child. So believe me when I tell you I know for a fact that you'll do everything in your power to take care of your girls. Without fail."

He watched me closely, letting my words process through his brain before he nodded slowly. "Do you ever think about having kids now?"

He asked and tilted his head, "I mean, before you met Kyson or even since? There are options out there for two dads, too."

I chuckled and shook my head. "I want kids again someday. But I don't know what Kyson's feelings are about it, and it's way too early to even approach that subject. So I guess you'll just have to keep Cora barefoot and pregnant so I can spoil my nieces and nephews for now."

He laughed and wagged his eyebrows, "I very much plan to fill our bedrooms with babies and you're more than welcome to spoil them senseless. But don't wait too long to talk about it with Kyson, I'd hate for you two to have totally different opinions on it and then suddenly have it become super messy with deeper feelings and time invested in something that's going in two different directions."

I nodded, "I hear you, man."

"Good." He said. "Now, let's talk about what the fuck we're going to do about our oldest child, Reid."

I groaned and rubbed my hands up and down my face. "I haven't had enough sleep to figure that puzzle out today."

On my way home from the office, I stopped and got some takeout from the Thai place near my apartment and felt the giddy tingles up my spine as I rode the elevator up. I didn't know if Ky was home or not, but I was eager to see him. Especially given that I left him naked in bed this morning after our first night together.

I walked into my apartment and set the bags down on the counter, and looked across the courtyard. It took me a while, but I finally found him sprawled out on the floor of his spare bedroom surrounded by fancy high heel shoes as he took pictures of them each before putting them in separate piles with other clothes.

I stood there for a while and watched him as he worked. His hair was down, and he was shirtless, wearing only a pair of black sweatpants and bare feet, and it was sinfully sexy. I took my phone out and typed out a message to him and then watched him as he got it.

Can I tear you away from your work for some Thai takeout?

He read the message and peeked over his shoulder, finding me standing in my apartment, and smiled brightly before replying.

Do I have to get dressed to come over?

I groaned and replied instantly.

It would only add time to my endeavor to get you undressed again. Coming.

Yes. You sure will be.

I turned away and started setting out the containers and a couple of minutes later, a knock sounded on my door.

"Come in," I said and wiped my hands on a dish towel as Ky walked in, wearing a pair of slide-on sandals and his black sweats, carrying a bottle of wine and a smile.

"It smells delicious in here." He said as he set the wine down and kicked his sandals off, but he made no move to come any closer to me and I could see the hesitation in his body language.

"Is something wrong?" I asked, leaning back against the counter, crossing my ankles.

His lips parted, and he ran a hand through his hair as he walked forward to set the bottle down on the counter. "I don't know how you want to handle things in the light of day." He said, sighing. "You left so quickly this morning that we didn't have time to talk. And the more time that passed without a word from you today," He shrugged, "I'm just not sure where your head is at."

I nodded but didn't move towards him like I ached to do. "Can you start by telling me where your head is at?"

His eyebrows rose, and he bit his lip before letting it pop free and taking a deep breath. "I enjoyed myself last night."

"As did I," I replied instantly.

"And... I enjoy spending time with you." He added slowly, with that damn hesitation again. He was afraid of putting himself out there.

"But?" I asked, sensing it coming.

"But..." He said, and then dragged his hand down his face. "I'm just nervous to get my hopes up, until you figure out what you are feeling."

Nodding again, I played with the belt loops on my slacks. "I enjoyed myself last night, Kyson." I said firmly, "More than I thought I was going to, to be honest. A part of me thought it would feel awkward and clumsy to be with you, or any man. And maybe with anyone else it would have, but with you," I said and leaned forward to take his hand, pulling him close and pushing his hair back from his face. "I've never felt more comfortable in my own skin before. Not once."

His green eyes glowed behind his dark lashes, and a smile tugged on his full lips. "Really?"

"Really," I confirmed, sliding my hands over the taut skin of his hips, and letting my thumbs run back and forth over the band of his sweats. "I enjoy spending time with you too, not just sexually, Kyson. That's why I wanted to feed you dinner and spend time with you tonight. I had no intention of going into the office today because what I wanted to do was spend the entire day lounging around and relaxing with you before the week started again, but my boss is a jerk wad when he wants to be." I joked, and Ky snorted lightly.

"Aren't they all?" He smiled and leaned into me. "How do you still smell so damn good after a long day of paper pushing?" He asked, and I poked his side with my thumb, causing him to jump and laugh. "Kidding!"

"So I don't smell good?" I teased, sliding my hands around his back to drift them up and down the tight muscles there as he smiled against my neck.

"No, you still smell damn near edible, I meant about the paper pushing, though to be honest I'm not sure what a corporate lawyer does, so it could be that."

"Hmm." I hummed and then groaned when his lips gently kissed the skin beneath my ear. I felt his smile again before he licked a trail up my neck and then sucked my earlobe into his mouth. "Kyson," I growled, sliding my hands down to his ass and squeezing. "If you're not careful, I'm going to be eating you for dinner."

He chuckled and bit my neck hard enough to leave a mark, and my hips bucked in pleasure. "Okay, okay." He laughed and pulled back, "Let's eat first." He stepped back and reached down to adjust himself and smirked at me, knowing how badly I wanted him.

"Tease."

"Only for you." He quipped and started rifling through dinner options.

"Hmm." I hummed and shook my head, laughing. "I'll be right back," I said, leaning down behind him to kiss his neck. "I'm going to go change out of my work clothes."

He looked over his shoulder and winked at me as I walked away towards my bedroom. I changed quickly, sliding on a pair of shorts, and forgoing a shirt since he was walking around looking like a damn snack without one.

When I came back out, he was sitting on a pillow on the floor in my living room with an array of dishes spread out on the coffee table. "Is this okay?" He asked, "I thought we could watch a movie or something."

"It's perfect, I'll grab the wine." I took two glasses from the rack and uncorked the bottle before pouring for us both and joined him on the floor. "Damn, this looks good," I said, as my stomach growled.

We ended up turning on a documentary about lost pirate treasure in the Caribbean and ate a ridiculous amount of delicious Thai food until we were both lounging back on the couch, stuffed, and satisfied.

My phone pinged on the table between us, and I opened it up and read the message, and groaned. "Fuck."

"What is it?" He asked, pausing the movie.

"I forgot they were painting in here tomorrow." I looked around at the ugly white walls and contemplated telling Saint to cancel it altogether, because I hated the idea of being disrupted for three days.

"That's right, you have to be out until Thursday, right?" He asked, remembering the conversation from the other day.

"Seems as much." I sighed. "I'll get a hotel room, but it means I won't be around the next few days."

He contemplated that for a moment before shrugging his shoulder. "Feel free to say no, but you could always just stay at my place for the three nights."

I ran that through my head, and he chuckled, holding his hands up. "Hey, I said you could say no. No biggie."

"It's not that I don't want to," I blurted, trying not to hurt his feelings. "It just seems like a lot rather quickly."

"Were you planning on sleeping here alone for the next three nights?" He asked.

I smirked and nudged him with my elbow. "Not necessarily," I said honestly. "It just seems like a lot of pressure on this," I motioned between us, "so soon."

He nodded and took a sip of his wine, and then turned to face me. "I get that, like I said, it's no biggie either way. Get a hotel room somewhere if that makes you feel more comfortable and then you can just play it by ear."

I was waiting for the anxiety and apprehension to grow in my chest at the thought of relying on Kyson for a place to stay, but it never came.

"Want to talk about what's going through your head right now?" He asked gently.

I smiled at his genuine curiosity and laid my hand on his knee as I took a deep breath. "I haven't allowed myself to rely on anyone in four years. It's honestly stressed me out to even contemplate it with anyone else."

"But?"

"But right now... I don't feel that usual anxiety." I replied.

"Is that a good thing?" He had a bit of hope in his eyes behind the gentle easygoingness.

"I don't think it's a bad thing," I admitted, and his shoulders relaxed a bit as he nodded his head.

"Okay, well, feel free to do whatever makes you most comfortable, and I promise not to take it personally either way." He turned the movie back on, effectively tabling the uncomfortable conversation for now.

We went back to eating and relaxing, and I was relieved to not feel any rift between us after that. When I was married, the slightest disagreement between us would lead Hope to nitpick and drone on and on about the topic until it resulted in a catastrophic argument that wouldn't end until neither of us had any energy left in us to even remember what it all started over.

God, it was so nice to feel peace in my soul now that I allowed myself to feel anything at all.

I sprawled out in the corner of the couch with his head on a pillow in my lap as we watched the show. I wasn't paying it much attention though because I was too busy sliding my fingers through his long dark hair fanned out on the pillow and watching it glide like silk. Tenderly, I danced my fingers over the sensitive skin at the nape of his neck and he groaned, tilting his head to the side to give me better access.

"You can do that every single day for the rest of my life if you'd like." He mused, sliding his hand over my thigh under the pillow.

"Never cut your hair and I will," I replied.

He looked up at me out of the corner of his eye, "Do you like my long hair? I would have guessed it to be a turnoff for you."

"Why would it turn me off?" I asked, turning the volume down on the long-forgotten show.

He shrugged his shoulders as he pondered it, "I don't know, you just seem like a man's man, so I guess I just assumed you'd find it too femme."

I tightened my fingers in it and pulled his head back to look up at me. He sucked a quick breath in as his eyes widened, looking up at me. "It's one of my favorite things about you physically, Ky," I said, tangling my fingers into it deeper and drawing a moan from his lips. "You're so responsive when I've got a good fistful of it."

He moaned as his eyes fluttered closed. "Tell me what else you like." He whispered, and I slid my free hand down his bare chest to his abs, trailing my fingertips over each ridge slowly, teasing him.

"You mean besides the fact that you have a body cut from stone, your tattoos that we've already discussed are my roadmap to Pleasureville, and the caramel in your voice when you moan makes my cock ache."

He swallowed quickly and licked his lips. "I think I've taken all the light petting and cuddling I can handle for right now, Dex."

I smirked down at him as my fingers reached his waistband, "And what is it you want to fill your time with now?"

"You." He said, groaning as I pushed my fingertips under his pants and against the head of his hard cock where it grew up under the band. His hips jerked as I pushed my hand in deeper, sliding it down the length of him until my fingers cupped his smooth balls. "I need you, in either of my holes, whichever one you choose, it's yours. I just need you." He panted, and I pulled my hand from his pants and pulled his head up off my lap.

"Take your pants off," I demanded, and he shoved them down, kicking them off as I drew him onto my lap to straddle me. His cock was rock hard, the head red and needy, with pre-cum leaking from the tip. "Was last night when I was inside of you the last time you came?" I asked as I leaned forward and bit his peck before twirling my tongue over his nipple.

He groaned and jerked in my arms as I wrapped my hand around his cock, fisting it and stroking it like he'd done the other day in his apartment while I watched. "No." He gasped, letting his head fall back as I stroked him.

"You jacked off today?"

"Yes." He panted, "In the shower after you left me all alone in bed with morning wood."

I growled and tightened my fist around him. "And what did you think about as you stroked your cock?"

"You." He gasped, looking down his taut body to where I was caressing him. The head of his cock rubbed against my stomach with each stroke and my hips flexed under him. My cock desperately searched for friction against his ass. "I thought about you, and how good it felt when you stretched me open last night."

"With my fingers or my cock?"

"Both!" He moaned. "Both felt so fucking good."

"I want to play with you again," I said boldly as his eyes rolled and his lips parted.

"Whatever you want, Dex, it's yours."

I rolled us until he landed on his back on the couch, and I stood up, towering over him as I pushed my pants down, freeing my cock and leisurely stroking it while he watched. "I'll be right back," I said and walked into my bathroom, grabbing a towel, and finding the bottle of lube I'd long ago abandoned there before grabbing the condoms I'd bought at the convenience store next door to the Thai place on my way home.

When I walked back to him, he lay with his legs spread and his arms fisting the pillow behind his head, breathing deeply like it was exerting great energy to not touch himself.

"You can just fuck me, Dex. You don't need to do anything extra." He said, tightening his hands around the pillow as I dropped to my knees between his legs and leaned forward to kiss his stomach. I kissed my way up his chest to his lips and pressed my hips forward until our cocks were rubbing together.

"I don't want to *just* fuck you, Kyson." I reminded him and flexed my hips, rubbing my cock up the length of his. "Rub us together," I demanded, and he quickly followed my direction, sliding his hand between our bodies and wrapping it around both of our cocks, stroking them together. "Just like that." I hissed as I buried my teeth in his neck before licking away the mark I left. I let him work us up together while I kissed him deeply, grinding against him like a man possessed, and then pulled away, kissing my way back down his body. "When I fuck you tonight, I want you on your back like this," I said, pulling his hand away from his cock and replacing it with mine, stroking him with long, slow pulls. "I want to see the look on your face when you come."

His eyes fluttered closed, and he groaned. "Please Dex. Fuck me right now. I can't take any more."

"Lift your legs," I commanded, and he bent his legs at the knee and pulled them wide for me, opening himself up. I coated my fingers with the lube as he slid the towel under him and then I poured some more on his tight hole. Sliding one in caused us both to groan as I swirled it around, feeling him tense around me.

I loved watching his face as I pleasured him, his skin flushed, and a sweat broke out on his forehead as I added a second finger and started spreading them to open him up for me.

"I wanted to make you come like this, but I don't think I can wait anymore," I whispered as I reached down to stroke his cock while I prepped his ass to take me.

He groaned and rolled his eyes. "Thank God." He panted.

I chuckled and added a third finger and then nodded towards the condom on the coffee table. "Put it on me."

He quickly grabbed the condom and tore it open with his teeth before reaching forward and grabbing my cock, stroking it briefly before slowly sliding the latex onto my length. I hissed as he squeezed me and twitched in his hand uncontrollably.

"Now Dex. Please, baby." He begged, aiming my cock down towards his ass as I removed my fingers from him. He pressed the head of my cock against his open ass, and I pushed my hips forward, easily sliding the head in past the tight ring of muscles. "Oh, fuck." He groaned and threw his head back onto the pillow as I pulled out and poured more lube on.

"That's exactly what I'm going to do, and you're going to take it so fucking good, Ky."

He swallowed quickly and relaxed his body as I lined back up with him and pushed in, bottoming out with one slow steady thrust until my hips pressed tight against his. "You're impossibly big in this position." He gasped, pulling me down to kiss him. He clung to my neck and shoulders as I started fucking him into the couch.

"You like it though, don't you?" I asked, biting his shoulder before pulling back up to look down at where I was disappearing inside of him. "Tell me how good my cock feels."

"Jesus." He groaned and dug his short nails into my stomach muscles as I slammed into him and pulled back out. "You're so big, so deep, baby." I grabbed his cock and stroked it where it lay hard and leaking on his stomach as I pounded into him, turning him into an incoherent puddle of pleas and moans. "It's the best I've ever had. I've never been fucked so good, Dex."

"Tell me what you were thinking about when you jacked off this morning," I demanded.

"I told you already. I was thinking about you stretching me open." His eyes were closed and his neck tensed as he pushed his head back into the pillow. "I'm close already, Dex."

"Don't come," I ordered. "Not yet. Not until I give you permission." I kept the pace up, dropping my hips so I could go deeper. "Did you like my fingers inside of you last night, rubbing your p-spot?"

"I can't wait." He gasped, "You feel too good." I let go of his cock and pulled out of him, sitting back on my heels as he popped his eyes open and stared at me in shock. "What the fuck?" He sputtered.

"I told you, no," I said easily, before reaching down and massaging his balls in my hands, pulling on them and chasing away his orgasm. "Answer my question."

"Yes. I loved it, it felt so good Dex." He reached down and fisted himself. "I have to come, please, baby. Please fuck me."

"No more jacking off without me," I instructed him, and he blinked in confusion. "If you jack off, I want you to ask me first. I want to know where you are, and what you're doing to yourself, and I want to know what you're thinking of when you come. Understand?"

"What?" He shook his head, slowing down his fist as he paused, stroking himself. "What if you're at work or somewhere important?"

"Then call me and tell me exactly what you want to do. I want to be a part of every second of pleasure that you find Kyson. Whether or not I'm here. "

"Oh, my God." He moaned, licking his lips and nodding his head. "Okay. Yes, okay. Now fuck me!"

I was already lining back up and slamming back into him, causing him to yell out in ecstasy as I bottomed out. I wrapped my hand around his cock again and laid forward, biting his neck and whispering dirty things into his ear as I pushed him closer to that orgasm he had been chasing.

"That's it." I moaned, feeling my balls tighten up as pleasure crashed over me. "I'm going to come." I squeezed hard on his cock as I fought to hold my orgasm off as long as possible.

"Yes!" He roared, throwing his head back again and his cock started spurting in my hand, coating his chest and my fingers with his release. His ass tightened almost painfully around my cock, and I filled his ass with my orgasm. I kept my face buried in his neck as he continued milking me and taking my pleasure in his until we were both still and empty.

He pulled me forward until my head was on the pillow under his shoulder and he wrapped his arms and legs around me, holding me close as we both fought to calm ourselves. My cock twitched in his ass, and he chuckled in my ear and tightened around me again. "If you want round two, you're going to have to use my mouth because my ass is useless for you right now." He joked quietly as he absentmindedly played with the hair at the back of my head.

"Hmm," I said, tilting my hips to pull my cock out almost all the way before pushing back into his relaxed body and he moaned, tightening around me instinctively. "I think you're more ready for round two than you let on."

We lay like that for a while until his come started drying on his stomach and chest uncomfortably. "I need to get cleaned up." He mused, and I leaned up off of him, feeling some of his release dry on my skin where I'd laid on him.

"Shower together?" I asked, slowly pulling my cock from his ass and sitting up.

"Sounds lovely." He said, taking my hand and following me to my master bathroom where he proceeded to not only take me for round two but also beg me for round three and four on his knees like a good boy.

Chapter 11 – Kyson

Dexter Chase was a one-in-a-million kind of man. And I was going to be a fucking goner if I didn't play my cards right.

It was Monday morning and his alarm had just gone off for work, interrupting the little sleep we'd gotten after our shower sex-escapades last night. His bed was like a dream and sleeping in his arms all night long felt so natural it was slightly alarming. I'd dated a few men long-term, but they never felt… serious. It was more out of convenience and for fun.

So when Dexter rolled back over to me and pulled me against his chest, kissing my neck and shoulder, I was left wondering where to go from here.

"For the first time in forever, I want to call in sick." He whispered behind me, and I smiled into the darkness around us.

"Are you feeling ill?" I joked.

"I am." He answered, sniffling and then fake coughing before tightening his arms around my chest, "I think I need a good dose of medicine to make me feel better."

"Hmm…" I droned. "I'm all out of cough syrup at my place."

"Well, then an orgasm should help cure what ails me." He rumbled behind me as he bit my shoulder and then reached down my body to grab onto my already rock-hard morning wood. "Seems you could go for one, too."

I laughed and pressed my ass back into his erection. "Won't you be late for work?"

"Seeing as how I took a second shower at two am, I don't need to take one this morning, so I have an extra twenty minutes."

"Twenty minutes, huh?" I asked, as his wet thumb pressed against my hole. "Hmm. What will you do with the other fifteen?" I challenged cheekily, and I was rewarded as his entire thumb pressed deep into me. "Oof." I groaned at the sudden invasion.

"Be careful." He warned as he pressed me onto my stomach and laid out on top of me. "Or I'll gag you while I fuck you."

"Mmh." I moaned and pushed my ass up into the air, inviting him where I wanted him most. "Promises promises, baby."

He didn't end up gagging me, but he did keep his hand wrapped around my throat most of the time that he was fucking my ass and that was just as good.

I stood at my kitchen counter making myself a cup of coffee when my front door opened and Dex walked in, wearing his freshly pressed cream-colored suit and caramel shoes. He wore a light turquoise button-up under it and he looked like he should be on a Greek island boarding a yacht, not heading out for a day in a high rise in NYC.

"God, you make me hard," I said over my shoulder to him as he walked forward with gentle power in each step until he was pressed against my back. He flexed his hips against me, and I felt the hard ridge of his cock down his leg as it stiffened between us.

"Same." He whispered and then kissed my cheek before leaning against the counter next to me.

"Would you like some coffee?" I offered the carafe to him and he nodded, so I took a travel mug from the cabinet and set it next to him. I'd been able to unpack most of my apartment yesterday while he was at work, and it was helping me feel like this place had the potential to be home for a while.

"Quite the array of coffee paraphernalia you got there." He said, eyeing up the different syrups and creamer choices I had laid out to choose from.

"Paraphernalia?" I snorted and laughed. "I like choices is all," I said, watching as the man poured the piping hot caffeine into the travel mug and then simply put the lid on it and took a sip from it. My mouth hung open as I stared at him in disgust. "Did you just drink that straight?"

He raised his eyebrows at me and leaned his hip against the counter as he brought the cup back up to his lips and took another unflinching sip of the bitter lava.

"You could have just said yes or acknowledged that you indeed were a psychopath. You didn't need to risk third-degree burns on your tongue to prove a point." I turned back to my choices with a smirk. I picked up the vanilla syrup and almond milk and went about mixing my morning cup of energy.

He stayed silent next to me and watched the entire process until I frothed the milk for the top and he groaned, rolled his eyes, and walked away with a smirk on his face.

I added ice to it and took a tentative sip, sighing as the sweet flavor awakened my tastebuds and my soul alike. "Gosh, that's good." I mused and then set it down. "Are you off to work?"

He nodded and put his hand in his pocket. "Does your offer still stand?" He asked, and I could see the reservation in his eyes.

"To let you stay here?" I asked, and he nodded. "Sure, the couch is pretty comfy, I think you'll be okay on it for a few nights." I tried to keep my poker face on, but at the last second, I broke out in a smile and a wink. "Of course, it still stands. Turns out I sleep pretty well next to you, even if you are a blanket hog."

He snorted and rolled his eyes. "You snore."

I gasped and scowled at him. "I do not. That's absurd."

The infuriating man just smiled back at me with that devilishly good-looking mystery on his face. "I'm just kidding. And I have to agree with you, I sleep pretty well next to you too." He opened my front door and grabbed a garment bag he left in the hallway and turned back to me. "Mind if I leave this here for now, at least?"

"I don't mind at all," I said with a smirk. "You can hang it in the bedroom." He headed to my bedroom but on his way by he stopped, sliding his palm against the side of my face, and leaning in.

"You're smirking at me."

My smirk grew into a full, shit-eating grin. "I am not."

He tsked, leaning in as he covered my lips with his and hummed against me. "You are, and if you aren't careful, I'll make you pay for that."

"Don't tease me, baby." I challenged, and he growled.

He opened his mouth to do just that, but my phone started ringing on the counter behind me. He pulled back and raised an eyebrow at me. "Saved by the bell." He kissed me gently. "For now."

He went on into the bedroom and I picked up my phone, seeing my sister Lauren's name on my screen, and I groaned before answering. "Isn't it butt crack o'clock on the west coast?"

She laughed, and then promptly yawned. "Yes, yes, it is. But we haven't been able to connect on the phone for the last few days and I hate that. So I got up early to catch you before your day started."

"Aw, Lo, you really do love me." I droned on dramatically and she laughed. Dexter walked back out of my bedroom and stared at me with that mystery in his eyes again, that made my knees weak. He had such a strong poker face, when he wanted to keep his feelings private, he was completely unreadable.

"Of course I do, dweeb. How's life?" She said as Dex picked up his coffee cup and nodded towards the door.

"Lo, hang on a second," I said, setting my phone down on the counter and hitching my eyebrow up at the man as he tried to silently leave me. "Forgetting something?" I asked him accusingly.

He smirked at me and then looked at my phone. "I didn't want to interrupt."

"Hmm, likely excuse." I deadpanned. I heard Lo gasping in shock and then firing a million questions into the empty receiver, but ignored her as Dexter sauntered back over to me.

He leaned down and gently kissed me, threading his fingers through my hair and groaning. "You taste sweet like vanilla." He murmured.

"Does that mean you could like Vanilla coffee after all?" I asked, sliding my hands down the incredibly soft fabric of his button-down shirt.

"From your lips, I like anything." He said huskily, and I moaned as he leaned in for another taste. "I have to go." He said finally, looking down at the phone again where Lo was still squawking. "Tell your sister hello for me. I'll talk to you later, have a good day."

"Bye," I said back dreamily as he walked out of my front door, winking over his shoulder on his way. I sighed and then picked my phone back up, "Sorry, where were we?"

She sputtered, "Uh, who the hell was that!"

I laughed and took my coffee to the couch, sitting back and relaxing for a no doubt very entertaining conversation with my twin sister. "Dexter Chase."

"The man from next door?" She all but screamed, "What the fuck did I miss in a few short days?"

I laughed again and dove right in, "Uh, well, when I went over there the other night to get my wine opened, the chemistry was off the charts."

"Clearly! It's what… six thirty there right now, and he was in your apartment talking about drinking from your lips! Holy fucking hell, Kyson! I'm fucking speechless."

"Uh, to be speechless, Lo, you have to stop talking." I joked.

"Shut up, you know what I mean! What are the chances that the sexy man next door is gay and available and interested and, from the sounds of it, totally into you?"

I groaned, "If only it was that cut and dry."

"What does that mean?" She asked speculatively.

"He's not gay." I blurted out. "He's straight."

"Um…" she paused, "Do you need a lesson in sexual orientation, brother? Because you're a man, and he's a man, which means he's gay, or at the very least, not straight."

"You know what I mean, Lo." I groaned. "He's never been in a same-sex relationship before, casual or sexual."

"Start at the beginning while I get coffee because this is too much to comprehend this early without it." She said and I could hear her moving around her apartment, getting her morning caffeine going.

"This is going to sound… crazy to you. I know that. But hang on for the ride anyway, okay?" I asked, and she hummed her agreement, though she sounded cautious. "You know our apartments line up across the courtyard, we can see directly into each other's space, and the first night I was here, I thought I saw someone looking out his window into mine, but it was too dark to know for sure. And then that weird super electric elevator ride up to our floor that night we talked on the phone happened and I went over to get my wine opened and it was the same thing in his apartment."

"But he's straight?"

"He always has been, but he admitted to being attracted to me and being confused by it because he has never been drawn to a man before."

"Right, and then you both had the mutual masturbation voyeur thing that night. So how did it change from curious attraction to drinking from your lips?" She rushed on.

I chuckled again, "I challenged him to act on his impulses to see if it was just something built up in his head or if he genuinely enjoyed it in action."

"And did he?"

"Yeah." I groaned. "He kissed me in the elevator, and I swear to God Lo, I've never felt something so powerful in all of my life."

"Powerful? How?"

"Like... divine intervention powerful. Like he was the man I was meant to kiss and no one else will ever compare."

"Holy shit, Ky."

"I know." I sighed, laying my head back with a stupid smile on my face. "He asked me out Saturday night and it was... magical. And we ended up coming back to my place and... well, you can figure it out from there."

She giggled like a schoolgirl, "No. No, I can't figure it out from there. I need more."

I laughed and shook my head at her boldness. "Uh, we had sex, Lo."

"You took his gay virginity on night one? You whore!" She joked and then sighed dramatically. "Was it great?"

It was my turn to sigh now. "I can't even put into words how strong the connection is between us. It feels... like I'm waking in the sunlight for the first time in years."

"Holy shit."

"Yeah."

"So, what happened after that?"

"We spent last night together at his place, and he might stay here the next few nights while they paint his apartment. Though he's reserved about putting pressure on our relationship so early, so who knows."

"Why is he reserved? Is he trying to keep things just sexual? He's not trying to keep you some dirty secret hidden in the back of his closet, is he?" She said, slipping into that protective sibling role she'd always taken.

"No, it's not like that, Lo. We went out to a super nice restaurant Saturday night, and he was so sweet and romantic. He's loved and lost in the past and he's reserved because of it. His last relationship was four years ago, he hasn't so much as kissed someone else since then."

"Wow!" She said, falling silent as she thought it over.

"Yeah, I know. I can't imagine going without physical contact for four years, let alone emotional support from a partner."

She snorted, "It's not like you've exactly been in healthy supportive relationships over the years either, Ky. You may have gotten the phys-ical contact out of your boyfriends, but you hardly got the emotional support either."

"Jeeze, thanks a lot. You know how to make a guy feel great about himself first thing in the morning."

"You know what I mean, Ky." She blurted. "You've dated some duds, so maybe the two of you could be good for each other if he's not looking for something casual and fleeting. Because you deserve to be the center of someone's world."

"Aw, are you going soft on me in your old age?" I asked, playing on the fact that she was seven minutes older than me.

"Ah fuck you."

"Oh, there she is." I joked, snapping my fingers, "There's the hard ass man's man I've called a sister my whole life." I laughed, and she snorted.

"Well, I'm happy for you, Kyson. It sounded like he was absolutely smitten with you. I hope it stays that way and he doesn't hurt you."

"Yeah," I said wistfully. "Me too."

We chatted for over an hour before I forced myself to get up off the couch and get to work for the day. I had meetings all day with clients for a couple of big events coming up and quickly lost myself in the creation and planning stages of my craft.

Dexter ended up staying at my apartment on Monday night, Tuesday night, and now it was Wednesday night. I was exhausted from a day of hell and wanted nothing more than to go home and lay in his arms, which presented a problem for me.

I wasn't that guy.

But with him, I somehow had become that guy.

Somehow I'd gone from the guy that dated unavailable men casually for years to the guy that turned a straight man gay and became a stage five clinger, desperate for his attention because he was so damn good at giving it.

Ugh.

My phone rang in my hand and Dexter's name came up, sending butterflies off in my stomach.

"Hello?" I answered as I opened the fridge, looking for something to eat.

"Hi." His deep voice rumbled through the phone and sent shivers down my spine.

"Hi."

"I miss you." He said in that same deep voice, and I shut the fridge, suddenly unable to rub two brain cells together to worry about food because they were mush in my head.

"I miss you too." I sighed.

"Can I stay with you again tonight?" He asked the same way he had each night that his apartment was under construction.

"I'd love that."

"I was thinking I could pick up some food on my way home and we could eat on the floor and watch a movie or something. And then cuddle."

Now my heart was mush. "You know, for a heterosexual man, you sure are good at all of this romance. It's very surprising."

He chuckled into the phone, "Anything in particular, you're craving?"

"Besides you?" I asked and paused for dramatic effect. "Pizza sounds good."

"Pizza it is then, I'll order it, and have it delivered before I leave. I should be home in about a half hour."

Home.

Brain mush.

"Okay," I said, trying to not sound so lame. "I'll see you then."

When we hung up I quickly stripped down and ran to the shower, washing off the grime of the day from running around the city, and changed into a pair of white cotton shorts before returning to the living room to pick up my work stuff I'd thrown down when I got home.

Within a few minutes, a knock sounded at my front door, and I opened it up, revealing the night-time doorman Saint, with a giant box of pizza and a takeout container with what I hoped was chicken wings given the amazing aroma wafting from it.

"God, that smells good." I groaned as I opened the door wide so he could bring it in and set it on the counter.

"Luigi's is the best in the city if you ask me, it was a good choice." He said with a gentle smile.

"Thanks so much for bringing it up," I said, grabbing cash from the cup by the door and tipping him.

"No problem. Have a good night Mr. Hart."

"Thanks, you too Saint," I said and opened the door again for him to leave. The elevator door opened back up and Dexter stepped out looking like a model straight out of Paris Fashion Week and I had to bite my tongue to suppress the moan that wanted to escape.

"Mr. Chase," Saint said, pausing in the hallway. "Your apartment is still being painted, sir."

Dexter nodded to him and smiled. "I know, I'm staying with Ky until it's done." He said easily, and the doorman looked between us curiously. "Have a good night Saint," Dex said, spurring him into motion again as he nodded and walked towards the elevator.

"Right, you too." He said as Dexter slid his hand against the door behind me and held it open, nodding for me to go in ahead of him.

Always a gentleman.

As I turned to walk in though, I noticed the way Saint stood in the elevator, staring with morbid curiosity in his eyes before Dexter blocked my view with his large body and shut the door.

"What is it?" He asked as he set his briefcase down on the table by the door.

"He just always seems surprised to see us near each other," I said, shrugging it off.

"He's just used to seeing me alone, and I'm sure it's odd to see me talking to anyone."

"You don't think it's because I'm a man?" I asked curiously.

Dex snorted, "Well, I'm sure he can tell we're involved, though he's too professional to comment on it."

"And that doesn't bother you?" I asked, watching him closely as he unbuttoned his suit jacket and shrugged it off.

"Should it?" He asked easily. "Does it bother you?"

"No. But I'm gay, I'm used to it."

He shrugged his shoulder and looked so unaffected by it; I almost believed it. "It doesn't bother me if he knows we're together romantically, Kyson. I don't care."

"Hmm." I hummed, and he closed the distance between us, sliding his hands around my waist and hitching me towards him as he lowered his lips to my neck. He inhaled deeply, like it was the first deep breath he'd taken all day, and I relaxed in his arms, unable to feel anything but comfortable in his embrace.

"I missed you." He said again as he stood up to his full height and looked at me. "Are you okay?"

I nodded and smiled at him, "Just a long day. I'm beat."

"Then let's get you fed and relaxed shall we?" He asked like it was the most normal thing in the world for him to take care of me.

And it felt normal.

And easy.

And too good to be true.

"I'm going to go change, I'll be right back." He said, kissing my forehead and heading off towards my bedroom.

I watched his ass as he walked away, loving the way his pants hugged it tightly and he looked over his shoulder at me, smirking like he knew he'd find my eyes glued to him.

I rolled my eyes at him and turned to get plates out of the cupboard and a couple of beers.

Warm hands wrapped around my waist, lying flat on my stomach as I put a couple of pieces of pizza on each plate. "I don't know what smells better, you or Luigi's." He whispered into my ear, and I laid my head back on his shoulder, inviting more of his attention. I felt his smile against my ear as he pushed my hair aside and kissed his way down my neck to my shoulder. "Never mind, it's you. You smell better." He growled, sliding one hand up my chest until it wrapped around the front of my neck. I moaned and sank into his arms even further as he worked me up into a tizzy of sexual need with light touches and gentle kisses.

"Forget the pizza, take me to bed." I panted, resting my palms flat on the countertop for support.

"Beg me to fuck you." He commanded, and my knees went weak. "Show me how bad you want it."

I turned in his arms and he crashed his lips against mine, fisting my hair and pressing me against the counter with his hips. His bare chest and stomach aligned with mine as his lips feasted.

I let him kiss all of my frustration from the day away until I was putty in his hands of moans and pleas.

I pulled my lips from his and kissed my way down his neck and chest before licking my way down his abs and sinking to my knees in front of him. "I need you." Panting as I pulled the waistband of his sweats down, revealing his bare, hard cock to me. It bobbed in front of my face, and I flicked the end with my tongue, drawing a growl from his lips. "I need you to consume me, make everything else disappear until it's only us, Dex. Please."

"Suck me. Take me deep into your throat and show me." He commanded, pushing my hair back off my face as I kissed the tip of his cock before spitting on it and taking him into my mouth. He groaned as I relaxed my throat and let his cock slide down deep into the back of my throat. "Shit Ky."

I popped my lips off of him and gasped for breath, "Fuck my mouth, baby. I need to feel you come undone."

He clenched his teeth and fisted both hands into my hair, holding me how he wanted me. "Take it. Take every inch down your throat." He hissed and pushed himself forward until his balls pressed against my chin. "Fuck."

I reached forward and rolled his tight balls between my fingers, massaging them as he fucked my mouth like a man possessed. He was close, I could taste his pre-cum getting thicker on my tongue with each thrust. Moments later, he tilted his head back and roared as his cock erupted into my waiting mouth.

I swallowed down every drop as he gave me everything I begged for until his hips finally stilled, and his fists loosened in my hair. I cleaned up every drop by licking his still hard length, and then I put my wet lips to his smooth balls. I sucked one into my mouth and swirled my tongue around it as he groaned, looking down his body at me.

"Stand up, I need you." He ordered, picking me up as he kicked his pants off and walked me to the couch. "You're so fucking good at that. I almost could live buried deep in your mouth."

"Hmm." I mused, kissing up his neck and biting his ear. "You'd miss my ass though, and you know it."

"Fucking Christ." He groaned and dropped me to my feet before twisting me around to bend over the back of the couch. "I want to eat your ass and then I'm going to fuck you so hard the floors above and below us will know exactly what we're doing in here." He growled, kissing his way down my spine as he kneeled behind me.

"Oh god." I groaned when he pushed my shorts down and spread my cheeks wide before running the flat of his tongue up from my balls to my ass, swirling it around the rim and pushing it in. "Are you sure you've never done this before?" I gasped.

He chuckled, reaching down to stroke my raging hard-on as he continued his pleasurable torture. His five o'clock shadow scraped against my sensitive skin most deliciously and I was nearing my orgasm in no time at all.

"Please fuck me," I begged. "Please. Please. Please. Don't make me wait to feel you stretching me wide open on that giant cock, Dex. I need it." I cried as I fisted the cushion of the couch in my hands, spreading my legs and pushing my ass back against his face even harder. His large hand came down hard on my upturned ass cheek, drawing another groan from my lips, and he moaned before doing it again. His hand covered my ass cheek, lighting it on fire with tingling pleasure as I cried out. "Again. Please give me more."

He pulled his tongue from my ass and replaced it with two fingers, pushing deep inside of me as he sucked one of my balls into his mouth and swirled it around exactly as I had for him.

I groaned loudly as cramps started in my calves from standing on my toes to open myself for him. "I'm so close, I need your cock, Dexter."

"You're so sexy when you beg me to fuck you." He mused, biting my ass cheek, which was already on fire, pulling more moans from me. "I'm going to make you feel so good." He promised.

I was on the verge of tears; actual fucking tears because of how badly he had me worked up without giving me what I needed most to push myself over the top. He twisted his fingers inside of me and hooked them towards my cock, rubbing them in small circles over my p-spot, and I roared in ecstasy as fire nipped my spine. "Yes! Just like that!"

Between pleasure and pain, torment and delight, I found myself lost when movement from across the room caught my attention.

"Surprise!" A female voice called out as my front door slammed open against the wall and my sister Lo jumped into my apartment before letting her eyes land on the scene playing out before her. "Oh, my god!" She screamed, dropping the bottle of wine she held. It fell and crashed against the floor into a million pieces as she covered her eyes and turned to run back out the door, running into the doorjamb on the way. "My eyes!" She screamed.

Dexter stood up from behind me and grabbed the throw blanket off the back of the couch, covering us both with it before my brain even comprehended what was happening. My apartment door slammed shut behind my sister as I unfolded myself from the back of the couch and turned to look at Dex in shock.

"Who was that?" He asked, with angry fire in his eyes as he dropped the blanket and pulled his pants back up.

"Lo," I said, still trying to come back down to earth now that the orgasm I was chasing ran away completely, leaving me fuzzy and confused. "My sister."

"Oh." He said, stilling as he looked back towards the door. "Oh, shit."

"Yeah." I quipped, pulling my shorts on. "I'd better go make sure she didn't break her face on the door frame." I headed towards the door, pushing my hair back, trying to make sense of it all.

"Careful." He said, grabbing my arm and stopping me seconds before I stepped on a piece of broken glass. "Hang on." He ran to the hallway closet and grabbed a pair of shoes for us both and the broom. After my feet were safe from the glass, I opened the door and walked out into the hallway, finding Lo squatting down against the wall by the elevator with her hands still over her eyes.

"Hey," I said, stopping a few feet away. "What are you doing here?"

"Are you dressed? Because I can't convince my eyes to open back up if there's even a chance that you're still naked." She rambled.

"I have shorts on," I said, crossing my arms over my chest and waiting for her to dramatically crack an eye open and look up at me.

"I just saw you and your boyfriend naked, having sex on the couch." She cringed and shook her head. "Oh my god, I just saw your boyfriend naked!" She gasped, covering her mouth with wide, crazed eyes.

I rolled mine at her and held my hand out for her, helping her stand up. "What are you doing here, Lo? Unannounced, I might add."

"We're in Jersey for three games, so I rode the train up to surprise you." She said, and then her whole body shook. "But I got the surprise."

I laughed at her and shook my head. "Well, I'm not going to apologize for what I do in the privacy of my home with the man I'm seeing. So if you're waiting for that, keep waiting."

"Stop it." She hissed. "I have to leave. I can't possibly show my face in there now."

I rolled my eyes at her again, "Come on Lo. Since when have you been so easy to scandalize?"

"Since you're my brother, and luckily from the side, I didn't see any of your..." she swung her hand down toward my crotch. "Stuff.

But him…" Her eyes rounded. "A king-sized blanket couldn't hide that thing swinging between his legs!" She hissed quietly.

I groaned. "Forget it. Wipe it from your memory bank and never speak on it again. Understand."

"I can't." She cried. "I can't unsee it!"

Just then my apartment door opened up and Dexter walked out, wearing a shirt and a pair of jeans, carrying his garment bag and brief-case. He smiled a reserved, polite smile towards my sister and me and nodded towards the elevator. "I'm going to get out of your hair for the evening so you can visit with your sister." He said and my heart plummeted into my stomach.

"What?" I asked, "Why? You don't have to leave." I stammered.

He just gave me a look, and I knew he wouldn't budge on this. "I'm sorry you walked in on that Lauren." He said genuinely to my sister with a curt nod before turning back to me. "I cleaned up the glass and tossed it in your recycle bin, so be careful when you take it out, so you don't cut yourself."

"But you didn't even eat the dinner that you bought." I tried again, desperate for him to stay.

He smiled and looked at Lauren, who still stood silently next to me with a look of pure bewilderment on her face. "I'll grab something on my way to the hotel."

I shook my head, grasping at straws. "Lo, can you give us a minute?" I snapped, and she picked up the duffle bag at her feet that I hadn't noticed before as I shoved her toward my apartment. "I'll be right there," I told her and then turned back to Dex. "You don't have to go."

He cocked his head to the side and leaned forward to kiss my cheek. "Yeah, I do. She came all this way to see you, so spend time with her."

"Dex." I tried again, but he reached behind him and pushed the elevator button.

"It's fine, Kyson. It's no big deal."

I pouted, and he smirked at me as the elevator door opened. "You're cute when you pout, but I'm still not staying." He said firmly, kissing me chastely on my lips before walking into the car. "Go enjoy time with your sister. Call me tomorrow."

"Hmm." I grumped, crossing my arms over my chest, but he just smirked as the doors closed, leaving me alone in the hallway. "Damnit." I cursed, walking back to my apartment, and stepping inside to my waiting and still blushing twin sister.

"I'm sorry." She said, cringing. "Did he leave because of me?"

I hummed and grabbed the plate I'd been filling before Dexter had ravished me against the couch, leaving me hard and so close to an orgasm I could taste it, but ultimately unsatisfied.

"No." I sighed. "He had a hotel to stay at, anyway."

"I'm sorry Ky."

"I know." I sighed and took a bite of pizza. "I'm just moody because I'm horny, ignore me."

"I would be mad if you ruined my chance of getting railed by that dick, too." She said with a sassy wink, and I rolled my eyes at her.

"We are not talking about his dick."

"Fine, then let's talk about everything else that's been going on, because I've missed you terribly." She said, and I relaxed in her presence, admitting defeat and accepting that I wasn't sleeping next to Dexter tonight.

"Grab a slice and let's relax," I told her, heading to the couch with my spoils.

Chapter 12 – Dexter

"You know, she's lucky she's fucking phenomenal for Maverick, or I'd be really inclined to toss her out a window."

I looked up from my computer to find Reid walking into my office, looking flustered.

"I'm going to need a bit more information than that." I deadpanned and leaned back in my chair.

"Cora." He huffed, tossing his arms out at his sides. "She's ordered me to be fitted for a suit for that stupid auction I've somehow been forced to take part in." He leveled his finger at me and scowled, "I still don't understand how you've gotten out of it by the way, even when I tell her no, she just smirks and talks like she didn't hear me."

I rolled my eyes at him, "Like you won't enjoy women throwing their money around for a chance with Reid Haskins for the night." I droned, and he deflated a bit with a smirk before flapping his hands around shaking it off.

"It's not the point. The point is, I have to let some man measure my inseam in her office in two minutes to participate in something I want no part of!"

I laughed and shook my head, giving in to his plight. "You act like you don't wear tailored suits every day, Reid."

"Tailored by my guy!" He scoffed, "I don't like strangers in my junk area."

I stood up and buttoned my suit jacket, shaking my head at him. "You willingly have let half of New York City's female population near your junk area, my guy. Why is this any different?"

He scoffed and crossed his arms. "Because I'm sober and miserable and my head is... fucking pounding." He sighed, running his fingers through his hair, and I saw the weight of detoxing from alcohol on him. His skin was pale and clammy, and he had bags under his eyes.

"Hey," I said, walking around my desk, grabbing a bottle of over-the-counter painkillers from my desk drawer, and handing them to him. "Take a deep breath and a few of those and you'll feel better in a little bit." He popped the top off the bottle and swallowed a couple of pills dry and then handed me the bottle, but I put my hand up. "You keep them, I think you'll need them the next few days." I had been so distracted lately with Kyson that I didn't even bother to check in with Reid to see how he was doing. But judging by the way he looked, it had been a rough few days for him.

"Fucking sucks." He groaned under his breath.

"I know, man, but it's for the best and you know that."

"Yeah." He grunted and then pocketed the headache medicine. "I guess I'd better report for my cavity search before she comes looking for me. Her pregnancy hormones have left her a bit on edge the last week or so. I don't know whether she's going to cry or throw something at me most days."

I laughed and slapped my hand on his back. "How about I come along for emotional support?" I extended my offer, driven by a sense of protectiveness, hoping to make things easier for Reid, considering the physical obstacles he had encountered in the last few days.

"Thanks, man." He said, and we walked down the hallway towards Cora's office. "Are you sure you only had to say no to her to get out of this?" He quipped as he pushed her door open and stepped in.

"Yeah, I guess my balls are bigger than yours." I chuckled and then nearly swallowed my tongue as I walked into Cora's office and came face to face with the sexiest man in the world. "Kyson?" I said out loud as my brain tried to process what I was seeing.

Ky kneeled on the floor in front of our friend Carter as he ran a tape measure up his inner thigh.

The room stood still as Kyson looked up at me with confusion on his face for a second before Cora stepped in, looking between us. "You two know each other?" She asked, hitching her hip out and watching me speculatively. "You didn't strike me as the kind of man to have a personal stylist, Dex?"

My mouth hung open, and I looked past her to Ky as he stood up, winding up his tape measure and watching me closely as he conducted business as usual. "We're all set here, Carter, thanks for coming in. I'll have the suit at the event Saturday afternoon." Kyson said, but I hardly heard him. I was so distracted by how good he looked in a sharp navy-blue suit. I didn't know he even owned suits, let alone could wear one that fucking good.

But who was I kidding, Kyson Hart could wear literally anything and look damn good doing it.

I'd left his apartment last night after his sister barged in on us unannounced and spent the night miserable and alone at a hotel.

Carter looked away from me to Kyson standing right in front of him and held his hand out, firmly taking Ky's to shake, and then he walked towards me. "Everything okay, Dex?" Carter asked, confused. "You look a little rattled."

"Yeah, all good." I struggled to say as Cora showed him the door and then closed it behind him and turned on us.

Reid took a seat on the couch by the wall, crossing his ankle over his knee like he was settling in for a movie as I tried to process what I was going to do.

"Dexter?" Cora asked. I stood unmoving and staring at Kyson as he looked down at his feet and grabbed for his things. "What is going on?" Ky's cheeks were red, and his jaw was tense as he turned to write measurements on a paper on the table.

My discomfort had offended him.

He thought I was going to pretend I didn't know him. Or at least cheapen how I did know him.

But he was wrong.

"Kyson is the man I'm dating," I said, staring at him firmly as his green eyes snapped up to mine in shock.

"Oh, my God." Cora gasped, covering her mouth for a second before she dropped her hand and turned to him excitedly. "I've only known you professionally as Ky, I never even correlated the two names together!" She said and then turned back to me. "Holy crap, Dex, way to go." She said, winking at me, and Ky chuckled nervously as Reid sat watching it all unfold.

"If you don't mind, I'm going to steal my boyfriend for a second," I said, stepping forward to grab Ky's hand and drag him towards me as I opened her office door. "We'll be back in a second."

"Wait," Cora said, reaching for Ky's arm as I propelled him through the opening. "Hold on." She said again, but I continued to drag Ky down the hallway towards my office as she yelled after us. "I have so many questions!"

"Exactly why we're running away," I yelled back, and Ky looked over his shoulder with wide eyes as I laughed at him.

"I'm working Dexter." He said finally, sounding a bit afraid as I opened my office door and then locked us inside. The door was opaque, and we were locked away in privacy, but I knew it would be short-lived if Cora and Reid had anything to say about it.

"I know," I said and then took a step towards him as he backed up towards my desk. "I just needed a minute with you."

His expression softened, and he closed the distance between us until he stood right in front of me. "I had no idea you worked for Maverick Jones." He said as his brows knitted over his eyes. "I would have told you I was working with Mrs. Jones on her charity event if I'd known." He said, and then uncertainty clouded his eyes. "Wait, are you in the bachelor's auction?" He asked.

"Am I single?" I asked him immediately, without pause.

"I—" He stammered. "I don't know, are you?"

I glared at him and took the last step between us and dragged his body against mine. I slid my hand through the hair on the back of his head, tangling my fingers in under his hair tie, and then lowered my mouth against his. He was stiff in my arms for a nanosecond before he leaned in against me and tilted his head how I liked. His lips were warm, and he tasted like his vanilla coffee, and I moaned and pushed my tongue into his mouth for more.

His hands moved between us, opening my suit jacket, and then his palms were sliding over my stomach, making my muscles twitch. "You smell so fucking good." He groaned as I dropped my lips to his neck. "Wait," He groaned, "We have to talk about this." But even as he said it, he tilted his head further to the side to give me better access.

"I don't feel single," I said firmly, as I pushed his jacket over his shoulders. He shrugged it off, and I tossed it onto my desk. "Do you feel single?" I bit his ear and sucked it into my mouth as his hips jerked and he rubbed himself against me. He didn't answer me, so I reached down and palmed him, stroking his hard cock in my hand. "Answer me, Kyson," I demanded, tightening my grip around him. "Do you feel single right now?"

"No." He gasped, but then pushed me back a step and took a couple of ragged breaths in as he fought for control. "God." He panted.

I pushed my hand through my hair and forced my hands away from his body as I took a deep breath to calm myself down, too. "I'm sorry." I apologized. "I didn't mean to get carried away."

He groaned and rolled his eyes at me as he walked back into my arms. "Don't apologize for that, ever." He sighed. "I just hadn't planned on getting ravished in the middle of the day when I got here today."

"Well, that makes two of us," I replied cheekily as I straightened out my jacket. "But to answer your question, that started all of this, no. I'm not a part of the auction."

"Good." He answered quickly and then groaned and cringed. "Not that you couldn't be if you wanted to be." He stammered on embarrassed. "I'm just saying that you can do what you want, we haven't labeled this—".

I gently pulled him back into my arms and hugged him, trying desperately to keep it tame because I knew we were both hair triggered close to fucking on my desk. "I thought dating was a label."

He huffed and poked my side. "You've been out of this game for too long, Dexter Chase." He chastised me and smiled. "Dating someone has so many levels of commitment it's nauseating to even think about."

"So let's define it then," I said easily, pulling him with me to my chair and sitting down, yanking him onto my lap. He came willingly, but looked less than comfortable at the moment. I hoped it was the conversation and not the proximity to me at the moment that was causing it. "What level of commitment do you feel is appropriate right now? You're the one who has been in the dating game more recently than me and, more importantly, you've been in the same-sex dating game *far* longer than I have."

He rolled his eyes and then turned in my arms, throwing his legs over the arm of my chair, and leaned against me more comfortably.

So it was the conversation and not me.

Good.

"This is brand new, Dex. And you're still not even sure if you're straight." He sighed as it pained him to say it. "And this world," he swung his hand around my office, "This big wig Fortune 500 businessman world isn't always easy going on men like me, so I understand if you don't want to join my club publicly. I just don't know what you do want, though."

I tightened my hold on him and forced him to look me dead in the eye. "I'm sorry if I haven't said the words out loud to you since that morning in the elevator when we first kissed." I started, as I tried to portray what I wanted to say correctly, "I didn't realize I had to, because I thought I was doing a good enough job showing you, but that's not a mistake I will not make again." Sliding one hand over his jaw, I cupped his face. "I'm bi Kyson. I realized that before our first date. And I'm not attracted to you simply for a fetishized reason or anything. I'm attracted to you because I genuinely believe there is some sort of cosmic force pulling us together and making me stupidly crazy with desire for you. And not just for your body." I dropped my hands to his waist and picked him up, setting him down on my desk before pushing his thighs apart so I could step forward. I growled deep in my chest as dirty images rushed through my brain of him spread open for me right here. "And believe me, I'm downright feral for your body." I leaned forward and kissed him gently, but pulled back as he tried to deepen it. "But I'm crazy about your brain and your personality too, Ky. Every conversation we have just drags me deeper into this complete admiration of you that I've been in since the first moment I spied on you through your windows."

He chuckled and rolled his eyes at my attempt to joke about our nonconventional beginning. "So what do you want this to be, then?" He asked, looking at me to define it.

"I want you," I said firmly. "I'm not interested in anyone else and I'm sure as fuck not interested in sharing you with someone, either." I hooked my hands under his knees and dragged him forward until his legs were spread as wide as they could go around my hips. "I want to take you out on dates and develop a relationship that can be built into something long-lasting."

His pupils dilated, and he licked his lips as I leaned in closer. "A relationship? You want an actual public relationship with *me*?"

I growled and pressed my lips flush against his. "When are you going to stop acting like you're the one gaining something from this?" I rolled my hips and deepened my voice to the tone that he always responded best to in bed. "I want you in every single sense of the word, Kyson. And I want you publicly, I want to hold your hand and kiss you and let those around us know that you're mine and I'm yours. I don't know that I'll ever be a scream it from the rafters type of guy, but I wasn't like that in relationships with women either."

He kissed me, sliding both hands around the back of my neck as I leaned forward and pressed myself against his crotch, drawing a moan from his lips. "Are you sure?" He gasped, barely pulling his lips back far enough to speak. "Because you're doing and saying everything a man like me has ever dreamed of hearing. And if you're not careful, I'm going to get stupid enough to let myself fall for you, and then you'll be stuck with me because I'm a clingy bastard when I want to be."

I laughed, feeling the mirth deep in my soul as I took his lips again in a soul-searing kiss. "If you're stupid enough to think I'm a good catch, I'm going to keep tricking you for as long as possible."

I kissed him again and felt that desire burning deep in my gut again and deepened it.

Seconds later, though, a banging on the door interrupted us. "Dexter! You have two minutes to bring my stylist back or I'm going to sell you in the auction!" Cora yelled from the other side of my door, and I groaned.

"You can't make me do anything I don't want to do." I fired back childishly, and she chuckled manically.

"If you aren't in my office in two minutes, I'm naming Reid as soul guardian of my daughter in my will!"

I shuddered at the thought and scowled. Kyson was watching me closely as I interacted with his Mrs. Jones, and I laughed at him. "Don't worry, she's not as scary as her name and portfolio makes her out to be."

He smiled at me and slid off my desk, righting his pants and button-up. "How long have you known Mr. and Mrs. Jones?"

I scoffed and grabbed his jacket, helping him slide his arms back into it, "I've known Maverick since college, and Cora, while only this last year, is probably the person I'm closest to in the group."

"The group?" He asked, straightening his tie, "Does that include the man that you were comparing the size of your testicles to when you walked into her office earlier? And the man that I was measuring at the same time?"

I rolled my eyes at him and adjusted my hard cock down my pant leg, desperate for some relief, and reveled in the way his throat worked as he watched me with desire in his eyes. "The only man I compare my ball size to is you when they're slapping together as I fuck you." I challenged, and his eyes fluttered closed.

"Dex." He whispered in pain. "I'm going to make a fool of myself around your friends if you don't stop talking like that."

"Fine," I said back, kissing him once more. "But just know that the entire time I was alone in my hotel room last night I was fisting my cock, thinking about how badly I wanted to be inside of you."

"Mmh." He moaned, and I led the way back down the hallway to Cora's office.

"Reid, the man I walked in with, is the CFO here and he's been a best friend to me for years too. He's... going through something right now that's making him moody and miserable, so just go easy on him. He's crass and angry and kind of wild. But he's single-handedly the most loyal person I know in this entire world."

His warm green eyes softened, and he put his hand on my arm as I reached for Cora's door handle. "I'm glad you have people like this in your corner, Dex. And I'm also kind of glad I get to meet them, even if it's uncomfortable for you."

I turned to look at him head-on again and let my tone drop to the seriousness of what I was trying to explain to him. "I'm not un-comfortable because you're a man and I'm bi, Ky. I'm uncomfortable because I haven't introduced anyone to them in years and I know they can be a handful and the thing I dread the most is them saying or doing anything at all to upset you. Because that would upset me."

He smiled gently at me and then winked. "I'm a big boy, Dex, I can handle myself."

I laughed and nodded as I swung the door open, "That you are."

When we walked into Cora's office again, I groaned when I saw Maverick lounged back on the couch next to Reid, looking smug as shit.

"What?" Mav asked innocently as I glared at him. "I was told we were meeting the future, Mr. Chase; I couldn't miss that."

Kyson stepped forward and extended his hand to Maverick as he stood up. "Mr. Jones, it's a pleasure to meet you." He said as Maverick grimaced.

"It's Maverick, please." He said and smiled over at me. "If you're dating Dex, you're one of us now, like it or not, so we can drop the formalities."

"I appreciate that, but I do still work for you and Mrs. Jones for the charity event."

"To be fair, everyone in this room works for me. My wife included. So, trust me, just call us Mav and Cora. Please."

"As you wish," Ky said and then looked over at me with a satisfied smile on his face.

Cora stepped around her desk again and nudged Ky in the arm before leveling him with a serious look. "I'm usually not one to threaten people, I'm kind of a softie by nature and leave the menacing threats to my husband, but I will tell you this once and never speak of it again." She said as the room fell silent around them. "Dexter is my very best friend; he has a heart of pure gold and there isn't anything in this world I wouldn't do for him. And that includes helping him hide a body, so don't hurt him."

"Jesus fuck Cora." I groaned and pulled Kyson away from her as he paled a bit. "Ignore her, the pregnancy hormones are making her ankles and her brain swell." I deadpanned, and she glared at me before glancing down at her perfectly slender ankles.

"Never mind Kyson, I don't like him so much after all." She said, and Maverick slid his hands around her waist, pulling her back into him as he leaned against her desk.

"She means well, man." Mav said, "She's very protective, is all."

"No problem. I get it." Kyson said, smiling again now that he realized it was all in jest. "My sister is the same way. It's good to have someone like that in your corner."

"Indeed." Maverick agreed, kissing the top of her head.

Reid stood up from the couch and sighed, "Okay, well, now that you've met the lovebirds, I suppose I'll just introduce myself." He held his hand out, and Kyson took it. "I'm Reid, and I suppose you'll be stealing my last friend from me, leaving me completely alone in the world."

"Oh, can it man." Maverick groaned, gently shoving Reid as I rolled my eyes and shook my head.

Kyson got to work, taking Reid's measurements for his uniformed suit for Saturday's event while Maverick and Cora asked him all about himself and what he saw in me. I relaxed back on the couch and felt calm happiness settle into my bones as my family accepted Kyson into our circle with open arms. Even Reid got less cranky around Kyson's easy humor and gentleness, and before long, he was laughing and joking like the old Reid.

The Reid we used to see before he started numbing his joy with alcohol, at least, and it was nice to see his clear eyes and easygoing nature again.

"What are you guys doing tonight after work?" Cora asked, as Kyson picked up his things and loaded them back into his bag. It was almost the end of the day, and I had a pile of work waiting for me on my desk and a million emails that had pinged my phone in the last few hours, while I hid out in Cora's office with my friends, who also seemed to enjoy avoiding responsibilities for a while. But I didn't want to deal with any of that right now.

Kyson looked at me to answer, and I just shrugged my shoulders. "We don't have any concrete plans."

"Good, then let's go out. I would kill for some mozzarella sticks from Pandora's and you owe me a round of Karaoke." She said, clapping her hands in front of her excitedly as she pulled her phone out, "I'll text Nat and let her know we're going."

She left little room for argument, but I caught Reid in the corner of the room, pulling on his tie as his skin paled just thinking about going to a bar.

"Uh- actually. We have plans tonight." I stammered, "Sorry, I forgot. Kyson's sister is in town for a few nights only." Ky looked at me questioningly, and Cora watched us closely. "Maybe next week? After the event is over, plus I'm sure Ky has a million things to get settled for it still."

"Um, yeah, I need to get everyone's suits ordered for delivery and then have to go over the dresses for you and your mother-in-law still." He said confidently, following along.

"Oh," Cora said, nodding her head. "Right, sorry." She deflated a bit.

"Next week, we promise," I said confidently, and she smiled. "Well, we will get out of your hair, I'm going to head out for the day, but I'll be in early tomorrow to make up for it."

Mav just shook his head. "Don't worry about it, I trust you to get your shit done, Dex."

I nodded and waited as Kyson grabbed his things and held the door open for him. When we were back in my office to gather my things, he watched me pensively. "Why did you say we had plans? Lo is at the game tonight and tomorrow."

I sighed and loosened my tie a bit. "Reid has a drinking problem he's trying to get ahead of. He's only a few days into his dry out and the last place he needs to go is the bar. If I made the excuse, he didn't have to."

"Ah." His eyes warmed as he nodded his head. "He's lucky to have you as a friend, Dexter." He said easily as I walked into his embrace.

"Maybe," I said, kissing him lightly on the lips. "But I'm not without my difficulties either."

He smirked at me, "You don't say."

I poked his stomach and grabbed my briefcase.

"Careful, or I'll make you ride home in a stinky cab." I threatened, but pulled him in for a kiss again, regardless. "Your sister isn't staying with you tonight?"

"No. She's in Jersey tonight and tomorrow and then off to some other state."

"And she won't be popping in unannounced?"

"No." He answered breathlessly as his eyes darkened.

"So I can spread you out on my kitchen counter like a thanksgiving feast and we won't be interrupted again?" I asked.

"Dexter." He moaned, letting his eyelids flutter closed as he bit his lip. "I was so fucking horny last night after you left me hard and wanting."

"Me too, baby." I groaned, "But don't worry, I don't intend to stop until we're both drained and exhausted."

"Take me home." He begged.

"If you insist," I said, kissing him once more on our way to our little slice of privacy and peace.

Later that night, I laid in bed with an exhausted and drained Kyson sprawled out across my chest as I ran my fingers through his hair. I was drifting off to sleep when his soft voice vibrated against my chest.

"Will you tell me about her?" He asked into the silent darkness.

"Who?" I asked, half awake and confused.

"The woman before me." He said, turning his head to look up at me, "The one who didn't love you as much as you loved her."

His green eyes were dark in the low light, but I could still make out the flakes of gold around the rim of them at this close distance. I kept my fingers moving through his hair even though my chest seized up tight at the thought of Hope. I hated even thinking about her in this space that had become a place of peace and pleasure with Kyson.

"What do you want to know?" I asked finally, trying to let him into my past, painful as it was.

"Anything you want to tell me about her."

"Why do you want to know?"

"Because I'm a firm believer that our past pain shapes us into who we are today, and if we understand how that shaping took place, we know how to heal it and keep it from happening again."

I raised my eyebrow at him and then looked up at the ceiling as I let that resonate in my head. "You sound pretty wise, you know that?" I asked him and he smiled at me, but said nothing else to get me out of telling him my sordid tale. "It's not a pleasant story."

"Tell me anyway. Please." He insisted gently, resting his chin on his hand against my sternum.

I took a deep breath and tore the band-aid off. "Her name was Hope," I whispered and then smirked. "Which is ironic because she had a way of sucking the hope right out of people." His green eyes didn't waver as he listened intently. "She was a bartender at a bar I went to all the time when I first moved here." I ran my fingers through his hair again to keep myself grounded. "She was beautiful and charismatic, and she entranced me from day one. But our relationship was fast-paced and turbulent every single step of the way. I thought that meant passion and fire, but it was really just toxicity and red flags." I groaned and looked away from him to look back up at the ceiling. "I proposed a few months in, and we got married a month later, even though everyone told me I was crazy to think she'd ever settle down," I said and he took a quick breath in.

"You were married?" He asked.

"For a couple of years before she left."

"Wow." He mused. "That must have hurt."

"That's not even the worst part." I groaned, feeling that familiar pain in my chest at the memory of my previous life.

"You don't have to tell me." He whispered, running his fingers over my chest like he could feel the pain radiating under my skin and was trying to soothe it.

"I want you to know." I admitted, "It's just that I never talk about it with anyone."

"Not even Maverick or Cora?" He asked, "Or Reid?"

"Honestly, I've talked about it more in the last few months than I have in the last few years, though I'm not sure why."

"Maybe it's because you're finding healing in it now." He tried. "Maybe enough time has passed to ease it for you a bit."

"Maybe." I pondered, "Though it's not a pain that will ever go away."

I opened my mouth to say the words and closed it a few times as I tried to say them out loud to the man that had engrained himself in my life permanently.

I took a deep breath and purged the deepest, darkest part of my pain to him and his understanding eyes. "She got pregnant not long after our wedding," I said and his entire body stilled on top of mine. His fingers stopped moving on my chest, and his own chest stopped rising and falling as he stopped breathing altogether. "A boy; we named him Sammy," I admitted and closed my eyes to the memories. "I've never known a love deeper than when I looked into the perfect innocent eyes of my son for the first time."

"You have a son?" He asked with a haunted look on his face.

"I *had* a son," I replied, pained. "Or at least I thought I did." I sat up, dislodging him from my chest until my back pressed against the tufted headboard of my bed and I ran my hand through my hair. "He was eight months old when I came home from work one day to an empty home and a note that said she regretted ever marrying me, and it had just been a means of escape for her to get out of a life she hated."

Kyson sat up in the center of the bed and stared at me in horror. "Oh, my god."

I nodded and continued. "The note said that she had been having an affair with a man the entire time we were together and that Sammy wasn't mine after all."

"No." He whispered, covering his mouth with his hand.

"The other guy gave her an ultimatum, either leave me or he'd leave her, so she packed up everything I'd given to her and took my son to go be with him. I fought her in court, I mean, I'm a lawyer for fuck's sake, I refuted the divorce and filed for full custody of him. But to be awarded custody, I had to take a paternity test to prove he was mine, even though we were married at the time of his birth and my name was on the birth certificate." I said and scrubbed a hand over my face in agony at the memory of getting the results back. "Turns out he wasn't mine after all. And I had no legal rights to him, regardless if I'd spent the first eight months of his life loving him as my own or not." I said and shook my head. "I lost my entire world when she took him from me, and I haven't seen him since. It wasn't even the loss of my wife that pained me at that point, I'd realized right away that I never truly loved her because I never truly even knew her. But when she took the only reason I had to breathe each day from me..." I shuddered. "She destroyed me."

He slid up the bed to sit next to me and reached for my hand. "I'm so incredibly sorry that you had to go through that, Dexter. I can't understand that kind of pain or comprehend how you've coped with that over these years." I squeezed his hand tight in mine and pulled him against my chest. "Thank you for telling me, though."

I hummed in agreement and took a deep calming breath in, letting the scent of his shampoo calm me. "Thank you for listening and meaning so much to me I wanted to tell you." I kissed the top of his hair, and he wrapped his arms around my waist.

He groaned, "Now I feel bad for being so whiny about being used as a sex toy by some rock star." He buried his face against my chest, and I chuckled, running my hand up and down his bare back.

"Well, I'd be whiny too if I realized I peeked years ago with a rock star and am now saddled to a boring, stuffy lawyer." I deadpanned, and he pinched my thigh and bit my peck under his cheek.

"You are the furthest thing from boring Dexter Chase." He said, turning and sliding his leg over my thighs until he sat straddling me. His bare ass nestled nicely in my lap and my cock instantly jerked to life beneath him. "In fact, I've never had a more fulfilling sex life before, to be honest with you."

"Really?" I asked speculatively. "How is that possible when I'm as novice as a virgin?"

He snorted, tipping his head back to laugh. His hair shook out behind him, and excitement danced in his eyes in the moonlight. "We both know you're not a novice about when it comes to your magnificent cock." He tilted his hips, rubbed my cock between his smooth ass cheeks, and bit his lip. "But sex for me is so much more than just a physical act between two people. It's deeper than that, it's a dance of two souls, two minds, and two personalities, and ours... they perfectly align every time we're together. It makes the sex so incredibly gratifying, each and every time baby." He leaned down and gently kissed my lips as my hands tightened around his waist, pulling him down against me harder.

I'd just fucked him less than an hour ago, but both of our cocks were hard as he ground himself back and forth in my lap.

"But—" He said and pulled back to look at me as he bit his lip pensively. "Speaking of virginity—" He droned on again and I raised my eyebrow at him.

"Yes?" I asked.

"Have you thought about bottoming at all?" Both eyebrows rose into my hairline as I let his words dance around in my head.

"Have I thought about being fucked in the ass?" I asked for clarification.

"Yeah."

"Yes," I answered truthfully. "Not before I met you, but the first time I saw your cock in person, I thought about it."

"And is that something you want to do? At some point?" He asked, sliding his hands down my chest to my abdomen and back up.

"I figured we'd swap at some point." I grabbed onto his hard cock where it lay against my stomach and slowly slid my hand up and down on it. "Why? Do you want to fuck my ass?"

"God, yes." He moaned and closed his eyes. "I do."

"I thought you were a bottom."

"I am, usually. I love being fucked, especially by your monster cock." He panted. "But I've been thinking about how good it would feel to take you, knowing it was your first time." He moaned and opened his eyes to look down at me. "I think I'm becoming obsessed with the idea of it."

"Then let's do it." I indulged him. "Work me up to it and let's do it."

He groaned and leaned down, crashing his lips against mine in a hungry, desperate kiss. His fingers grabbed onto my hair, and he tilted my head, pushing his tongue deep into my mouth and I sucked on it as his cock jerked in my hand. This dominant side of him was new, but not surprising, either. He was a masculine guy; I knew he had some alpha in him, and I was finding it hot as hell to be a little manhandled.

Interesting.

"Lay down." He said, sliding down my legs to the bottom of the bed as he grabbed my ankles and yanked me onto my back.

"Whoa," I said, laughing, but it dried up on my tongue when I saw the intensity in his eyes as he pushed my thighs apart and stared down at me.

"Do you want to be on your back with your knees to your chest or on your stomach with your ass in the air?" He asked, getting straight to the point.

"Uh—" I stammered, "Stomach I think." Before shaking my head, "Wait, what exactly are you going to be doing to me?"

He smirked down at me before laying out on top of me and lowering his lips to my ear as his cock rubbed against mine. "I'm going to lick and finger your ass until you explode."

I groaned, flexing my hips up against him for more friction before I pushed him up. "Stomach." I flipped over on my stomach, and he grabbed a pillow and a towel, propping them up under my hips. Instead of aiming my cock up towards my stomach under me though, he pulled it down, pinning it under my groin, between my legs.

"Spread your legs for me, baby." He said, as he laid his warm hands on my ass and spread my cheeks.

"Fuck." I groaned and widened my thighs as I laid my forehead against my arms and tried to calm my erratic heartbeat.

"If it's too much, just say so, and I'll stop. I promise." He said confidently, as he grabbed the lube from my end table and kneeled between my legs. "But I think you're going to love every second of this."

"Mmh," I groaned as he leaned down and kissed the base of my spine, "I love every single thing you do to me, Ky. I trust you."

"You have no idea what that means to me, baby." He purred and then kissed each of my cheeks and spread them again before spitting directly on my hole. He hummed as he leaned in and ran the flat of his tongue up from my balls to my spine and I jumped when he pushed firmly against that forbidden place. "Relax."

I took a deep breath and pushed my ass further into the air and opened myself up more. He swirled his tongue around me again and moaned, vibrating against my sensitive skin. "Fuck." I groaned when he pushed the tip of his tongue into me, twisting it around and then pulling it back out. I heard the snap of the lube top open and then cold liquid poured down the length of my cock seconds before his hand wrapped around it, gliding up and down in time with his tongue. "Kyson," I growled in pleasure.

"Yeah, baby." He said. "I'm right here." He bit my cheek as more lube poured against my asshole, and I tensed again at the foreign feeling. His fingers followed the liquid, and he pressed the pad of one finger against the loosened opening of my asshole. "Let me in Dex. Relax and push back against my finger, baby." I did as he said, and his finger slid in painlessly. "Good boy." He praised me and then chuckled as I groaned.

"I'll show you a good boy." I challenged. He may have some alpha in him, but I didn't have any submissive in me.

"Oh, I'm sorry." He hummed, leaning forward to kiss my spine again as he pumped his finger into me and stroked my cock at the same time. "Should I call you daddy instead?"

I groaned again, but this time in pleasure. "Kyson," I warned, fisting the blankets under my head as my body pushed back on his finger quickly because his slow progression was torturing me.

"Hmm." He smiled against my skin. "I guess we both liked that." He straddled my thigh and rubbed his hard cock against me under him and quickened the pace of his finger and his fist to match. "God, it's so fucking hot watching you take me inside of you, even if it is just one finger."

"Another." I gasped, "Give me more."

"Yes, sir." He groaned and added another finger with his next thrust and I moaned loudly, arching my back further.

"God, yes." I hissed. "I'm so close."

"Your giant cock is nearly purple it's so needy."

"Needy for you."

He chuckled and quickened his pace. "I'm yours, Dexter Chase. You own me and my desires. But right now, I want to own yours." He said and turned his wrist, twisting his fingers inside of me until they pushed forward, and a warm buzz of pleasure spread out from my spine to the tips of my toes and fingers. "That's it, baby." He praised as he rubbed on what I could only assume was my p-spot.

Noises I'd never made before fell from my lips as Kyson pushed me over the edge of unexplainable bliss. "Please," I begged in desperation.

"Give it to me, Dex, give me every drop of that come." He hissed in my ear as his hips continued to grind himself against my leg. The head of his cock was pressing against my ass cheek. The triple stimulation of his fingers inside of me, his fist around my cock, and his length thrusting against me pushed me over the edge and I roared my release into the pillows as he worked me through the orgasm and down the other side.

"I'm coming." He moaned, and his cock erupted, covering my thigh and ass with his come to mix with my own until we were both gasping and sated.

"Holy fuck." I sighed, looking over my shoulder at him as he started cleaning us up with the towel and then crashed on the bed next to me with a goofy smile on his sexy face.

"Ditto babe." He mused. "Fucking ditto."

Chapter 13 – Kyson

"**I**'m freaking out," I said into the phone as I wedged it against my shoulder so I could continue to steam the Gucci dress hanging in front of me.

"Ky, take a deep breath. You've worked *far* bigger events than this one before. You've got this." My sister's voice was doing nothing to calm my nerves, though.

"I know that, but there is literally so much money on the invite list tonight it's ridiculous." I sighed, "And these people are Dexter's friends. There's a level of expectation to make him proud that I've never felt before."

"You have everything all prepared. You're ready, Ky." She reminded me and I took a deep breath.

"You're right," I said and relaxed the tension in my shoulders. "I've got this."

"Damn fucking right you do." She cheered, and I smiled.

"Okay, I have to go. It's almost time for Cora and Marsha Jones to show up to begin hair and makeup and then the bachelors will be here to get dressed."

"Call me tonight if you want to tell me how it all went, but just remember to relax and enjoy yourself as a guest after you get everyone else ready." She reminded, and I smiled.

I couldn't believe I was attending the Jones Memorial charity auction as a guest. People each spent hundreds of thousands of dollars at the event every year and the guest list included names I'd only ever dreamed of meeting before. But what I was most excited about for the evening was being on Dexter's arm as his date.

Our first proper date amongst his peers and his official coming out night.

I didn't know who was more nervous, him or me.

But I had hours of fittings to get through first before I could even worry about our evening.

"Oh, my god!" Cora shrieked from the doorway to the large dressing room I'd been given as she looked at the outfits laid out. "Oh, my freaking god." She repeated with a dreamy smile on her face. "Kyson! These dresses! These tuxes! They're fabulous!"

I smiled graciously at her as she walked in, laying her bag down before running her manicured nails down the dress she was going to wear tonight.

"Is this one mine?" She asked with an excited smile on her face.

"That's the one, it's fit for a queen and it's going to fit you like a second skin. I promise."

She had been so worried about finding something to fit with her growing belly that didn't make her feel like a stuffed sausage, but would accent the new life inside of her. And I'd found just the dress.

"I'm so excited to dance the night away!" She sing-songed and then sat down in the stylist's chair in front of the mirrors. "And I'm so eager to get to spend the evening with you and Dex! And help you network with all the elite attending tonight."

"Thank you again for inviting me! I've dreamed of this event for years and to not only get to style it but attend it, is a once in a lifetime opportunity for me and my career."

She waved her hand at me and scoffed. "I planned on waiting until Monday to talk to you about this because I didn't want to add any pressure to your shoulders tonight, but what the hell." She said and motioned for me to come to sit next to her in the other stylist's chair. Trepidation crawled up my spine as I sat down and looked at her. I'd only known her for a few weeks and at first, I was incredibly nervous to be working with the infamous Jones family, but she had been a dream so far. She was so sweet and gentle and surprisingly down to earth for a billionaire. She reached across the space and took my hand in hers. "Kyson, Dexter is family to Mav and me and, by extension, you're a part of our family now, too. And nothing makes me happier than surrounding myself with good friends and family in both personal and professional aspects. So assuming that tonight goes well with your designs and your dressings, I want to offer you a contract as an exclusive stylist for the entire Jones family."

My eyes rounded, and I heard a ringing in my ears as her words settled in my brain.

"What?"

She smiled at me brightly. "Your primary job would be to make sure I looked as good as possible for every event I attend, and on top of that, you'd take care of mine and Maverick's wardrobes. And you'd be in charge of every event like this." She motioned to the glam room around us. "You'd still be free to work with other clients as you desired too, you wouldn't be exclusive to us only, but we'd use only you for our needs. You'd have a set salary from us regardless if we had events for you to help with or not and then for each event you did style, you'd receive an added stipend."

"Oh my God, Cora, I don't know what to say." I stammered to get the words out clearly.

"Say nothing just yet, wait and see how tonight goes and how you feel about it, and as I said, Monday morning we'll meet, and we can talk numbers and terms if you're interested."

"I'm interested!" I rushed out and then smiled, embarrassingly. "I mean, it would be a dream to be your stylist full time. Your closet alone would keep me satisfied for the rest of my life, before even adding Maverick's to the mix. I'd love to work with you."

"Good!" She said, clapping her hands. "I hoped you'd be interested. Gosh, I'm so stinking excited!" She cheered and then took a calming breath, and I did the same. "I have to be honest with you though, my motives are kind of selfish for asking you to be at my side. This world we live in is so dog-eat-dog and cutthroat, and I've avoided it for the last decade by existing in the shadows, but now that I'm married to Mav and expanding our family, I can't hide anymore. And it's hard to know who I can trust and who is genuine, but since the first moment we talked on the phone, I've felt such a calm comfort in your presence, and knowing that Dexter trusts you, just makes me so much more comfortable with you." She rushed on. "But please do not think that this job is entangled in your relationship status because it absolutely is not, if things don't work out between you and Dex, it will not affect your employment status with me. I'm more than willing to keep things separate if necessary."

"I don't know how I'll ever express my gratitude to you, Cora, but I will try."

She patted my hand again before relaxing back in her chair and rubbing her belly over her sweater. "Just be genuine and kind to me and my family and we'll be even."

"Deal," I said and then the door to the dressing room opened up and Cora's mother-in-law, Marsha Jones, walked in looking regal and elegant in a sundress.

"Well, darlings, what do you say we get glammed up and dance the evening away with our handsome men?" She said in a flourish and Cora and I smiled at each other.

"Let's." I agreed, standing up and getting to work.

Hours later, Cora and Marsha dressed to divinity, while the bachelors matched in their black and cream matte tuxes, and the champagne flowed as the guests started arriving at the lavish affair.

I was in awe as I walked out into the event space in the extravagant retro hotel ballroom. Crystal chandeliers, champagne-colored silk walls, and low candlelight adorned the room, giving it a 1920s glam dancehall style.

I stood by the entrance and adjusted my matte black suit jacket over my blood-red silk shirt. Forgoing a tie, I left the collar open and my leather cross necklace on display for an edgier look. I kept my hair down tonight and the loose waves fell gently beneath my collar.

I may dress the top one percent, but I still dressed as if Johnny Depp and David Beckham had a love child, and I was the product.

It was me, and I didn't apologize for it.

I walked over to the bar and ordered a drink to calm my nerves after a long, chaotic day. The bartender had just laid my Tom Collins down on the bar when I felt Dexter in the surrounding air.

The hair on my neck stood up and my skin prickled seconds before his body pressed against my back and his breath touched my ear. "You are hands down the sexiest person in this room tonight."

I smiled into my drink, letting the cool gin swirl on my tongue before I looked over my shoulder at him with a sultry glare. "That's because the guests have barely started arriving yet."

Dexter slid his hands around my waist and turned me to face him, letting his eyes roam down my body to take it all in. "Doesn't matter. No one holds a candle to you."

"Have you looked in the mirror tonight? You're a downright sin." I said, pushing him back to look at him. He wore a black suit with leather lapels and a crisp white shirt underneath. His pants hugged his muscular thighs and tight ass so snugly that just looking at him made my mouth salivate. "God, Dex."

He smirked at me and leaned in for a kiss, lingering against my lips. "How did everything go today?" He pulled back and leaned against the bar next to me.

"It went well. Really well, actually." I said with a smile, and he squinted his eyes.

"What exactly happened to make you smile like that?" He asked.

I took another sip of my drink and let it swirl around in my mouth. "Cora offered me a job, styling them full time."

He raised his eyebrows, and a smile teased his full lips. "And what did you say?"

"I said yes, emphatically like a fan girl, and then remembered to try to seem mildly interested and mysterious, but the damage was already done. She knows I'm on the hook."

"Well, if you want, we can talk about it more and I can help you make the best decision for you, terms of employment wise."

"Wouldn't that be a conflict of interest? I assumed you'd be drafting up the contract on their side."

"I'll have one of my junior lawyers draft it up, and I'll review it from both sides to make sure neither of you is leaving anything on the table. I'm a fair man."

"Hmm." I mused, leaning closer to him. "I'd hope so. I only like to be fucked in the bedroom, not in business."

He smirked and took my drink from my hand, downing the rest of it. "Speaking of fucking." He growled. "It's been way too many hours since I was inside of you."

"Dexter," I warned, as his eyes darkened mischievously.

"Just give me fifteen minutes." He hummed deeply. "I'll make you feel so good, baby."

"Dex," I whined, leaning into him further, close to giving in to the promise of his cock.

"There the two lovebirds are." A voice called out, and I backed up quickly as Maverick and Cora walked up to us. Dexter chuckled at me and slid his arm around my back, pulling me back against him.

"Stop acting like we just got caught doing something we shouldn't be." He said into my ear before turning to address his friends. "Hey, guys. The place looks great." He said to Cora with a gentle smile.

She beamed up at him and looked around the room. "It really does." She gushed. "This was my first enormous event to coordinate as Mrs. Jones, and it's come together perfectly."

"Careful Angel, don't jinx yourself." Mav chided good-heartedly and kissed her head.

She elbowed him and leaned against his side. "I know. I'm just so stinking happy." She squeaked, and I laughed easily. Her good mood was infectious, and she'd kept me light and worry-free most of the day with it.

"Kyson, everyone looks amazing tonight. You've outdone yourself." Maverick said with a nod in my direction, and I beamed brightly at the compliment.

"Thanks, everyone has been great. They all made it easy."

"Everyone except Reid," Cora said quietly with a sad look on her face.

"He's going to be fine. It's just hard right now for him." Mav said, rubbing her arm affectionately.

"Has anyone seen him lately?" Dex asked, looking around the space that was quickly filling up with the world's most elite.

"Not since getting him dressed," I said. "That was about an hour ago."

"He's probably lying low somewhere until he's absolutely needed," Maverick added.

"Maybe," Dex said, but I could still see the worry in his eyes for his friend.

I leaned into his side. "Maybe you should go look for him and check on him," I whispered, and he glanced at me before nodding his head.

"I think you're right." He replied. He leaned over and kissed me, lingering lightly against my lips. "Don't let anyone steal you away while I'm gone."

I smirked and rolled my eyes at him. "I won't."

"Go with him," Cora said, nudging Mav. "Ky will stay with me, won't you?" She asked me, and I quickly nodded in agreement. "I'll be fine." She reassured Mav as he looked less than certain. "Oh, come on, no offense boys, but Kyson looks more menacing and dangerous than the both of you combined with his sultry dark looks and bad boy appearance."

I'd learned in my short time knowing the couple that Maverick had made some mistakes in the past with Cora, and he harbored a lot of guilt over them. And his guilt sometimes came out as overprotective-ness, especially now that she was getting to the end of her pregnancy. But regardless of what happened in the past, he was a doting and loving husband, and it didn't take an expert to tell that the couple was destined to be together forever.

"I got her," I said to Maverick, and then nodded to Dex. "Go check on Reid."

"Okay." He said, kissing me again and then walking away with Mav in search of the elusive friend in need.

Cora winked at me and slid her arm through mine. "What do you say we go mingle and introduce you to some big names?"

I grinned down at her and covered her hand with mine. "I think you're quickly becoming my favorite person." She chuckled and nodded in agreement.

"We're going to be best of friends, Kyson Hart. I can tell."

And I believed her.

Cora had stayed true to her promise and had introduced me to people who I'd only ever dreamed of seeing in person from afar before, and I was shaking their hands and making their acquaintance.

I have more than a few business cards in my pocket and more offers of 'call my people and we'll work together than I could comprehend.

I'd worked so hard over the years to make myself known and my client list spoke for itself. But adding even one or two of the names I'd met tonight to it would propel me even further up the ladder and solidify my career for quite a while.

"I can't believe Madeline Ace was so nice to me." Cora stage whispered as we walked through the crowd. "She's hands down the rudest person I've ever met before. I think it's because she was so attracted to you though, did you see the way she looked you up and down like a snack." She said, and I laughed.

"You forget you're the queen tonight Cora, I suspect any person in this room would bend over backward for your affection tonight."

"Hmm. Maybe." She mused, nodding and smiling at a governor she'd introduced me to earlier, though for the life of me I couldn't remember his name or what state he ruled over.

I looked around the room for Dexter or Maverick, but still didn't see them and was getting worried. As I scanned the room, my eyes faltered over a familiar pair of black ones staring at me from a few feet away, getting closer by the second.

"Oh, fuck." I groaned, pulling Cora to a stop as my body froze up like ice. Dread burned down my spine as I watched the man that had introduced me to my sexuality before exploiting it walk towards us.

"What is it?" Cora asked quietly as she looked around. But I didn't have a chance to warn her as my ex stopped in front of us.

"Kyson Hart." He drawled in his honey-smooth voice as he looked me up and down. "What a fucking pleasant surprise."

"Trevor Kingsley," I said back plainly, trying to act like the man had no effect on me. He had shaggy black hair and bottomless black eyes to match his black soul. But to the rest of the world, who didn't really know him, he looked sinfully sexy. Dark and dangerous, with his black and gray tattoos covering almost every inch of his skin, including his neck and fingers.

Fingers that had once been something I craved to feel against my skin. But the thought of them now made my throat burn with acid.

He wore a black shirt open to the middle of his chest with an array of golden chains hanging over his inked chest and a pair of maroon jeans, ripped and distressed, and the overall look screamed rockstar sex god.

And that was exactly what he was, and the entire world knew it because he had never tried to hide his sexual exploits from the public, regardless of the ramifications it had on his partners afterward. He had never cared about others' feelings. Mine included.

He smirked at me and licked his lips with a wild glint in his eye for a while before turning to Cora. "Mrs. Jones." He said, nodding his head. "Thank you for inviting me to your swanky affair. I'll be honest, I wasn't planning to stay long, the guest list at these things is usually too stiff and boring for me. But I think I might change my plans now that I know Ky is here."

"You two know each other?" She asked, looking from me to him and back.

"In a past life," I answered firmly.

"Oh, come on," Trevor said with a boisterous laugh, attracting the attention of everyone around him. "It wasn't that long ago, baby." I looked away from him, trying to find an exit strategy, but he had always read me like a book. "Trying to run away already, Ky?" He smirked and bit his bottom lip seductively. "You always had a thing for being chased."

"Don't act like you actually remember anything about me." I bit out, hating the way the anger came through my voice. "We both know you don't remember your conquests after you come off the high."

Cora's arm tightened around mine as she tried to step in. "If you'll excuse us, Trevor,--"

He cut her off, though, fire burning in his eyes as he took a step towards me. "We both know what we had was more than just some conquest, Ky. Because I was your first, and you were the only man I've ever loved." He said boldly, and the air in my lungs evaporated.

"What's going on here?" A deep baritone voice rumbled behind me, and my eyes fluttered closed as a groan escaped my lips. I looked over my shoulder as Dexter and Maverick came to a stop on each side of us, flanking Cora and myself in with their dominating presences.

Dexter had heard Trevor's words and judging by the tick in his jaw, he was fucking enraged by them. "Are you okay?" He asked me, finally pulling his menacing glare from my ex.

"Yeah, I was just leaving," I said firmly, letting go of Cora's arm and ushering her towards Maverick. "I have to go check on the lineup," I added, trying to calm my erratic heartbeat. "Come with me?" I asked softly, trying to soothe the fire burning in Dexter's eyes.

"Yeah." He said, looking back over to Trevor with disdain, before sliding his hand around my waist and turning away. Trevor's eyes squinted as he watched us clued into our relationship and his shoulders stiffened like he was preparing for battle. Dexter nodded to Mav. "I'll catch up."

Maverick watched the entire thing with fascinating curiosity in his eyes and a smirk on his lips, nodding to Dex. "Oh, I can't wait." He said.

"Ky, wait a second," Trevor said, but I ignored him and walked away, pressed tightly to Dexter's side as my entire body vibrated with nerves.

When we were across the room and headed down the hallway to the dressing room, Dexter finally spoke. "Are you okay?"

I nodded my head but kept walking until we were in the silent and empty room with the door shut behind us. "That fucking piece of shit." I cursed, pacing the glam room that had brought me such joy only hours ago.

"Was that the man you told me about? The one who used you before he got famous?" He asked, where he leaned against the door with his arms crossed over his chest.

"Man is a stretch of the word." I spit out in frustration and then sighed.

"What happened before I got there?" He asked.

I shook my head and threw myself down in the chair at one of the vanity stations. "I saw him with only a few seconds before he was on us, or I would have cut and run to stay out of his presence, I swear," I said, trying to assure him I wasn't looking for Trevor's attention tonight. If the roles were reversed, I would be a jealous catty bastard right now.

"I know Ky, I don't doubt you." He said evenly, not swaying a bit.

"Good." I sighed again. "He came up to us and Cora asked if we knew each other when he called me by name, and he spits some bullshit about knowing me well and was just overly familiar with me and I told him to cut it and to stop acting as he knew me at all anymore. That was when you walked up."

"When he said that he had been your first and that he was in love with you? That's what you mean?" He asked and I could feel the barely restrained anger in his voice.

"I didn't know he would be here," I said. "I haven't seen him in four or five years."

"But you broke up long before four or five years ago, didn't you?" He asked.

It didn't sound like much of a question.

"Yeah," I answered honestly as he watched me closely.

"And when you saw him last, what happened?"

Bile rose in my throat as I contemplated my answer, shame and grief washed over me at my stupidity and loneliness back then.

"We hooked up."

His eyes were dark blue depths of emotion as he watched me from the other side of the room. "You left out the fact that he was your first and that you two were in love when you told me the sordid tale that night."

I could feel his anger again, and it felt like he was aiming it at me, so I became defensive. "The same way you neglected to tell me you'd been married and fathered a child with the woman you described from your past, too." I bit out and then regretted it instantly.

His jaw clenched as he stood up off the door and adjusted his suit.

"I'm sorry," I said quickly, rubbing my forehead. "I shouldn't have thrown that at you, I'm just frustrated with myself right now."

He nodded his head and looked down at his feet. "I have to get back out there; the event will start soon." He said, pulling his sleeve up to check his watch.

"Please don't be mad at me," I tried, standing up and walking to him. "I didn't know he'd be here. And I didn't know he'd approach me like that."

He stayed still and stonewalled for a minute as he looked at me and then sighed and relaxed his shoulders. "I'm not mad at you, Kyson. I'm mad that there is someone else out there that knows what it's like to feel your skin against theirs." He pulled me in until our foreheads were pressed together and slid his fingers into my hair, holding me captive against him, which was exactly where I ached to be. "Someone that knows what it feels like to be the center of your attention and affection, because my God Kyson," He groaned, "It's fucking heaven and hell all wrapped into one. Believe me."

He captured my lips in a searing kiss that spoke volumes above what we couldn't say at that moment. I held onto him as he tortured my lips with his teeth and teased my body with his hands until I was aching to climb him like a tree and fuck him right there against the wall. Through the door, the emcee announced the event was beginning and asked everyone to take their seats, causing Dex to pull back and growl.

"We'll finish this later." He promised and gently kissed my lips, "I'm going to erase every other touch from your memory until only I exist inside of your head and your heart."

I leaned into him, "You already have." I said.

He smiled at me, but I could see he didn't believe me. I'd prove it to him one way or another.

When we walked back out to the event, we quickly found our table with Maverick, Cora, Maverick's parents, Marsha and Christopher, and an empty seat for Reid. Dexter and Maverick both kept looking around the event space through the first few rounds of auctions for their missing friend, and I could tell Dexter was getting more and more agitated as time went on.

When I turned to look around the space myself, dark hair on a tall, muscular set of shoulders caught my eye, and I looked to see if it was Reid. But it was Trevor, and he was watching me over the rim of his liquor glass with mischief in his eyes. I glared at him with what I hoped was menace and then looked away.

The emcee was announcing the next lot in the auction, a five-night stay at a chalet in France courtesy of Maverick's parents, and I tried to focus. The auction was changing over from items such as vacations and spa trips to the bachelor part after the next five items. We needed to find Reid or Cora was going to have a stroke. She was chewing on her lip anxiously as the big event got closer with still no word from him.

Just then, I saw him walking from the room towards the back entrance to the outside bar. Instead of telling Dex, I decided maybe a fresh face would help convince Reid to play along for the evening. "I'll be right back," I whispered to Dex and stood up, excusing myself from the group.

He grabbed my hand with worry in his eyes, "Where are you go-ing?"

"I saw Reid headed outside. I'm going to go talk to him and make sure he's all set."

"I'll go with you." He said, putting his napkin on the table and starting to stand up.

"No." I hurried on. "Let me go. I think he's heard it enough from you three lately. Maybe a fresh voice will help him."

He didn't look convinced, but Cora patted his arm as she and Mav looked on. "Let him go. He's got that gentle easiness that Reid may respond to, who knows?"

I smiled at her and then gave Dex a peck on his cheek to ease his temper that was no doubt building at being told no, "I'll be back in a jiff."

I raced off before he could tell me no because, let's be honest, he was going to tell me no. Especially because Trevor was still out in the crowd and Dexter knew he couldn't control him from the table. But luckily for me, I'd already seen where Trevor sat and avoided that entire area on my way out the back entrance to the terrace.

As soon as the humid night air hit me, I took a deep breath and went on the hunt. But I didn't have far to go because Reid sat at the empty outside bar with a crystal glass of amber-colored liquor sitting in front of him.

He had his head in his hands, looking down into the glass as I approached and when he heard my footsteps, he snapped his head up to look at me, in fight-or-flight mode.

I held my hands up, pausing my advancement on him until he relaxed in his seat. "I don't want to hear a word." He said gruffly, looking back down into his glass. I silently pulled the stool next to him out and sat down, unbuttoning my jacket.

"I didn't plan on saying anything," I said calmly. The bartender walked over and asked for my order, "Tonic water with lime, please."

"Don't be dry and boring on my account." Reid deadpanned from next to me, still holding his head. "It's miserable being sober."

"Are you sober?" I asked as my drink appeared.

"Painfully so." He hissed.

"How long has it been?"

"Eight days."

"That means the hardest part is nearly over," I said easily. "It's usually weeks two and three where things ease up a bit on the physical side of the battle, anyway."

He looked up at me out of the corner of his eye in question. "How would you know?"

I shrugged my shoulder and took a sip of my cool water. "Because I used to like vodka too much," I said, and he sat up to look at me better as I continued. "But when I drank it, I got mean. And after I was mean, I got sad. And when the vodka and the sadness mixed, I needed to take an upper to combat those two downers. So I added cocaine into the mix to balance out." I took another sip. "But I think we both know someone high on hard drugs and liquor is anything but balanced."

"So let me guess, you're going to tell me you know how I'm feeling right now and that it will get easier and all the other self-help bullshit that's been spit my way." He snarled at me.

I raised my eyebrow at him in a challenge. "No. I have no clue how you're feeling because when I detoxed I was doing it off of so many things at once I had it way worse."

He scoffed and slid his fingers around the rim of the glass. "Kay. Thanks for the talk. You can go back to your perfect boyfriend now and tell him you had a heart-to-heart with his buddy like he asked. I'm sure he'll fuck you good and long tonight for the effort."

"I plan on getting fucked good and long tonight regardless of you, thank you very much. But if you want to do yourself any favors at all, you'll find something to fill the time you used to spend drinking or you'll give in and take that drink in front of you. But you won't just stop at one, you'll keep going until you're so fucking shit-faced that you won't even recognize yourself in the mirror." I said, drowning the rest of my water. "And if I know anything at all about any of this," I motioned to the bar, "It's that the hardest fucking day is the one after you slip up. Do you think it's hard right now? Try doing it tomorrow after waking up hungover and miserable, because you won't have just alcohol in your system. You'll have regret, shame and despair and a million other things weighing you down that will only make it that much fucking harder to start over."

I laid down a tip for the bartender and stood up, figuring maybe I'd overstepped with Reid. "I can't do it." He said, catching me as I started walking away. I paused, and he looked up at me with those sad dark eyes that I'd seen in Cora's office the other day when she'd invited us all out for drinks. "Even work events are loaded with booze, I can't get away from it."

I sat back down on my stool and turned toward him. "Some people never gain the ability to be around it in social settings again, and maybe you'll be one of them. There's nothing wrong with that."

"Except my fucking job requires me to schmooze with these people at these events all the time."

"Some people can't do it, but that doesn't mean that will be how you are," I said, and he turned to look at me again. "I've overcome my addiction to it, but I still drink wine in moderation, hardly ever having more than a glass, and I've never had a slip up of overindulging since I got sober." He looked like he didn't believe me. "You are the only one who can choose how you handle this from now on, Reid. But you don't have to wallow in self-pity about it along the way if you don't want to."

He stayed quite a while, looking back down at his drink before pushing it away. I reached over, picked it up, and slid it down the bar to the bartender, who promptly poured it out. "I was out of line for saying that about you and Dex. I should thank you for coming out here to talk to me, not throwing that in your face. Though to be honest, it has nothing to do with your taste in partners, I would have given you shit if you were into women, too. It's just how I am."

"I get it," I replied, because I did. "Believe it or not, I've been the shit starter before." I chuckled humorlessly.

"I can't go up on that stage and parade around like I'm fucking perfectly fine right now. Because I'm not." He shook his head. "I'm not."

"Okay," I said, putting my hand on his arm and nodding. "Okay," I reassured him as I tried to figure out what he was going to do about the auction.

The coordinator for the event opened the doors, sticking her head out with panic in her eyes. "There you are! Thank God!" She gasped, rushing across the terrace to Reid. "We have less than two minutes before you go on. The auction has started. Let's go." She grabbed his arm and started pulling him off his stool.

Terror filled Reid's eyes as he looked from her to me and I felt it in the pits of my soul because I remembered how fragile my grip on sanity was when I was fresh in the sober world. "Wait," I said, rubbing my fingers over my forehead in frustration, trying to figure out a way to get him out of this whole thing. An idea struck seconds before my good sense shot it down, but the seed had been planted. And I didn't have another option in front of me, and he was out of time. "I'll do it."

"What?" They both asked in shock.

"I'll do the auction," I said, standing up as dread filled my bones, nearly causing me to panic as I thought about how pissed Dexter was going to be at me. "Under one condition." I pointed my finger at Reid and leveled him with my most menacing glare.

"Anything." He rushed on with desperate eyes. "Anything you want, it's yours if you do this for me."

"You cannot let Trevor Kingsley win me," I demanded.

"The—" He paused. "The rockstar?" Confusion marred his features.

"Gentlemen!" The coordinator snapped her fingers. "We do not have time for this!"

"Promise me!" I snapped at him as the tiny but feral woman dragged me towards the doors.

"I promise." He gasped, following us. "Thank you!" He called out as the woman hauled me behind the stage and towards the steps.

"Jesus fuck." I muttered, taking a deep breath and running my hands through my hair as I walked up onto the stage.

Here goes fucking nothing.

Chapter 14 – Dexter

I scanned the crowd again, looking for Kyson or Reid, but still came up empty. "Where the fuck are they?" Maverick hissed from next to me as he panicked. "I swear if he makes Cora look bad up there, I'm going to wring his neck."

The crowd started clapping in congratulations for the poor bastard that had just been won by a woman twice his age with a yellow hue to her aging skin and more money than she could spend in the rest of her short lifetime.

Cringe.

"Alright," Cora said from the stage where she stood next to the emcee with a look on her face that could only be described as deer in the headlights. It was Reid's turn, and he was the last bachelor of the night, but he was nowhere on stage. "Uh- our next bachelor this evening—" She paused, looking around.

"It's not his fault." A voice hissed from behind me and we both turned to see Reid standing there, hiding from Cora on the stage.

"What the fuck are you doing—" Maverick started.

But Reid held his hand up to him and turned to me, repeating himself. "It's not his fault."

"What isn't his fault? Who?" I stammered in confusion, but dread was already sliding down my spine at the fact that Reid was here, yet Kyson was not.

Commotion from the stage grabbed our attention, and we all turned to look as Kyson walked hesitantly up onto the stage to stand next to Cora, leaning down to whisper in her ear.

"No." I bit out and took a step forward, but Maverick grabbed my arm and pulled me backward.

Cora's face lit up as she nodded to him and then walked forward. "Ladies and gentlemen alike, do we have a treat for you."

"I'll kill you." I snapped at Reid, and he rolled his eyes.

"He offered. He made me promise not to let that singer from Death's Gate win him, though." Reid said, cocking an eyebrow at me. "Care to tell me what that's about?"

I ignored him though and looked back up at the stage, locking eyes with Ky as he found me in the crowd.

Cora continued. "We've had a slight switch in the lineup tonight, but something tells me a bit of a bad boy for an evening never hurt anyone before, what do you say?" She cheered, and the crowd erupted in shouts and claps. Women and men alike cat-called Ky on the stage, and he looked around the room, giving a slight nod before looking back at me. "Kyson Hart is the hottest stylist in all of NYC right now, and soon to be the entire nation. He's got that bad boy vibe and a heart the size of Texas!" The crowd cheered again, and he widened his eyes at me once again. "Alright, our highest bid of the night went to Carter Washington for twenty-five thousand dollars, but I think Mr. Hart here is worth so much more than that, so ladies and gentlemen, get your checkbooks out and let's start the bid at twenty-five thousand!" She yelled.

"Twenty-five." A woman from the front called instantly, and I groaned.

"Twenty-six." A male voice called, and I turned to see Trevor Kingsley standing at the side of the stage with a smug look on his face as he bid on a man that was no longer his.

"Twenty-six," Cora said, but even I could hear the dread in her voice as she acknowledged his bid.

"Thirty," I called, glaring at her, and then looking at Ky and nodding. No one else was going to win him, even if I had to clear out my entire bank account to make sure of it.

"Forty," Trevor replied instantly. Everyone in the room was volleying their heads back and forth between us as the war was declared.

"Forty-five," I responded.

Kyson looked downright pale, standing under the bright lights as his hands tightened and loosened into fists repeatedly. His stress was unmistakable.

"I've got twenty thousand towards the bid," Reid said from between me and Mav. "It's the least I can fucking do."

"Fifty," Trevor responded, smirking at me across the dancefloor as it cleared to leave us both in the center of the affair.

"Fifty thousand to Trevor Kingsley," Cora said, looking back to me with the question in her eyes.

"Sixty-Five." I shot back, glaring openly at the piece of shit trying to steal what wasn't his anymore.

He smirked at me, raising his glass, "One hundred thousand dollars."

The crowd gasped and awed at the outlandish bid and in any other circumstance, I'd have walked away. No person was worth a hundred thousand dollars for one evening. But Kyson wasn't just a person.

He was my fucking person. And I'd pay millions to keep him safe from a man that had used him and made him feel small before.

"Wow!" Cora praised, trying to keep the event light and drama free. "A hundred thousand dollars is an incredible amount of money for our charities. Thank you, Mr. Kingsley." She nodded to me. "Mr. Chase?"

"Whatever the cost, I'll cover what you can't," Maverick whispered. "You're not losing your man to that piece of shit."

"I know I'm not," I replied, never wavering or taking my eyes off Kyson on the stage, and I knew my eyes were the only thing giving him strength. His lips pulled up in a gentle smile at me and his shoulders relaxed. "Two hundred."

"Sold!" Cora cheered! Pointing her hand at me. "Sold to Mr. Dexter Chase, who just so happens to be Mr. Hart's incredible boyfriend." She added with a wink and the crowd oohed and awed at the romance.

When he realized he would not win the auction, Trevor looked like someone had reached out and struck him across the face. Thank God Cora called it when she did, or I have no doubt he would have tried to snake his way back into Kyson's world, whatever the cost.

Maverick clapped his hand on my shoulder and smirked at me. "That's a hell of a tax write-off my man."

"I don't care," I said, walking away and heading toward the stage to claim my prize. Cora talked on, explaining more about the charities and the events still left for the night as I walked around the back of the stage and met Kyson.

"Thank God." He groaned as soon as he saw me in the dark alcove. I grabbed his jacket and pulled him against me, crushing him in my arms.

"What the fuck were you thinking?" I asked, fisting my hand in his hair to pull his head back to look at me.

"I panicked." He admitted. "I wanted to help Reid; he was so desperate." His cheeks reddened as embarrassment filled his body. "I didn't know what else to do, I'm sorry."

I leaned forward, crashing my lips against his, and felt him soften in my arms, relaxing my anger. He opened for me, and I eagerly tasted him, backing him up against the side of the large stage. Decorations and décor hid us in the darkness, and I took advantage of that. "You. Are. Mine." I growled against his lips as I flexed my hips, rubbing myself against him.

He moaned and begged for more, pulling me closer to him. "I'm yours." He panted. "You literally bought me tonight, and I never thought that would be sexy before. But for some reason, the idea of being owned by you is making me so fucking hot right now."

"Let's get out of here," I said, pulling my fingers from his hair and sliding them down his jaw. "I have special plans for you tonight, and you can't say no. Because, as you pointed out, I own you."

"Yes." He panted with a devilish smile on his face. "I'm yours to use, baby."

"Well, that was quite a show you two put on back there." A voice called out from behind us, and I looked over my shoulder. "Though I think I'm enjoying watching this one more."

Trevor Kingsley stood at the edge of the darkness, watching us with grotesque fascination in his glassy eyes. I turned around and faced him as Kyson adjusted his rumpled clothes behind me.

"What do you want?" I asked him plainly, ignoring pleasantries and manners since he was obviously not polite enough to give privacy to a couple in a dark corner.

"Well, I'd been planning on fucking Ky for old times' sake tonight." He said, swallowing down the rest of his drink. "But maybe I'll make it a two-for-one deal." He winked at me and licked his lips. "What do you say, *Dex?*" The way he said my name made my skin crawl. "I bet you'd like my cock in your ass as much as Ky does."

"Get out of here." I bit out, taking a menacing step towards him. "Consider yourself lucky for even being able to hold on to the memory of Ky, because you'll never touch him again. So get fucking lost."

"Aw come on man, no need to be so uptight," Trevor said, looking past my shoulder to where Kyson still stood as his hand slid in mine and tightened it.

"Trevor just stop," Kyson said. "That time has passed."

"But think about how good we were together, baby," Trevor replied, taking a step forward, but I slid to the side, blocking him with my body. He talked around me, "You used to beg so prettily for me. And the things you could do with your mouth…" He groaned, letting his eyes close like he was remembering the feel. "You always were a good fuck toy, Ky. But you'll never be anything more than that. So why even try to blend in with these rich bastards? You can dress yourself up and pretend you're some fancy piece of shit now all you want, but you're still just a pathetic toy that's bent over every backstage couch on the east coast for a line of coke."

"Fuck off." Reid appeared around the corner, grabbing Trevor's shoulder and hauling him backward before throwing a fist directly into his face. The sound of his nose breaking under the weight of Reid's fist was deafening. "You're a pathetic piece of shit and Ky's ten times the man you'll ever pretend to be." Trevor fell backward onto the floor, holding his bleeding face as Reid shook his hand out. "Fuck, that hurts worse the older I get."

I laid a hand on Reid's shoulder, pulling him back as he went in for another punch and stepped between them. "Don't do it, man." I looked over my shoulder at the sniveling, pathetic man on the floor. "He's not worth it."

Maverick appeared with a few security guards seconds later. "Heard there was a commotion over here." He said, looking down where Trevor was spewing curses at Reid and me and nodded to security behind him. "Take out the trash, would you boys?" Security stepped forward, grabbed him, lifted him off his feet, and carried him out the side door.

"You'll regret this, Kyson!" He yelled as the doors slammed shut behind him. "I'm going to sue your fucking boyfriend and ruin his life!"

I looked back over at Kyson where he stood with a shocked look on his face. "Mr. Jones—" he stammered, "I'm so sorry. I didn't mean to cause a scene."

Maverick waved him off and held his hand out for him to shake, which he did cautiously. "No one disrespects our family, Kyson. And you are a part of our family now. So don't worry about it." He said, "Besides, security knows to throw him out on the front steps, directly at the feet of the paparazzi that have been camped out there all night. I'm sure they'll eat up a disgraced rockstar like starving men eating a steak. He'll be laughed right out of New York by the morning."

"Thanks, Mav," I responded, shaking his hand, and then looked at Reid. "You too, Reid. I appreciate it."

He shook his head and laid his hand on Ky's shoulder. "Not nearly as much as I appreciate you two. Now get out of here. Take your prize home and enjoy the rest of your night." He winked at Ky, who rolled his eyes with good humor and leaned against me.

"Let's go home." He said, and I could hear the arousal in his voice.

"Let's."

The elevator doors opened to our floor, and I pulled my teeth from Kyson's neck. "Go to your place and give me a few minutes, then come over," I instructed him.

He looked at me through the haze of arousal and nodded. "You have five minutes. That's it. I'm too needy to give you any more."

"That's all I need, baby," I responded, kissing his lips and walking to my place. "Keep your curtains shut, no peeking."

"Yes, Sir." He threw over his shoulder with a wink as he went to his door and walked in.

I rushed around my apartment, getting the last few things I needed ready for the night, and went into the bedroom, stripping out of my evening wear to my boxer briefs, and then started lighting the candles.

I may not have experience with male relationships, but romance didn't know gender or labels. It was universal.

A couple of minutes later, a knock sounded from the front door, and I opened it, revealing a completely naked Kyson holding a rose between his teeth.

I leaned against the door and let my eyes rove over his delectable body and smirked at him. "And what would you have done if someone had gotten off the elevator on the wrong floor?"

He shrugged his shoulders at me and smiled, "Made their night?"

"Hmm." I hummed, reaching forward to grab his erection that bobbed between his thighs and pulled him into my home by it. He groaned as I took the rose and tossed it on the counter, and then pushed him against the door. I lowered my lips back to his neck where I'd been sucking and biting in the elevator and continued my assault as I stroked his cock. He thrust his hips forward, pushing his cock into my hand, and held onto my biceps as I worked him over. "Tonight is going to be intense," I whispered. "We need a safe word."

He panted and shook his head. "Why? What are you going to do that I wouldn't like?"

"It's not about liking it or not, Ky. You're going to love it. But it's going to be a lot. And it could get overwhelming."

"What is it?"

"You'll have to wait and see," I said with authority, and his eyes fluttered closed. "What's your safe word?"

"Uh—" He stammered. "I don't know, I've never used one before."

I kissed my way down his neck and chest until I was crouching down in front of him, leaving a trail of wet kisses down the center of his abs, pausing directly above his aching cock. "Think of one Kyson. Something you wouldn't scream out during sex normally. But something you can remember."

I sat back on my heels and gently laid a kiss on the end of his leaking cock, tasting his come and savoring it as I swirled my tongue over the end.

"Corkscrew." He gasped as I engulfed his cock with my mouth, and I pulled back off of him with surprise.

"Corkscrew?" I asked, trying to keep the smile out of my voice, but failed.

"It's what brought me to your door that first night. It's what started it all." He looked down at me with a sexy smile on his lips as his dark hair fanned out around his face.

"Corkscrew," I repeated and then nodded my head. "Okay." I stood up and kissed him hungrily. "I'm going to make you beg for it tonight, Kyson. And I'm going to make you crazy with need before I give it to you."

"Jesus Dex. I'll beg you right now if that's what you want, baby. I'm already desperate for you."

I smirked and turned away, pulling him behind me into my bedroom. He paused in the doorway and took it all in. Candles were lit on every surface of the room and black satin sheets covered the bed.

"Wow." He whispered with an excited smirk. "You did all of this for me?"

"For us," I said, leading him to the bed and grabbing a sash of satin off of it in blood red. "Close your eyes."

He watched me for a moment before slowly closing his eyes and allowing me to tie it over his eyes, blinding him.

I took a deep breath as my body thrummed with excitement at having him at a disadvantage and at my mercy. "Lie down," I ordered, and he slowly laid back in the center of the bed with his head on the lone pillow in the middle. I ran my fingertips down his thighs to his feet, and his muscles twitched and jerked beneath me. I kissed his calf and then his ankle as I reached for the hidden tie and gently fastened it around his ankle before he noticed what I was doing. When it tightened, he jerked, feeling the resistance holding his leg wide open, and he gasped.

"Dex?"

"Shh," I commanded, grabbing his other foot, and running the edge of my thumbnail over the sensitive flesh in the arch of his foot. "Spread your legs." He did as I told him and I fastened it with the tie, tightening both to keep his ankles spread to the outer corners of my king-sized bed. "Good boy." I praised and his cock throbbed, leaking a large drop of come onto his stomach. I leaned up onto the bed and licked it off his skin, pulling a groan from both of us before moving up to his wrists.

"What are you going to do to me?" He asked in a breathy whisper as I tied one arm up over his head towards the corner and walked around to do the other.

"Tying you down and torturing you with pleasure."

"Mmh." He moaned as I ran my fingers down the inside of his bicep. "Are you a Dom in secret?" He asked, "Waiting for the right time to come out of the dark and surprise me?"

I chuckled and kissed his chest. "If I'm a Dom, I'm a pleasure Dom."

"Fuck yes." He hissed as I sucked his nipple into my mouth and bit it.

"Well, with a side of pain to mix with the pleasure."

"Oh, my God. I'm going to explode in record time."

I smiled against his skin as I worked my way down his body with my mouth. "I'm going to suck you so good, but you're not allowed to come. Do you understand?"

"Yes." He panted.

"What's your safe word?"

"Corkscrew." He replied instantly.

"Good," I said, fisting his cock and swirling my tongue around the tip again before sucking it into my mouth with lots of pressure. He groaned and his hips flexed at the sudden sensation as his limbs pulled on their restraints. "Do you have any idea how sexy you look all tied up like this?" I pushed my head down, so his cock went down my throat until I gagged and pulled back up. "At my mercy." I dropped my lips to his smooth balls and sucked on them, one at a time, until he was panting and wiggling under me in pleasurable agony. "Beg me for more, Kyson," I demanded as I pulled up off of him and hovered over his cock.

"Please Dexter, give me more. I'm so fucking close. Please give me more."

I nipped the inside of his thigh before lowering myself down again to suck his cock as my fingers rolled his balls.

"Tell me what Trevor did to you in bed that you liked the most," I said, watching him up his body as my words penetrated through the arousal in his head.

"What?" He gasped. "Why the fuck do you want to talk about him right now." He jumped when I bit the tip of his cock before pushing it all the way down my throat until my lips kissed his stomach and pulled back off. "Holy fuck." He cried. "Dexter."

"Tell me."

"No." He refused, shaking his head back and forth.

"Tell me, Kyson," I demanded once more. "I won't tell you again."

"Dex, please." He begged, shaking his head again. "I don't want him here."

"I need to know what he did that you liked." I fisted his cock and twisted my hand around the head of it with quick, powerful pulls that drove him wild.

"Oh god." He moaned, flexing his hips. I pulled off and stood at the end of the bed, silently watching him as he realized I left him. "Dex! Why did you stop?"

"Because you are disobeying me," I said easily as I leaned over to blow out a candle next to the bed, letting the smoke waft towards him. I knew he'd think I was calling it quits, and he panicked.

"Wait!" He gasped, "Don't stop. Please, for the love of everything holy, please don't fucking stop, baby." His chest heaved as he fought for control. But I needed the control tonight.

I'd lost control earlier when he put himself up for auction with his possessive ex in the room and I'd nearly lost my mind.

"Tell me."

"I–" He groaned. "I can't."

"Why?"

"It's not relative anymore. Please, just let it go."

I picked the candle up off the end table and held it over him, but he couldn't see it thanks to the blindfold.

"Last chance. Tell me."

"Dex—" He tried, but I warned him. I tipped the candle over, letting the liquid wax pour out over his hip as he let out a hiss and a yelp. "Fuck!" I poured a line of wax across his lower abdomen, dripping it dangerously close to the crown of his cock where it lay twitching against him as he moaned in ecstasy from the pleasurable pain. "Degradation!" He all but screamed.

I lifted the candle to stop the dripping as he panted. "Degradation?"

"He degraded me. It was his kink." He rushed on.

"But you told me that was your hard limit," I said, setting the candle down on the table and watching the flush of shame or pleasure crawl over his skin.

"It is. He ruined it for me." Ky said, shaking his head back and forth. "He made me crave it. I fucking loved it, but he was cruel and toxic."

I watched him closely. "What did he do?"

"No, Dex."

"Kyson," I growled, and he groaned, flexing his hips as I grabbed onto his cock and rubbed it.

"He used me. In front of others." He said, moaning as my hand tightened around the crown of his cock just how he liked. "He'd make me small and pathetic for everyone else to laugh at."

Anger coursed through my body as I imagined Kyson allowing someone to do that to him in confusion and shame. "You're not pathetic," I retorted. "Or small."

"Yes, I was Dexter. And I enjoyed being used. That was the worst part."

"It's not wrong to enjoy being a toy or feeling used in a healthy consensual relationship Kyson, stop wearing that shame. It's not yours to bear."

"How would you know?"

"Because degradation is something I've played with before. I know how powerful it can actually make a person, a sub, feel if done right." He panted, and I tore the blindfold off of him, making him squint into the golden candlelight. "I can make you feel good, Kyson. With or without it."

He closed his eyes and battled with himself before simply nodding his head. "Use me Dex."

"Safe word?" I asked him, as my skin prickled with anticipation.

"Corkscrew."

"Good boy." I praised, and he grinned.

"That's the opposite of degrading me."

"They're one and the same if it's done right, baby," I growled against his lips before taking them in a passionate kiss. Moving down, I unfastened his ankle tie from the bedpost and slid it around the bottom of his foot before tying it to his wrist, folding his knee up towards his side. I repeated the process with the other one until his legs were both spread and pulled back, opening his ass and cock to my wandering hands. "I'm going to make you feel so good, so cherished," I assured him. "You're the absolute start and finish of my world, Kyson Hart," I promised as I kneeled between his legs and lowered myself down until his still hard cock was lined up with my mouth. I sucked on him, pulling long groans and pleas from his lips as I worked him up. "I'm positively obsessed with you. You know that, don't you?"

"Are you?" He panted, fighting the restraints.

"Painfully so." I took him back down my throat, coating him with my saliva before pulling off and then sucking his balls into my mouth and humming.

"Shit." He cursed, trying to flex his hips, but he was unable to lift them very far in the precarious position I had him tied up in.

"Do you like being at my mercy?" I asked and slid my tongue down over his exposed ass, swirling it around and pushing it in. "Do you like being helpless to me?"

"Fuck yes." He hissed.

"Do you trust me to pleasure you without fail?"

"Yes." He repeated, panting like he'd just got done with cardio.

"Good. Because that's exactly what I'm going to do. I'm going to use your body for my pleasure and yours at the same time. Because you're such a little slut for everything I give you." He groaned and come leaked from the tip of his cock. I pushed two fingers into his ass, using my saliva to lessen the burn, but it wasn't as good as lube. And that had been the point. "You're such a little slut for my mouth and my fingers, aren't you?"

"Yes!" He cried. "Yes, Dex."

"Who do you belong to?" I asked him as I pushed a third finger into his ass and curled them forward as I sucked him deep again before popping off. "Who does your ass belong to?"

"You baby. Only you, no one else." He looked down his body at me as I kneeled up between his spread legs. "Please Dexter, please give it to me, baby. Own me, I'm so close."

"I say when you can come, Ky." I reminded him as I found his p-spot and pressed hard on it, rubbing my fingers back and forth over the spongy flesh inside of him.

"That feels so good."

"You're such a needy whore." I groaned, "Your ass is strangling my fingers, desperate for more." He thrashed his head back and forth as I pleasured him with my fingers and my words. "I think I'll keep you tied up like this all the time. Open and ready for me to use whenever I want to like a slave. I can just imagine coming home at the end of the day and your needy asshole just being on display for me like this. And you completely restrained, unable to tell me no." He licked his lips and watched me with crazed eyes as I looked down at his sexy body. "I'm going to tie you down and use you whenever I want, however I want." I promised him and his body shivered.

"Please. Just fuck me already, I need your giant cock forcing its way inside of me." He begged.

"Who's cock is this?" I asked, squeezing him as I poured the lube over it, letting it slide down to his puckered ass as my fingers pushed it in deep. He mewed, tossing his head back and forth as he fought to keep his orgasm at bay. "Tell me who owns this ass and cock and I'll fuck you like a good little slut. And I'm taking you bare tonight too. I'm going to claim your ass as mine with my come."

"You!" He bellowed. "They belong to you, I'm yours. Please fuck me now! Please, I'm so desperate for it." He cried, and I lined up, slamming into his helpless ass in one punishing thrust. "YES!" He screamed, throwing his head back into the pillow and letting his cry for more out into the room around us. The veins in his neck bulged as I railed his ass with my cock in deep, dominating thrusts, leaving no question who owned him.

"Good boy." I praised him as his eyes rolled and his entire body tensed. I kept up the painful pace of fucking him into the mattress, even as I pushed myself towards my orgasm way faster than I'd planned. It felt so fucking good to slide into his body at the angle and pace fit to please me, because I knew the entire experience was pleasing him. "So fucking good." I stroked his slick cock with my fist as I fucked his ass, and he did nothing but lie there and take it because I took away every other option when I tied him up. "You're perfect Ky. So sexy like this, so perfect for me."

"I'm coming." He gasped, looking down at his body where I fisted him. "More!" I reached forward and laid my free hand on his throat, restricting the blood flow to his brain, I pushed him into ecstasy, and he exploded underneath me seconds later. His eyes were positively feral as he stared up at me as I choked him and fucked him hard, pushing myself over the edge as I filled his ass up with my come.

"Take. Every. Drop." I growled with each thrust as I emptied my balls of copious amounts of come. "Fuck." I groaned sagging against him in fatigue for a second before I leaned back up off of his used body and gently pulled my cock from his body, watching every centimeter slide free until the head popped free and my come dripped out of his gaping hole before it clenched back up, locking it all up inside of him. "That's the sexiest thing I've ever seen in my life." I praised, shaking my head back and forth in wonder.

I looked up at his body and paused when I saw he had his eyes closed tight and he was chewing on his bottom lip. "Ky?" I asked, but he didn't acknowledge me. "Baby," I commanded, but he still wouldn't open his eyes and look at me. I quickly grabbed his ankle and undid one tie, gently lying his leg down on the mattress before reaching for the other one as tears started pouring from the corners of his closed eyes. He was fighting to contain his emotions and my heart seized in my chest as I worried I'd hurt him. "What's wrong?" I asked, reaching up and undoing his arms. "Talk to me!" I yelled in panic.

When both of his arms were free, he covered his face and his shoulders shook with silent sobs as I stared down at him, afraid I'd pushed him too far. I felt gutted, raw, and exposed as I watched him lose it. I leaned down over him, and he wrapped both arms around me, pulling me tight against his body and I rolled us onto our sides, so I didn't crush him, and held him tight as he silently cried against my neck.

"I'm sorry," I whispered over and over. "I'm so sorry, Ky. I pushed you too far, I should have stopped. You should have safe worded out." I felt like the worst kind of monster for reading him wrong in a time of vulnerability when I'd felt so confident in our connection.

He finally calmed down and his breathing slowed, but he kept his arms and legs tight around my neck and legs as he whispered. "Thank you."

"Thank you?" I asked, pulling back, forcing him to let go of me enough so I could see his face. His cheeks were red and tear-stained as I pushed his dark hair back to look at him. "Talk to me before my heart seizes up completely here," I begged. "Please."

"You gave it back to me." He said, shaking his head and closing his eyes as more tears fell. "You gave *me* back to me." His chest shuddered as he took a breath and then he tried again. "He took the part of me that trusted anyone enough to give up everything and let them use me like that. And I hadn't realized how badly I missed it until just now. I thought I hated that whole side of sex, but what I hated was how he did it. Because he never cared about me when he used me, but you..." He paused, opening his eyes to look into mine. "You cherished me." His lips opened and closed as he rambled and then he stopped, taking a deep breath, and started again. "You cherished me, Dex, in a way I've never been cherished before. And you made me feel the most cared for

I've ever been before. All while calling me a slut and using me to feed that dirty, dark side that has been hungry and unsatisfied for years." He said with a snort. "How the fuck did you do that?"

"I just paid attention Kyson," I answered easily, running my fingers through his hair and taking a deep breath to calm my anxiety now that I knew he was okay. "I just did everything my heart called to me to do."

"I guess that's the difference between fucking and..." He stopped, blushing.

"And making love." I finished for him, and his eyes snapped to mine in surprise.

"Yeah. I'm falling for you Dex, it's true. But I didn't think that making love could be like that. I thought it was just when two people had slow, passionate, loving... sex." He looked over my shoulder with wide eyes. "But my God."

"The pace and position don't matter when it comes to using your heart, Ky," I said, leaning forward and kissing him gently. "And I'm falling for you, too." I kissed the tip of his nose and then slid from the bed.

"Uh-oh." He quipped, watching me get up. "You fuck me to tears and take off?"

I rolled my eyes at him over my shoulder as I walked into the bathroom and cleaned up, coming back with a warm washcloth and towel. I kneeled on the bed behind him and gently cleaned him up as he watched me with warm green eyes. "Aftercare is just as important as the fun stuff."

"You really are a Dom, aren't you?" He asked with a cheeky smile.

I shook my head. "No. But let's just say I know a Dom, and I've learned a few things from him over the years."

He raised an eyebrow at me as I dried us both off and climbed back into bed. "Who?" He asked when I didn't offer the information back up. "Come on, tell me! Who's giving you sex advice that literally just blew my head off?"

"Reid," I said, and his eyes nearly popped out of his head.

"What! No way!" He gasped as I pulled him into my arms and laughed at him.

"Yes, way. Though it's been a few years since I've seen him in action with a true sub. It's actually quite... mesmerizing."

"Mesmerizing?" He asked as he pondered that for a while. "I always assumed he was a fuck 'em and leave 'em kind. Don't Dom and Sub relationships take a while to build, and take nurturing and whatever to make it safe and healthy?"

"Yeah, they do. And he used to do that a lot, but he had a few duds in a row and he kind of walked away from the relationship thing and just aimlessly fucks his way around now. I think that's why his drinking got so out of hand."

"Do you think a Dom/Sub relationship would help him get his head back on square?"

"One hundred percent," I answered honestly, with a sad smile on my lips. "I never really understood it back then, because I'd only had casual relationships up to that point myself, but looking back now, he was a totally different man when he had a sub to lead and train."

"Well, that solves it then." He said, snuggling in against my neck.

"What does?"

"We're going to help him find a new sub." He replied, yawning and smiling against my chest.

Good lord help Reid, because Ky was going to help him find a new partner whether he wanted one or not.

But a small part of my brain told me that someone in the lifestyle could actually be the answer to his self-destructive tailspin.

Chapter 15 – Kyson

Monday afternoon I walked into Hawthorn Tower for a meeting with Cora to sign a contract of employment as the exclusive stylist for her and Maverick full-time. Dexter and I had talked at length about it yesterday as we lounged around his apartment. Talking about finances with a guy you've only been seeing for a few weeks wasn't exactly the most comfortable thing to do, but he actually brought a bunch of good ideas to the table, and we ended the conversation in a good place.

I was excited about this new opportunity because I would stay in the city more often if my primary clients were located here, which meant I'd be staying close to Dex more often. And after Saturday night's sexual breakthrough, I was all too eager to stay close to Dexter Chase.

I used to think that Trevor had ruined my previous enjoyment of a little degradation with my praise, but turned out that he had just ruined my enjoyment of him. Granted, his toxic use of my kink against me wasn't the only thing he had done to achieve that, either.

But Dexter had cherished me and shown me I did like being used when I was used by someone that cared for me.

And gosh, did I care for him too.

It had only been a few weeks, but we'd bonded and connected in a way that words couldn't describe. And I was head over heels for him and I didn't try to even play it cool anymore, he knew I was a goner.

As I got off the elevator in the main reception area on the top floor, I felt a bit of disappointment knowing that Dexter wasn't here right now and that I was probably going to miss him while I was here for my meeting. He and Maverick were across the city doing a deal with one of Maverick's other companies, but I'd see him tonight when he came over for dinner and a movie, so I just had to be patient.

"Mr. Hart!" The main receptionist said with a cheery smile on his face. "Saturday night's event went so smoothly, and all the bachelors looked incredible. Including you." He said with a wink, and I felt an awkward blush cover my cheeks as I smiled at him.

"Thank you. It was a great evening all around." I said and then nodded my head towards Mav and Cora's offices. "I have an appointment with Mrs. Jones."

"Of course." He said, blushing himself, "Go right on back. Slade is there waiting for you."

"Thank you," I said and headed down the hallway to the waiting area outside of the main offices.

Slade, Maverick's assistant, led me right into Cora's office and shut the door behind us on his way out.

As soon as I saw Cora behind her desk, I cringed though, because she didn't look so good. "Hey. Are you alright?" I asked cautiously.

She looked over at me and rolled her eyes dramatically, pushing her blonde hair back from her face. "I have the worst heartburn in the world's history." She complained, leaning back in her chair and rubbing her belly. "If this baby girl doesn't come out with a full head of hair, I'll be disappointed."

I smirked and shook my head. "I wonder if she'll be blonde or brunette. Though I'll bet anything she'll be the prettiest little girl in the world either way."

She smiled at me and motioned for me to sit across from her. "I agree, but I'm biased." She said and cringed a little, putting her hand on her stomach. Before I could say anything about it, she moved on, grabbing paperwork, and handing it to me. "Here is the contract that Dex had drafted up with the terms that we were thinking."

I read it over and suppressed the smirk that wanted to grace my face, as I was trying to keep my poker face in place. But every single thing I wanted in terms of employment was met and even exceeded in places like compensation, time off, and benefits, including a company car to keep me mobile and available to them whenever. "This all looks great, Cora," I replied.

"Thank God, because I don't think I have it in me to play hardball today, so I would have conceded to give you whatever you wanted to ensure your employment here." She said with a grateful sigh, leaning backward again.

"Are you okay?" I asked, putting the contract down on the desk and leaning forward on my elbows. "You look a bit washed out and uncomfortable."

She smirked and shook her head. "I think I overdid it Saturday night. I danced so much that my feet were swollen into balloons by the time I got home. This end of pregnancy life is not for the faint of heart, I'll tell you that."

"If you're sure," I said pensively. "I know Mav's not here, so I want to make sure you're okay before I take off."

She smiled sweetly at me and nodded. "Have time for a late lunch?" She asked hopefully.

"You haven't eaten yet?" I looked at my watch, it was almost three pm. "No wonder you don't feel good. Let's get you some food." I said, pulling my phone out. "What are you feeling like?"

She moaned, "Bar food." And then giggled. "How about Mc-Cauley's?"

"Perfect." I opened the food delivery app and ordered us a smorgasbord of fried food and relaxed in the chair as she chatted about the success of the charity event and the next one that she was planning until her phone rang.

"Ooh, maybe our food is here already." She said happily as she picked up her office phone. But as I watched her, I saw the color leave her face, and cold steel replaced the blue in her eyes. "Let her back to Slade and then get security up here." She slammed the phone down.

"Is everything okay?" I stood up as she did. She smoothed her blood-red Gucci dress down over her belly and grabbed a tube of lipstick from her desk.

"No. Everything is not fine." She said with a menacing voice that made my skin prickle. "The woman that Maverick cheated on me with in high school and then dated years later, just showed up at reception, requesting to see *my* husband." She bit out and I grimaced. "Oh, and she was my best friend at the time, too. Fucking cunt."

"What are you going to do?" I asked as she applied the matching red lipstick and puckered up. The pairing made her look regal and cunning and quite a bit intimidating even at five-foot nothing and pregnant.

"I want to punch the bitch in the face for even showing up here. But I suppose I should keep my hands to myself, considering." She said, sliding her hand down over her belly. "But I'm going to find out what she wants and then kick her ass out onto the street."

"Should you call Mav?" No way would he want her getting upset this late in her pregnancy or at all, for that matter.

"No time." She said and then walked to her door, pausing with her hand on the handle and taking a deep breath. "Do not punch the cunt. Do not punch the cunt." She repeated in a mantra before she opened the door and walked out with her head held high.

"Shit." I groaned as I grabbed my phone and shot a text to Dexter.

S.O.S. Mav's ex is at Hawthorn; Cora is meeting with her...

I followed Cora out to the reception area outside of her office and cringed when I saw the woman standing by Slade's desk. She was dressed in a low-cut black leather top paired with a white mini skirt that left zero to the imagination about what she had thanks to plastic surgery. Her eyes squinted angrily as she watched Cora walk towards her. My phone pinged in my hand, and I read Dex's reply.

Sarah? Fuck. I'll send Reid. Mav's going to lose his shit. DO NOT LEAVE HER SIDE! She'll knock Sarah's teeth out, given the chance.

On it.

"Sarah," Cora said with audible disdain. "What are you doing here?"

The woman smirked and looked Cora up and down. "God, you got fat." She smirked and my blood boiled as she flipped her hair over her shoulder and continued. "I'm visiting Maverick, no need to insert yourself where you don't belong."

"You're the one that doesn't belong here. You need to leave." Cora replied coolly, keeping herself composed. Kudos girl.

"Whatever Cora. I'm not here to see you. And Mav always sees me when I visit." She said with an evil gleam in her eyes. She was trying to bait Cora and I could tell my pregnant friend was on a very short fuse, so I stepped in.

"Maverick is not in the building right now, so you can leave a message with his assistant and leave. I'm sure if he's interested in what you have to say, he'll call you back."

Her eyes snapped to mine again. "Who are you?" She looked me up and down and I visibly cringed as she eye fucked me.

"Ew," I responded, unable to hold it back, and a fire burned in her eyes at my diss.

"Sarah." Reid's voice called out from behind us as he all but ran down the hallway. "Leave."

He stopped on Cora's other side and put his arm around her shoulders, pulling her back a step before pushing her towards me.

"What is with the guard dog shit, Reid? I'm just here to see Maverick. You know I visit when I'm in the city, this isn't new."

"But Maverick is married and no longer interested in you, that has changed. So you need to leave."

"No!" She yelled, drawing the attention of others in the offices as she turned on her ex-best friend. "You don't get to swoop in after all these years and act as if you fucking belong here." She said menacingly, pointing a finger at Cora. "This was supposed to be mine. Not yours!"

"Fuck off." Cora snapped. "You were never more than an easy whore and you know it."

"An easy whore that he proposed to." Sarah snapped, and the room fell silent.

"Ah fuck." Reid grunted, scrubbing his hand over his face. "Sarah, fuck right the fuck off."

Security came off the elevator and rushed over to the group of us standing in the lobby, about thirty seconds too late though.

"No, he didn't," Cora said in an almost haunting voice. "He didn't propose to you."

The other woman smirked, knowing she had hit her mark. "He didn't tell you?" She said with feigned regality. "He planned such an elaborate and romantic proposal, getting down on one knee and professed how much he needed me and loved me and wanted to create a future with me. We were planning our wedding together, Cora. He was going to marry me, not you. He chose me."

"Then why didn't he in the end?" Cora snapped, taking an angry step towards her, but I grabbed her hand and pulled her to a stop.

"Think of the baby," I whispered, sliding my hand around her back and holding onto her as her entire body vibrated with anger.

"I got cold feet, so we took some time off," Sarah said with a shrug and then glared at her again. "And then you swooped in and stole him from me!"

"I stole him?" Cora erupted, red-faced. "You stupid cunt. Get out of my office and stay the fuck away from my husband or I swear to God I'll make you regret the day you were ever fucking stupid enough to mess with me." She stepped forward again, but I pulled her back a couple of feet, knowing she was going to make a break for it if I didn't get her out of there.

I signaled to security. "You heard Mrs. Jones, get this woman out of here and put her on a trespass list so she's not allowed access to this building again. I'm sure Mr. Jones will not be happy to hear she was upset at all." I said with a pointed look and security stepped forward, grabbing Sarah by the arms, and hauling her away in a fit of anger as she screamed Maverick's name over and over, like he was going to come to her rescue.

Reid turned and helped me gently pull Cora back into her office as she spit impressively vile things about the other woman in anger. "Cora, take a deep breath," Reid said, trying to get her to sit down, but she paced her office in anger and frustration.

My phone rang in my pocket obsessively, and I finally pulled it out and answered it.

"Yeah." I snapped.

"What's happening?" Dex's concerned voice rang out.

"We just got Cora back into her office and security is escorting Sarah out."

"What happened? What did she say?" He rapidly fired as I rubbed my hand over my forehead. Cora was pacing angrily but then stopped, standing stone cold still as she turned to Reid.

"She's lying, right?" She asked him and he froze. Seconds passed and then nearly a minute and I knew the answer without him saying it. And my heart sank in my chest for Cora's sake. "No." She whispered with a horrified look on her face as she crumbled.

"Dex, I got to go," I said.

"No! Kyson!" He called out as I hung the phone up and crossed the room.

"Cora, have a seat." I tried looking over my shoulder at Reid for help when she refused, batting my hands away from her.

Reid was pale and looked regretful as he watched our friend crumble under the weight of knowledge. "Tell me it's a lie, Reid." She tried again, but he just shook his head.

"I don't know Cora."

"What do you mean, you don't know?" She gasped, staring at him. "How do you not know if your best friend was planning a wedding with the girl that destroyed my life?" She screamed.

"Stop," I ordered her, holding her shoulders square to make her look at me. "This is not Reid's fault," I said firmly, and she blanched a bit at my tone, but I had a sister who handled stress and emotions the same as Cora was right now, and I knew how to handle it. "Now take a deep breath, damnit," I said next and was a bit surprised when she relaxed her shoulders and did exactly as I said. "Whatever happened back then is in the past and getting upset about it right this second will do nothing but harm you and your baby. And you know that. The only person who can answer your questions is your husband, who no doubt is rushing across the city as we speak to get here. So just take a couple of deep breaths, relax, calm down, and wait for Mav." I said calmly and motioned for Reid to pull the chair over for her to sit in. "Good girl," I said when she gently lowered herself down into it. "The past does not matter, Cora. I understand why you're upset right this second, but everything can be explained and discussed carefully, and you can come out the other side of it for the better."

She looked at me with hesitation, but already the color in her cheeks was returning to normal and she wasn't breathing as rapidly.

"You're damn good in a crisis," Reid said, pulling up the other two chairs for himself and me to sit in, and I nodded to him. "Twice now you've been the savior in the room." He mused.

"I pride myself in being calm in emergencies."

"And that was a fucking emergency." Cora quipped with a guilty look on her face. "Thank you." She said finally, and I nodded. I didn't need to say anything else to her, she knew I was right.

My phone continued to ring non-stop in my pocket and I answered it again. "Yes, Dexter." I groaned, and Cora smirked.

"Where is my wife?" Maverick's angry voice bit out through the phone, causing me to jump and sit up straight like I'd been caught with my hand in the cookie jar.

"Uh- she's right here, Mav," I said. "Hold on." I held the phone out to her tentatively, but she rolled her eyes.

"I don't want to speak with him right now. I'm calm and okay right now, but I won't be if I talk to him." She said loud enough for him to hear. We could all hear him yell from the other end, though I couldn't quite make out the words he was saying, but he was less than pleased with that answer.

I sheepishly tried to hand the phone to Reid, but he held his hands up like it was a bomb. "No way in hell, man. Sorry."

"He's your friend." I hissed.

"He's her husband." He responded, still shaking his head.

"Oh, my god." Cora gasped, and we both snapped our heads back to her as she bolted up out of the chair and bent over to look at the floor. "Oh, my god!" She repeated, staring at a puddle of clear liquid dripping from her thighs.

"Holy fuck." Reid cursed, standing up and backing away. "Is that-?" He asked as she looked up at me with fear in her eyes.

I heard Mav all but screaming through the phone at the commotion on our end. "What's happening? Cora!"

I slowly slid the phone to my ear in a daze, "Mav, I think Cora's water just broke."

"Put me on speaker." He demanded, and I could hear the noise of traffic in the background of the phone along with Dexter's voice.

I put the phone on speaker and wrapped my arm around her waist as she seized forward with a groan. "Mav." She cried as she grabbed onto my arms, squeezing them tight. "I think I'm in labor. I've been in pain all day, but just thought it was heartburn."

"It's okay, baby. You're okay." He tried to reassure her through the phone.

"It's early." She cried, and I tossed the phone to Reid so I could hold on to her more as another spasm rocked her forward.

"It's not that early. The doctor said she expected you to go early because you're so small. You're full term." He said calmly, though I imagined he was anything but. "Kyson."

"Yeah," I called out. "I'm here, and so is Reid."

"You need to get her to Wilson Hospital immediately. I'm across the city, I won't make it to the office in time to get her to the hospital with this fucking traffic."

"Got it," I answered. "Dex, are your car keys here?"

"Yeah," Dexter answered. "In my desk. Reid go get them."

"On it." He said, tossing the phone back to me and running from the office.

"Can you walk?" I asked Cora as her blue eyes welled up with tears in fear and pain. She shook her head no and cried silently. "Shh, you're okay. I got you." I said soothingly. "Stay right here," I said, leaning her against her desk as I rounded it and grabbed her purse, and threw her phone in it. "Anything else?"

"No." She said and then groaned, gripping her belly.

"Mav, how far out are you from the hospital?" I called.

"Twenty minutes." He answered instantly. "Can you get her there in time?"

"Yeah, I got her. Just get there safely and in one piece, okay?" I said calmly, rushing back around the desk and swinging her up into my arms in a bridal carry. "I got you, Cora. You're going to meet your baby girl today." I said soothingly and headed for the door.

Reid met us in the hallway, and Slade held the elevator for us. "I've called down and security has been notified you're on your way down, you'll have a free path to the parking garage."

"Thanks, Slade," Reid said, slamming the lobby button. "How are you doing, Cora?" He asked, and she just hummed and groaned in response. "Good. Got it. Doing great." He sighed in anxiety.

"Kyson?" Dexter called out through the phone.

"Yeah?" I answered.

"You've got this. Keep your head on straight and I'll meet you there, okay?"

I nodded my head, fighting my own array of anxiety-ridden emotions, and then grunted. "Yeah. Got it."

I was in such uncharted territory it was unreal.

I was a gay man, for crying out loud. I knew absolutely nothing about women and pregnancy and babies past the knowledge that I never met a baby I didn't like and could envision myself someday having a little one in my arms myself.

But as far as the process of actually bringing one into the world... nope. Clueless.

Security waited for us in the lobby, keeping spectators as far away as possible as we headed to the garage and to the VIP parking spots by the door, thanking my lucky stars that Dexter's car was close because, with each groan and moan from Cora's lips, she sank further into her own head and even I knew that meant the pain was getting worse.

"Hang on, darling," I said as I gently set her down in the front seat. "We're only a few minutes away."

Reid jumped in the back seat, and I got behind the wheel and tore out of the parking garage as Maverick tried to talk Cora through the breathing techniques they had learned from her doctor. Even Dexter chimed in with tips as I fought through the midday traffic to the hospital that was blessedly only a few blocks away.

As soon as the car came to a stop at the curb of the ER, Reid ran inside screaming for help as I helped Cora out of the car and back into my arms. "It'll get towed." She finally said, looking over my shoulder at Dexter's car that I left sitting abandoned in a fire lane.

"Something tells me Maverick will buy him a new one," I said, and she snorted before moaning through another contraction.

A nurse met us at the entrance and escorted us upstairs to the maternity ward and directly into a private luxury suite that Maverick had called ahead about.

They said I was good in a crisis, but he was even better thinking to call the hospital to notify them.

I laid Cora down on the bed and the nurses rushed into the room and started hooking her up to machines and checking her as Reid and I tried to leave to give her some privacy. "Please stay!" Cora said, grabbing my hand and pulling me closer to the bed. "I can't do this alone. Please don't leave me."

"I won't," I said, preparing myself mentally to see something I never thought I'd ever witness in my life.

"We're almost there, baby," Maverick said through the phone I still clutched in my hand. "Five minutes Cora. Hold on for me."

"Okay—" She said, but it ended with a painful scream as she squeezed my hand in a death grip.

Reid paced back and forth at the end of the bed, not looking where he shouldn't be, but not leaving her side either. "You've got this girl." He said as he ran his hand through his hair. "Fuck, I need a drink." He whispered, and I felt for the guy. Not exactly how he envisioned spending his Monday afternoon, I'm sure.

"You're doing great Mrs. Jones." The doctor said as she gowned up and pulled a stool up between Cora's legs. "Baby's head is right there, Cora. What you're feeling right now is the ring of fire. Just breathe through it like we did in class, okay?" She asked as she grabbed all of her tools and supplies. Nurses buzzed around the room, preparing it in efficient order. "You must have been in labor all day without even knowing it. Some women would call you lucky."

Cora groaned and squeezed my hand again. "Those women probably had time for pain relief!" She cried as I grabbed a washcloth from the nurse and put it on her sweaty forehead, pushing her hair back to help cool her.

"You're doing so good, Cora. She's going to be here in no time." I said, and she smiled up at me as the contraction relaxed.

"I'm so excited to be a mom." She said wistfully. "I feel like I've waited my whole life for this."

"Well, you don't have to wait any longer." The doctor said, "You're ready to push, okay?"

"No." Cora gasped, "Mav isn't here yet. He can't miss this; it was his dream to be a dad. He can't miss the birth." She looked at me with wild eyes, but I didn't have any tips on how to keep a baby in while we waited for the dad, so I just nodded to her and squeezed her hand back.

"I'm here!" The door burst open, and Maverick ran to the other side of the bed and Cora cried with relief. "I'm right here, baby." He said, kissing her forehead and looking over at me. "Thank you, Kyson, thank you so much."

After stepping back and releasing Cora's hand, I found myself completely captivated by the entire process when she started pushing with her next breath. Dexter's hands slid around my waist and pulled me back to the wall behind the head of the bed so the nurses could get close to her. "Have you ever seen a baby be born before?" He whispered into my ear, and I melted into his powerful arms, letting my body relax for the first time since Cora's phone rang in her office.

"No," I whispered back, as Reid joined us at the head of the bed, staring at the wall and patting Mav on the back.

"I would leave, but the nurses have their equipment blocking the door." He said with a grimace. "But I'm not looking."

Dexter snorted at him, and Mav grinned like a dad about to meet his baby for the first time, oblivious to the impropriety going on with three men, two that were gay, and none of us the father of the child, in the room with a woman giving birth. But it was too late to leave now.

The doctor and Maverick were cheering Cora on as she pushed with all her might, and I was sucked back into watching the most incredible thing in the world.

"That's it, Cora, one last push." The doctor said and then caught the baby as she was born, wrapping her in a blanket and laying her down on Cora's chest.

"Oh, my God!" Cora cried, hugging her baby girl in shock and complete awe. "Hi, little angel." She cooed and Maverick watched on with tears in his big, manly eyes.

"Welcome to this crazy world, baby girl." He said, covering the baby's head with his giant hand. "We love you so much already."

"Amazing isn't it?" Dex whispered in my ear, and I nodded silently, wiping away the tears that had fallen down my cheeks without my notice at some point.

"Incredible." I sighed and then turned to look over my shoulder at Dex. He stared down at the little babe on Cora's chest and had a longing in his eyes that was unmistakable.

He missed his son.

"She's beautiful, Cora," Dex said gently, and she looked over her shoulder at us and smiled happily. "Just like her mama."

"Thank you both for being here." She said, reaching out and taking Dex's hand, and squeezing it before looking back down at her baby. "I can't believe I just had a baby with you three in the room." She laughed lightly and then winced as the doctor pushed on her stomach.

"Okay, let's give them all some space for a while. We'll be outside." I said, pulling Dex and Reid out of the room, who were as entranced with that little girl as the rest of us were now that things had slowed down a bit.

When we got out to the large waiting room, we all collapsed into the chairs and smirked at each other. "Holy fuck." Reid said with a shake of his head. "That was un-fucking real."

"Pretty life-changing, huh?" Dex asked, sighing and shaking his head.

"Yeah." Reid replied with a faraway look on his face before he shook it off. "I'd better get back to the office and man things for a while."

"You can stick around for a bit." Dex tried, but Reid was already standing up and ordering a car on his phone.

"Nah." He shook his head. "I'll just be in the way. I'll stop back by later when things calm down. Let me know if they need anything, I can grab it later."

"Reid..." Dex tried.

"Later guys." He walked away without a backward glance, and Dex fell back down into his chair.

"What was that about?" I asked, leaning over against his arm.

He shook his head as he ran his finger over his bottom lip in question. "Damn if I know."

Chapter 16 – Dexter

Annabelle Lucy Jones was born three weeks ago and to say I was smitten with the little blue-eyed sassy angel would be the understatement of the century. After the chaos of her birth calmed down, Cora confronted Mav about what Sarah had spewed at the office about them being engaged and planning a wedding together.

I had to jump in and side with Mav, assuring Cora that they were never actually engaged and that Mav never proposed to her. It was just another one of Sarah's lies to stir up drama and heartache for others. Reid couldn't confirm because he was overseas working on a deal, which allowed the fear to take root.

Of course, cuddling her precious newborn helped her let go of things.

Annabelle was just simply that perfect and had that calming effect on everyone she met.

Maverick worked from home as much as he could, only coming in for meetings he simply couldn't avoid before rushing back home to be with his wife and newborn.

Every time he stepped out of the house for anything, he made sure someone else stepped in while he was gone. Though he tried desperately not to make Cora feel like he thought she couldn't handle it, because to be honest, she was hands down the best mom I'd ever seen before.

She was kind and calm and her nurturing demeanor thrived with a baby to care for, but she always welcomed help or conversation while she went about her additional duties. Kyson spent a lot of time at their penthouse during the day when Maverick needed to leave, blaming it on needing to work on their wardrobes or planning outfits for future events, but really it was because he was obsessed with Anna.

I'd never thought I would ever describe a man as nurturing or fatherly by nature, but Kyson was born to be a dad.

It was as simple as that.

And the more times I would go to Cora and Mav's place after work to pick him up or something and I'd see him with his bright tattoos and rock star dark features all tame and calm with that precious little girl in his arms, the more my love for him settled into my soul.

Yes. I was in love with Kyson Hart.

Who would have fucking guessed?

Not me.

Nonetheless, it was easy to see why standing in the doorway to Anna's nursery with the fast setting fall sunlight shining in through the wall of windows as Kyson sat in the plush, white rocking chair. He crooned a lullaby and gently ran his fingers over her soft, dark brown hair. And I knew I was unapologetically in love with that man. Though for some reason I hadn't told him that yet. Like if I told him, he'd run the other way when I knew, deep in my soul, that he'd never leave me.

"...when the stars go blue." He finished in a gentle, warm singing voice. He looked up, sensing me, and smiled brightly at me where I stood leaning against the doorframe. "Hi." He whispered.

"Hi," I said back, walking into the room and kneeling next to the chair to kiss Anna's head.

"Cora's taking a shower." He murmured, like he had to explain why he was soaking up baby time.

"Hmm," I replied, leaning forward and taking his lips with mine. I pulled back a half an inch and pressed my forehead to his. "Do you have any idea how deeply in love with you I am?" I asked him and his breath hitched, as he leaned back further to look at me.

"Maybe half as deeply as I am with you?" He responded with a smoldering ember glowing gold in his green eyes. "Do you swear?"

I nodded my head slowly. "I don't know why I thought I needed to wait for the perfect time to tell you. But I guess this felt like the perfect time."

"I love you." He whispered, tilting his head to the side, and pressing his cheek against my palm as I slid my fingers into his hair, tucking it behind his ear. "So much Dex."

"I love you." I smiled, kissing him again before pulling back as Anna stretched in his arms and cooed. She opened her eyes and looked up at us before smiling brightly, singing the song of her people in joyful sounds. "Uh-oh, you woke her up." I joked, letting her take my finger in her palm and squeeze it. "Cora's going to fire you from nanny duties."

He swatted me playfully, "There isn't a force in this world that could keep me from this little girl." He turned to Anna and smiled at her. "Isn't that right, darling? You'd never let anyone keep you away from Uncle Ky, would you?"

I watched him with her and shook my head to keep my mouth shut because the part of my heart that had been severed and frozen when Hope took Sammy away from me was dangerously close to healing and I was on the verge of saying something foolish to Kyson about it.

Like, *want to have a baby with me?*

To be honest, it was all I'd been able to think about lately. Not exactly just adopting or surrogating kids with Ky someday, but marrying him and building a life together. And it was terrifying.

Baby steps.

"There you are," Maverick said from the doorway, rolling up his shirtsleeves as he walked in. "Give me my baby." He said gently and Kyson stood up to hand Annabelle off to her daddy, who had spent far too long away from her today at work.

It was such a mental trip to see my best friend in this new gentle role, given his ruthless and dominant alpha characteristics, I'd known our entire friendship.

"I'm ordering dinner if you two want to stay," Mav said, never looking up from his babe.

"Nah," I said, answering for us and gaining a glare from Ky at turning down the offer. I chuckled and pulled my man against my side. "We have plans tonight, but I appreciate it, Mav," I said surely as Ky looked at me guessingly because he had no idea what my plans were yet.

But he'd find out soon enough.

It was a Friday night, and it had been a long ass week, and I needed to spend some quality time with my boyfriend and unwind.

"No problem." Mav looked up finally. "Thanks for your help today, Ky. I appreciate you; I couldn't focus at the office if I didn't know you or my mom was here keeping Cora company in my absence. Now go have fun, you two lovebirds."

"We'll see ya," Kyson said, allowing me to pull him from the room as Mav sank into the rocking chair, already ignoring us again.

When we got into the elevator, Ky turned towards me, "So, are you going to tell me what our plans are, or did you make that up just to get me to leave?"

I chuckled at him before letting my smile turn predatory as I backed him up against the wall, caging him in with my body and pressing against him from head to toe. "Oh, I have plans for us tonight, baby. I'm just not going to tell you what they are until you're so desperate for it you beg me to."

His pupils dilated, and his hips flexed, rubbing himself against me through his jeans. "Is that so?" He asked, sliding his hands up my stomach and chest before grabbing ahold of my tie and pulling me in further to him. "And if I'm the one who wanted to be in charge tonight?" He asked against my lips before flipping us around and pressing me into the wall. "Would you tell me no?"

"Never." I groaned against his lips as he reached down to palm my aching cock as it grew down the leg of my suit pants.

"Good, because I have plans for you tonight. And I promise you," He licked my lips. "You'll be the one begging before long." The doors to the elevator opened to Mav's private parking garage and Ky pushed off the wall and walked out with a wink over his shoulder as I groaned in agony.

"Well, fuck me running." I cursed, chasing after him.

"Relax," Kyson commanded from behind me as he kicked my legs apart and stepped into the space. "Let me in."

"Kyson," I growled, fisting my hands, and laying my forehead against the cold granite countertop in his kitchen. "I'm trying."

"Not hard enough." He said and then his hand came down hard on my ass cheek, the echo splitting through the quiet air of his apartment. I reared up and hissed at the sensation, but he pushed me back down onto the counter with his hand between my shoulders. "Take it." He growled, and I groaned as he pushed the silicone plug in deeper, the widest part cresting past the tight ring of muscles in my ass before the small neck and flared end locked it into place. "Good boy." He praised, leaning down and kissing my spine. "Such a good job, baby."

"Fuck off," I grunted, standing up and pushing him back.

Turned out Kyson had some alpha in him in the sack when he was comfortable, which hadn't happened until we got together, and we battled more often lately for the top dog spot.

But I always came out on top because my guy talked a big game, but if I wanted to put him in his place, I knew exactly how to do that, and he melted in my hands every single time.

We had been working me up to take his cock the last few weeks, starting with his fingers and then small toys and plugs, but the one I was suffering through currently was the biggest. Coincidentally, about the size of his cock.

The last plug in the line of torture devices he had bought to prep me.

Well, torture and suffering were a stretch of the imagination because we both knew I loved every second of our experimenting so far. I was just too conditioned to be so masculine that I had a hard time showing my enjoyment of it because it made me feel inferior.

Or so my therapist and Kyson both told me, anyway.

Being vulnerable and letting Ky top me was more than just a bodily experience. It took so much mental preparation and willpower it was exhausting. But every time that he had pushed me into a submissive role, I'd enjoyed myself immensely.

But then something always still forced me to turn around and manhandle him into being the bottom again so I could be alpha once more.

I guess it's not being an alpha if someone else has to let you do it, but it worked so far.

I grabbed Ky and pushed him against the fridge behind him and settled my hand around his throat as his chest rose and fell with excitement. "I'm still the boss," I growled into his ear, tightening my hand around his throat before reaching down and grabbing his hard cock. We were both stark-ass naked in the middle of his kitchen after I fucked him into the mattress for an hour when we got home from Mav and Cora's.

But my time on top was short-lived because he had bent me over the counter and worked the damn plug into me so I could adjust. My cock was blazing hot, and it swung between my legs, hardening with every push and pull of the plug from my movements.

"You can be the boss, but I'm still fucking your ass tonight." He challenged, green eyes blazing as he grabbed my cock and started stroking it in sync with my hand on him.

"Maybe." I groaned as he cupped my balls.

"Don't act like you're not enjoying yourself right now, being so full and stretched so wide." He slid his fingers under my balls and my legs bowed when he pressed against the plug end. "You're going to come so hard when my cock rubs your p-spot for the first time Dex." He moaned, leaning forward now that my hand had gone lax around his throat in my delirious haze of pleasure, and kissed my parted lips as I moaned.

"I need to come again before we do that." I hissed. "I'm too feral right now."

"I know, baby." He purred, relaxing his grip on my cock to be gentle and tender. "Let me take care of you and then give yourself to me. Just let go and let me do all the work."

"Yes." I tightened my grip around his throat again and pressed my body flat against his. "Bed. Now."

"Yes, sir." He moaned and took off running to the bedroom as I stalked after him.

Every single step had the fucking plug moving around and rubbing against that magic spot inside of me that Ky had shown me. My skin was on fire, and I felt a bead of sweat drip down between my shoulder blades as I walked into his bedroom.

He was on his knees in the center of the floor at the end of the bed with his tongue sticking out, waiting for me and my cock, and I groaned at the sight.

"So fucking perfect." I fisted my cock and slapped it down onto his flat tongue and pushed it down his throat in one fast movement. He gagged and lurched, but pulled me tighter still until his nose pressed flat against my stomach and he looked up at me. "Fuck." I pulled back out, and he gasped for breath, but grabbed both of my hands and brought them up to his head, tangling them in his hair.

"Fuck my throat, Dex. Pull my hair and take everything you need from me."

And I did just that. He twirled his tongue around the head of me and then lowered himself down so I could easily slide straight down his throat, and I started thrusting. Long strokes brought me from tip to balls in his mouth and he took every fucking thing I gave him. "I love you." I hissed, tightening my grip on his hair as I was overcome with the need for him. "Never anyone but you."

He smirked around my cock as tears streamed down his face from the punishing fuck I was giving his mouth, but he wanted more. He loved being used and praised at the same time and I was giving him both the best way I knew how.

He reached around me and pulled on the plug as I bottomed out again and I threw my head back, bellowing into the ceiling as he tugged it free and then pushed it back into me without warning. "Kyson!" I warned as I gripped his hair so tightly I was sure it was pulling out in my hands, but he just did it again, pulling the wide base of the plug out until just the tip stayed in and then pushed it back in as I pulled out of his mouth. I was essentially fucking myself on and off the plug with each thrust of my cock into him, and I lost my ever-loving mind in ecstasy.

Sounds and sights ceased to be separate senses, and my body tightened from the hair follicles on my head to the soles of my feet as I started ejaculating. "Fuck. Fuck. Fuck." I gasped as I filled his throat with my release, stilling my hips as the plug pulled out completely. I sagged to my knees in front of him, sucking air and twitching as every nerve in my body misfired erratically.

He wrapped his arms around my neck and held onto me as I came down from the magic he had created inside of me. "I've never seen anything sexier than that, Dexter." He hummed, kissing the side of my face and neck. "Even when you topped, you gave yourself to me, baby."

I chuckled exhaustedly and pulled back to look at him, shaking my head. "I have no delusions Ky, you may have been on your knees, but you just topped from the bottom."

He smiled guiltily at me. "Did you hate it?"

I shook my head again and crawled up onto his bed, dragging him up with me. "I feel like I just saw a glimpse of the sunshine for the first time in my life."

I laid on my back and he laid his head on my chest, kissing his way down to my nipple and sucking it into his mouth before moving to the other one. "Well then hang on tight baby, because I'm going to take you into space and drop you on that big fucking fireball they call the sun."

I moaned in response, feeling relaxed and sated, which was exactly how I should have felt the first time I took a cock inside of me.

"Safe word?" He asked as he rolled me over onto my stomach like a limp rag doll.

"Ass fucker." I quipped, and he spanked my cheek for it painfully. "Oof."

"Serious, Dexter."

"Corkscrew," I answered truthfully, and he hummed his approval as he kissed his way down my spine. I grabbed the pillow and laid my head on it, literally not caring that I was about to be impaled with a cock for the first time in my life; I was that satisfied.

He grabbed a towel and the lube and got everything prepped as I lounged, relaxed and watched. He poured the warming lube over my loosened hole and worked his fingers in with little resistance, and I was surprised by the tendrils of pleasure crawling through my cock from the sensation after such a mind-blowing orgasm. I watched as he coated his bare cock with the lube and straddled my thighs. "Are you ready for me, Dex?" He asked, slapping the head of his cock against my ass.

"Yeah, baby," I replied, arching my back to make the angle right for penetration. He pushed the head of his cock in past the ring of muscles and I groaned, instantly feeling the burn of being stretched. "Shit." I tightened my hold on the pillow as he pulled the head back out and poured more lube on me.

"Hold still." He demanded, and I did my best as he pushed back into me, painfully slow. "Oh, fuck." He grunted as he buried himself inside of me. "Mother of—" He cursed.

He put both hands on the small of my back right above my ass for leverage and, on the next thrust, buried himself in one quick burst.

"Kyson." I panted, looking over my shoulder at him, and moaned when I did. He was the picture of perfection. His dark hair hung wildly around his face as he stared down at where he was entering me with an inferno burning in his eyes. The bright teal and purple in his tattoos were almost glowing in the low light against his tanned skin and paired next to the dark leather and gold of his bracelets and necklace—god, he was striking. "So full," I grunted, feeling his balls slap the tops of my thighs, and I reached around to grab his hip as he fucked me.

"Do you like it?" He asked between clenched teeth.

"Yes."

"Does it feel good?"

"So good."

"Thank fuck." He grunted, "I need more." He leaned forward until his chest pressed against my back and he wrapped his hand around my throat, pulling my head back to kiss me passionately. "I need to fuck you hard, Dex." He pulled back from my lips and laid his forehead against the back of my head. "I want to make sure you know who you belong to."

"Yes." I hissed. "Do it. Fuck me hard."

"I'm trying to keep my cool but—"

"Don't," I begged, bringing my knees up to my sides and slowly rising onto them as he moved with me, buried deep. "Fuck me like you need me. Fuck me like it's the last time you'll ever do it again and take everything you need, Kyson. I can take it."

"Dexter." He moaned as his hips surged forward like he couldn't control himself. "You feel so good. And knowing that you trusted me with this—" He moaned. "Fuck."

He reached down under me and grabbed my swollen cock, stroking me quickly as he savagely pumped into me. "Yes." I dropped my head and held still as he used me for his pleasure while giving me mine back.

"You take me so good, baby." He slapped my ass, "I'm going to do this again, you know. I'm going to fuck you just like you fuck me."

"I'm close." I panted, pushing back on him with each thrust.

"Come, baby." He commanded. "Come for me and I'll fill you up."

"Yes!" I roared as my cock jerked in his hand. "I'm coming." His thrusts sped up to jerks and jolts as he chased his orgasm, filling me with his hot come. It was such an odd sensation, feeling his hot come brand my insides as he orgasmed, but I loved it.

I tossed the towel and fell onto the bed as he collapsed next to me. Both of us panted, catching our breaths. I felt the fatigue settle into my bones as my body came back down and when I felt him giving aftercare, I simply hummed and nestled deeper into the pillows that smelled like him and me combined.

His lips pressed against my shoulder as he snuggled into me, pulling the blankets up over us. "I love you, Dexter Chase. More than anyone else I've ever met before."

"I love you."

Chapter 17- Kyson

"How long do you have left on your lease?" Dex asked as we sat at his breakfast bar drinking coffee and eating breakfast.

"Uh—" I paused, chewing my granola bar. "Well, I just moved in four months ago, so eight more months."

"A year." He said, staring off out the windows as he processed that.

"Why?" I watched him as he looked over at me and took a sip of his coffee.

"Because I want us to move in together." He said so matter-of-factly that I was sure I misheard him.

"Move in?"

He smirked and set his phone down on the table, abandoning the emails he had been answering. "Yes, move in together. Live together in one apartment instead of having two to choose from, but only ever staying in one at a time."

"Right," I responded, nodding my head.

"You don't want to move in together." He said, not actually asking it like a question.

"That's not what I said." I hurried on, setting my cup of coffee down on the countertop between us.

"You didn't say you wanted to either." He pointed out. His face was expressionless, but I could see the tick of his jaw muscles under it all, and I knew I'd struck a nerve with my lack of enthusiasm.

"You caught me off guard, that's all, Dex."

"How off guard was it, though? I haven't slept alone except for that time I stayed at a hotel while your sister was in town or when you were out of town for work since we first met." He stood up, pushed his stool in, and walked to the sink to rinse his still half-full cup out. "If we spend every day together anyway, what does it matter?"

"It doesn't matter, Dex," I said, standing as he started gathering his things to no doubt make a hasty exit.

"Right." He looked at me and sighed. "I have to go." He walked over to me and kissed my forehead, but ignored my pouting lips, which only made me frown more. "We can talk about it later."

"I leave for L.A. tonight." I reminded him. "My flight leaves at seven. I'll probably be leaving for the airport about the time you get home."

"Right." He repeated and took a deep breath. "Well, then we can table the conversation for now." He leaned in again, laying a gentle kiss on my lips before sighing. "I'll be home in time to see you off."

"Okay," I said, hating that there was an elephant of tension in the room with us suddenly. "I love you," I blurted, and he gave me a half-one-sided smile that didn't reach his eyes.

"I love you too." He turned and walked out of the apartment, leaving me confused and angsty as I tried to focus on the busy day I had ahead of me.

But I could only think about Dex, and how hurt he had looked when I didn't jump at the idea of moving in with him right away. The honest to God truth was that I'd love to live with Dexter full time, there was nothing I'd like more. I was just so confused by his approach to the subject that I was trying to read his riddle instead of reacting how I should have. And that made me sad because I'd hurt his feelings.

I sighed and forced myself to go about my day, finalizing purchases and deliveries for Cora and Mav, as well as other clients for the upcoming award show. I was sitting on the floor of my apartment looking at my phone, trying to figure out what to say to him to make it all better when I decided to just write it all out in a letter and leave it for him to read once I was in the air tonight.

I took out a pad of paper and pen, leaned back against the wall, and started writing all of my feelings and emotions down in ink for him, so he didn't wonder or doubt me anymore after tonight.

When I was done with the letter, I folded it up and put it in a rich red envelope and drew his name across the front and set it aside while I finished packing my suitcase.

I was supposed to be gone for four days, the longest I'd been away from Dex since we got together four months ago, and I hated the idea of it. Twice I picked my phone up to call and cancel my travel plans, claiming I was sick or there was a death in the family, but I resolved myself to go this time and just decline any future travel like this.

The day went by, and I checked my phone to see it was almost time for Dexter to come home. I had to hurry and get to the airport. I wheeled my suitcase and backpack over to Dex's place and went in, waiting for him to get home. Taking the letter I'd written him, I slid it into the junk drawer in his kitchen, knowing he wouldn't find it unless I told him to go looking for it. I'd poured my heart out, ripping open every wound I'd ever had and bled out on the pages for him. And I couldn't help that small part of my brain that was telling me he was going to come home and wash his hands of me, ending our relationship and it would kill me if he opened the letter while I was still around, so I kept it hidden until the right moment.

I was lying on the couch, scrolling social media, when a soft knock sounded from his front door, startling me. I sat up, looking over the back of the couch, frozen with uncertainty.

Who was visiting Dex that he didn't tell me about?

Was he expecting someone?

I got up and another knock on the door vibrated through the quiet space, this time louder and more assertive than the first. Maybe it was Saint or another doorman with a delivery or something. As I walked around the couch towards the door, my anxiety rose through the roof, like my brain knew something I didn't.

"Dexter. Open the door." A female voice called out from the other side of the wooden door, and I froze with my hand on the handle. "I heard you walking to the door Dexter, please just open up."

I turned the doorknob and opened the door, revealing a striking blonde on the other side with a suitcase next to her. "Can I help you?" I asked, as her eyebrows rose to her hairline.

"I'm sorry." She stammered, looking at the number next to the door and then up and down the hallway around her. "I think I have the wrong apartment." She said with a smile, "I'm looking for Dexter Chase." Dread formed in my gut. "Do you know him?"

"Yes," I said, straightening my spine. "This is his apartment."

She blinked in silence for a second, letting her eyes roam over my long hair tied back and the tattoos covering my arms beneath my rolled-up black Henley. "Uh—" She said, rubbing her fingers over her forehead and shaking her head with a tight smile on her lips. "I'm confused. Are you his roommate? Or a friend?" She said.

"I'm—" I started and then I saw a bit of movement behind her legs, causing the words to die on my lips. Bright blue eyes peeked out around her and stared up at me in open curiosity before ducking back behind her when they caught me looking back. I stumbled back a step as realization dawned in my sluggish brain. Pain radiated through my chest as I looked back up at the woman, who stared at me in confusion. "You're—" I couldn't finish the sentence.

She stiffened her spine, picking up on my shock, and stuck her hand out to shake. "I'm Dexter's wife, Hope."

It's true what people say when you experience a catastrophic event, that your body and brain disassociate from each other, leaving the two entities completely separate. I heard her words but couldn't grasp what they meant as I looked back down at the blue eyes that peeked back at me from behind her. "And you must be Sammy," I said, gentling my voice and trying to reign in the cyclone of emotions raging through my body. Even if he wasn't biologically related to Dex, he had the same crystal blue eyes, and if it hadn't been for his dark brown hair, he would have looked identical to the man who loved him as his own for years now.

"Is Dex home?" She asked, cutting me off and pushing her son behind her again. "We've traveled all day to get here."

"Of course." My lips said, as only my manners kept me from telling the woman to kick rocks before Dexter got home and had to face her. "Why don't you come in, he should be home from work in just a few minutes." I stepped back and held the door open as she wheeled her large suitcase in with Sammy holding her hand tight in both of his until they both stood in the open kitchen, looking around. "Can I get you some water or something to eat?" I asked, on autopilot as I moved towards the fridge.

"No, thanks." She said, keeping her eyes on me before dropping them onto my suitcase against the wall by the door. "So how do you know Dexter exactly?" She asked again, this time more forcefully, like she couldn't wrap her head around any explanation for my presence here.

I opened my mouth to answer truthfully as the front door opened and we all turned to watch as Dexter himself walked through the front door with his briefcase in his hand. He wore his trademark light cream designer suit, with a light teal button-up underneath that made his eyes glow next to his tanned skin. My chest ached to look at him, knowing the pain that was about to assault me. He looked at me across the space and then Hope cleared her throat across the room, drawing his attention as he snapped his head in her direction. She smiled brightly at him like they were reconnecting after a long trip apart or something.

Watching the array of emotions cross his handsome face nearly gutted me right on the spot.

Confusion.

Shock.

Anger.

Fear.

And then the worst of all... longing.

He opened his mouth to say something, but then slammed it shut, whipping his head back around to look at me with wide eyes. "Ky." He said, taking an involuntary step towards me but stopped, turning back. "Hope?" He asked in a whisper. "What are you doing here?"

My heart felt like it had imploded in my chest as I watched him physically, unable to decide which direction to walk.

To me.

Or to her.

She watched us with accusation in her eyes before she readjusted the bright smile on her face and shrugged her shoulders and looked down at her son, who was staring openly at Dex. "Sam and I want to come home, baby." She said like she was asking him about the weather, something so mundane and ordinary, instead of something so life-changing.

I watched in silent misery as Dexter looked down at the little boy he had loved and lost like a physical part of himself, and I could feel the pain he'd felt when Hope took him away.

Because I felt it at that exact moment.

Because I knew I'd just lost the only man I'd ever loved.

I couldn't compete with his love for a child that he had longed for over the last four years.

I dropped my head to hide the tears that pooled in them as I picked up my phone and keys off of the counter, taking a tentative step towards the door when Dex whipped his head around to look at me. His mouth opened and closed again as panic shined bright in his perfect blue eyes, but he didn't say a word.

And God, the silence was deafening.

"I have to go," I said, dropping my head again as I picked up my backpack and threw it over my shoulder, and popped the handle on my suitcase up.

He looked back to Hope and then to me, but I just opened the front door and walked out of it as he tried to figure out what to do.

Because that was answer enough for me.

His apartment door shut behind me with a thundering click as I slammed my finger into the call button on the elevator, praying the car was still here on this floor from where Dexter had just gotten off of it, but the ticker showed it was back down in the lobby.

I nearly collapsed to my knees in agony when I heard his apartment door open down the hall and then his quick steps as he ran after me. "Kyson wait." He begged, but I shook my head, unable to look away from the ticker over the door showing the elevator was still seven floors away and crawling up to me. "Please don't go." He said, slamming into me as he palmed my face in both of his hands, forcing me to turn to look at him. "I don't want you to go."

"Did you know she was coming?" I asked, feeling the tears break over the line of my lashes and slide down my face. I hated being so vulnerable at this moment, but this was my worst fear to come to life.

My newly bi-sexual boyfriend was going to go back to his wife, even if he didn't know it yet, and there was nothing I could do about it because I physically couldn't compete with her.

"No." He gasped, shaking his head. "I haven't spoken to her since the paternity test came back, sealing my fate."

"Then why is she here?" I bit out angrily.

"I don't know." He shook his head again, looking haunted and pale. Nothing like the strong, sure, and steady Dexter Chase I'd come to know. "I don't know Ky, I promise you."

"Then tell her to leave," I said plainly, and he reared back like I'd slapped him.

"It's not that simple." He tried grasping my hands in his as the elevator door opened for me to get on. "I can't just kick her out Ky. Sammy—" He said as his voice broke with emotion.

I stared into his blue eyes, and I knew we were over. I pulled my hands from his and picked up my bag again, turning away from him. "Then let me make it simple for you," I said, without a clue where my strength and defiance were coming from when everything inside of me was breaking into unrecognizable pieces. I walked into the elevator and hit the button for the lobby as he leaned forward on the door in agony.

"Don't go, baby. Not like this, let's figure this out." He begged desperately, but I couldn't even look him in the eye. It hurt too much.

"The worst part about a breakup is not knowing your last kiss was your last until it's too late to savor it," I said and swiped angrily at the fresh tears that fell on my face as the doors closed between us. I looked up at the last second to see his gutted face as the doors shut.

I sagged against the wall and utterly lost it. We went from him asking me to move in with him, to him not even being able to choose me over the woman that had a baby with someone else and left him.

What good was loving someone if they never loved you back in the same way?

Chapter 18 – Dexter

"**I**'m sorry," I said into the phone. "Please call me back, Kyson. I love you."

I ended the message, pacing the hallway, as it felt like my body was literally being torn in two different directions.

I walked back to my apartment door and paused outside of it, trying to figure out what the fuck was going to come out of my ex-wife's mouth when I walked back in.

And then there was Sammy.

My God.

He was four now, a full-grown human being, no longer a baby. He had no idea who I was, but he once had been the center of my universe and I didn't know how to act around him now.

What hurt me the most years ago was leaving one day, without even knowing I was looking at him for the last time before she stole him from me. I left for work that fated morning, kissed him goodbye as he sat on the floor of our living room, surrounded by his noisy toys, talking gibberish, and drooling happily, and then I never saw him again.

Until now.

And that was the only reason I turned the handle and walked back into my apartment instead of racing down the stairs and chasing Kyson to the airport to make this better.

I needed closure with Sammy before I could prove to Kyson that I was worthy of him.

I needed my son, even if it was to say goodbye. Or I'd never be whole again.

I shut the door behind me and looked at Hope, where she sat on my couch behind Sammy as he kneeled at the coffee table with a stack of paper and crayons spread out haphazardly. Years ago I'd imagined seeing him like this in this living room, but that dream had been ripped away from me, until today.

"What are you doing here?" I asked Hope again, loosening my tie and pulling it off as it threatened to strangle me alongside my anxiety.

She patted him on the head before walking across the room to me, and I let my eyes take her in. She was thinner than the last time I'd seen her, her once bright honey blonde hair was now flat and lackluster, and her eyes didn't sparkle like they used to.

She watched me look her over and a knowing smirk pulled her vicious lips back, and I knew she thought I was admiring her.

But the only thing I could see now was how different her feminine body was from Kyson's. How every strand of his dark brown hair glistened as he moved under the bright lights of my kitchen while hers looked like muddy water, or how his muscles rolled under his brightly colored skin like a motion picture in an olden time movie theater and hers looked dry and stretched too tight over protruding sharp bone ends.

Hope stopped a couple of feet in front of me and tilted her head to the side. "Who was that man?" She asked gently, but I could hear the jealous bite behind it. She had always been jealous of any person I came in contact with, and I guess that had more to say about her character than mine, given that she was the cheater, and I was the loyal lap dog that never even looked in another's direction the entire time we were together.

"I don't owe you a single explanation right now, Hope, so cut your shit." I snapped at her, shocking her and irritating me as I felt my blood pressure rise with my anger.

I looked over her shoulder to where Sammy drew with his back to us, expecting him to look at us at my outburst, but he never even acknowledged us. Like the venom in the room was nothing new for him.

She pursed her lips and crossed her arms before relaxing her shoulders and sighing. "You're right baby," She tried, gentling her voice in a way I used to think was submissive, but now I could see it for what it was, manipulation. "I'm sorry, it's just been a long day traveling from Texas to get here." She laughed like something about that was funny. "But we're here." She said, taking a step forward with a hopeful expression on her face. "That's what matters now."

"No, it's not." I jerked away as she reached forward to touch me. "I need a fucking drink."

I walked to the cabinet and blindly grabbed a bottle of liquor and poured three fingers into a glass and tossed it back before refilling my glass and turning around to face her. "Where is Trey?" I asked her bitterly and watched as Sammy snapped his head up to look at us at the mention of his father's name.

So that caught his attention, but my anger didn't.

"In Texas." She bit out with a sneer. "But I don't want to talk about him, I want to talk about us."

"There is no us!" I snapped in a hushed tone, pointing my finger at her with my glass still clutched in my hand, "You made sure of that when you took off and severed all of my rights to him!" I pointed to Sammy, who had gone back to ignoring us.

"I made a mistake." She rushed on, walking across the kitchen until she was right in front of me. "I'm sorry. Okay, Dex? I'm so sorry, I never should have left. The grass was never greener, and I was a fool for thinking I could be happy with that piece of shit." She said as tears filled her eyes. "I messed up. I know that now, but at the time, I thought I was doing what was best for me."

"Best for you?" I yelled. "How was ripping our family apart, best?"

"You never loved me!" She cried back, hushing her voice. "You never fought for me. You worked crazy long hours and came home to play with Sammy and spoil him senseless, but you never showed me any attention!" She grabbed onto my arms desperately. "I needed your attention Dexter; I was drowning in loneliness and boredom, and you never cared."

"I was right here!" I shook her off and walked away, turning back to point at her again. "I was right fucking here, Hope. Every day and night, while providing for us so you could stay home with him and raise him and keep him safe from that crazy world out there!"

"I know! And I thought that was what I wanted, but it wasn't Dexter. I wanted passion and fire and all-consuming love," She shook her head, "I wanted you to burn for me."

I scoffed at her. "Like you burned for me?" Rolling my eyes and drinking off my glass again. "You were too consumed with your affairs to care what happened inside of these walls, Hope, and you know it."

"There weren't affairs, Dex, just him. I made the mistake one time."

"Shut up." I glared at her, "Don't you dare show up on my doorstep after four years and lie to my face. I have friends throughout the court system here Hope, I know you petitioned three other men for proof of paternity when you were proving to the courts that he wasn't mine." Gipping the glass in my hand as the anger and pain from that time in my life burned renewed inside of my gut. "You lived here because out of the four possible men that could have fathered him, I was the best off and I gave you the security you wanted. But you were the one that stepped out and ruined us, don't blame me."

She glared back at me before looking at Sammy. "You have no idea how hard it is to be a parent, Dexter. You have no idea how fucking hard it is to commit yourself to someone twenty-four-seven. Every single second of every single day belongs to him," She sneered, lowering her voice. "I don't get a second to myself. Not one fucking second to take care of myself."

"Cry me a river, Hope. You made your bed, don't complain to me because you have to lie in it now." I said, taking a deep breath, looking back at the boy I'd envisioned spending the rest of my life loving and caring for, and hated how that love and longing still burned inside of me. I still loved that little boy, even if he didn't know who the fuck I was or how bat-shit-crazy his mother was. He deserved so much better than us.

"Please Dex." She said, sighing and leaning against the counter. "I don't want to fight with you. I just—" She paused, looking over at Sam. "I just want to do right by him."

"Then be a good mother to him, regardless of what man you're with at the time. Be good to him." I said, trying to call to that good mother I'd always seen in her when he was a baby.

"I'm trying Dex. But it's hard." She looked so defeated and worn out. "It's just so hard."

I took a deep breath and forced myself to calm down and think clearly about this whole situation, even as I calculated in my head how far Kyson was getting away from me the longer I stood here to deal with Hope. "Did Trey hit him?" I asked her squarely, already knowing that he hit her without her saying it out loud.

She looked over at Sam sadly, "No. Never." Before looking back over at me. "Only me."

"Did he see it? The violence?"

"Not really, no. He learned early on how to ignore most of the yelling and fighting." She shook her head and covered her face with her hands as her shoulders vibrated with silent sobs. "I'm so pathetic."

I didn't bother to negate that, because I simply didn't feel like making her feel any better about herself at this moment. I couldn't spare the energy for her when I needed it for Kyson and Sam. "So now what?" I asked her. "What are you going to do, to do right by him?"

She took a calming breath and wiped at her tears before straightening her spine and looking me square in the eye. "I just need a good night's rest, and then I'll figure it out." She smiled at me softly, "You know me, I'll figure it all out one way or another."

"Hmm." I hummed, not agreeing with her. I watched Sam as he pulled one piece of paper away and set it to the side before starting in on another drawing with a bright red crayon. I walked around the kitchen island and gently sat down on the couch to his side and watched over his shoulder as he let his imagination run wild. He drew big buildings with lots of windows in them, one by one adding detail and switching colors to draw yellow cars in front of the buildings. "Is that New York City?" I asked him gently.

He paused drawing and looked over his shoulder at me, letting his eyes roam over my face intently before turning back to drawing. "The lady on the airplane said the city had a big apple." He chewed on his lip as he drew the buildings in red again. "Apples are red, sometimes green or yellow, but mostly red."

I looked over at Hope as she sat down in the armchair with a tired smile on her face. "He's so fricking smart it's exhausting sometimes." She chuckled.

I looked back at the drawing and smiled. "New York City has a lot of super cool things. Like the Statue of Liberty and Broadway." He snapped his head back over his shoulder to look at me.

"Broadway is in New York?" He gasped, "Like where Hamilton is performed?"

I looked up at Hope and she had her head laid back in the chair, looking like she was asleep already. "Yeah, bud, lots of musicals and plays are performed all over the city."

"How cool." He said in a quiet voice so full of wonder and room for knowledge.

"Are you hungry?" I asked, looking at the clock on the wall.

"Starving." He said plainly as he added an American flag to the top of one of his buildings. "The plane had peanuts, but peanuts are disgusting." He paused his furious coloring and looked over his shoulder at me again. "Unless they're smushed into peanut butter. Then they're good."

I felt myself smile for the first time since arguing with Kyson this morning before work and felt that pull to this little boy that I'd felt when he was a newborn and snuggled safely in my arms. "Peanut butter is the best," I said enthusiastically. "Especially on apples or paired with raspberry jelly."

"-Raspberry Jelly." He added at the same time.

My heart lurched in my chest at how much I still loved him and ached for him to be mine, even after all these years.

The world was cruel and unjust.

But I refused to waste this time I was getting with him right now.

Too much time had already been stolen from me and Sam, and if I was only going to get a few more hours or minutes with this little boy while his mom rested before she took him away from me again, then I was going to soak it up while I could.

I gently laid my hand on his dark brown hair and ruffled it, painfully aware of how it glowed with golden strands like Kyson's. "How does pizza sound for dinner?" I asked him, swallowing back the lump in my throat. Grief and joy had no business feeling so similar to each other in my heart at the same time.

"I love pizza!" He said, standing up and turning to face me. "Can we really get one? Like delivery?"

I smiled at the bright wonder in his eyes. "Yeah Sammy, we can get one." I stood up and held my hand out for him. "We can even order two if you want."

He jumped up, pumping his fist in the air. "Awesome!" He cheered and slid his tiny hand into mine, holding tight as we walked to the kitchen to get the delivery menus.

I picked him up and put him on the counter as I opened the drawer I kept all the takeout menus in and paused when I saw the blood-red envelope sitting on top of them with my name scrawled across the front in Kyson's elegant handwriting.

"Did you change your mind?" Sam asked next to me, and I looked up at him. "Trey changes his mind a lot, too." He said with a blank expression on his face.

I picked up the envelope and ran my finger over my name before sliding it into my pocket and grabbing the menu for Luigi's out of the pile and handing it to Sam. "Nope, just trying to decide which toppings I want on my half." His megawatt smile made everything else melt into the background as he opened the menu and looked at all the pictures of pizza creations. The envelope felt heavy in my pocket and my fingers kept brushing over it as I tried to focus on his excitement.

I had to be present with Sam right now, but that didn't mean I didn't long to have Kyson happy and in my arms and at my side while I did it.

Chapter 19 – Kyson

I fell face-first down into the bed in my fancy hotel room and groaned at how bone weary and tired my body felt from everything that happened at Dexter's apartment before I left.

The further the plane took me away from him, the more I was sure I'd made a mistake by leaving him in his time of need. I hated how my insecurities had made me feel so inadequate and made me run fast and far away as he struggled.

I was hurt because he hadn't chosen me with certainty five seconds after seeing his ex-wife and lost son for the first time in years. And that was so selfish of me.

Of course, I knew that now, but I'd expected a decision from him on the spot and ran when he couldn't give that to me.

"I'm so fucking stupid." I groaned into the pillows.

I was the worst kind of selfish.

I rolled over and pulled my phone out of my pocket and pulled up Dexter's contact thread I had muted in the cab on the way to the airport in New York.

Thirteen missed calls.

Seven voicemails.

Forty-seven texts.

I groaned again and scrubbed my hand over my face as I fought the urge to call him back and apologize to him for leaving like that.

Because there was that part of my heart that was hurt still, even if I knew it was wrong and selfish of me to expect so much from him in a split second.

I sat up and tore my jacket off and kicked my boots off before peeling my shirt off and headed towards the bathroom, turning the shower on hot and letting the steam fill the room around me.

Maybe a scalding hot shower would clear the stupid out of my head and leave me able to think straight past my bruised ego and sore heart.

A loud banging rang out from my door, and I almost moaned in anticipation of how good the wine I'd ordered from room service at the check-in desk was going to taste as I drank the entire bottle in the hot shower, forgoing a glass altogether.

I opened the door, not even caring that I wore only my black jeans, and then cursed out loud at the man standing on the other side with my bottle of wine.

"Fucking hell," I grunted.

"Is that any way to greet your very best friend in the whole wide world?" Reid deadpanned, "I even brought your ridiculously expensive bottle of wine that some little twat was going to expect a twenty-dollar tip for delivering it to your door." He pushed his way into my room, and I let the door swing shut behind him. "You should be thanking me."

"What are you doing here?" I asked, running my hand through my hair in frustration. I was too tired for this.

"Dexter called me. I was in LA for meetings today, so I called Cora, and she knew where you were, and ta-da!" He held his hands out. "Here I am, like your very straight, annoyingly sober fairy godfather."

"What a pathetically tragic fairytale I've ended up in." I grumped as I grabbed the bottle of wine that he put down on the counter and then cursed when I realized I didn't have any way to open it.

Reid pulled a corkscrew from behind his back and winked. "Told ya." He said, grabbing the wine and opening it. "Fairy godfather." It had to be a corkscrew, didn't it?

"Hmm," I said, taking the bottle from him as he leaned down to smell it.

"I was just smelling it." He carried on, oblivious to how a simple kitchen utensil was sending me down into a tailspin of depression because it was how I had met Dex, to begin with. And it was also the safe word we used when we had rough and experimental sex. "I actually don't even like red wine." He continued as he walked further into my suite and threw himself down in a chair.

"You have poor taste then." I protested.

He smirked and then he fell serious as he looked up at my disheveled appearance. "You okay?"

I put the opening of the bottle to my lips and tipped it back, drinking down a large portion of it before coming up for air. "Perfectly fucked." I saluted him with the bottle and walked away. "I'm going to drink the rest of this in the shower, I'll be perfect by the time I get out. Feel free to show yourself out before I get done." I told him over my shoulder.

"Does red meat or pork pair better with that wine?" He called out, ignoring me as he grabbed the room service menu.

"Leave Reid." I declared, but he ignored me as he mumbled about the options available.

I shut the door to my master bedroom and then stripped out of the rest of my clothes as I headed towards the shower. I stood under the scalding water, letting it run over my head and down my back as I held the bottle against the wall, taking pulls off of it as it settled into my stomach and my senses.

I don't know how long I stayed in the steamy bathroom, wallowing in my pity, but the wine bottle was empty, and I couldn't seem to care about the tepid temperature of the water anymore by the time I turned it off in a haze and stepped out.

The wine was definitely worth the price when it got you that drunk, that fast.

The three glasses I had on the plane over probably had primed my drunk pump, but that was neither here nor there.

I knew I was straddling a narrow ledge of sobriety as I used the alcohol to numb my pain, but I needed the pain to just let up for a fraction of a second so I could think clearly.

I got dressed in a pair of joggers and a sweater and walked back out into my living room, hoping that Reid would have disappeared while I was gone, but he sat on the couch with his shoes off and feet up on the table, flipping through the tv guide.

"I'm drunk, and I plan on drinking more as the night goes on." I declared to him from across the room. "So if that's going to be too hard on you, feel free to check out now. No hard feelings."

He barely paid me any attention as he turned on some classic western movie. "I'm good."

I scoffed at him and rolled my eyes, but didn't bother to add anything to it. On the table by the wall, there was an array of room service plates laid out and a couple of bottles of water and orange juice. "Where's the wine?" I inquired, lifting the lids off some plates and hating the way my mouth watered at the choices he made. I didn't want to eat when I was so fucked up emotionally, but I had eaten little through the day and knew it was the responsible thing to do.

He hooked his finger over his shoulder, and I saw a fresh bottle on the counter, uncorked with a glass next to it. "I figured maybe with this one, you could try to actually taste it on the way down." He stated with a smirk, and I flipped him off.

I grabbed a plate with a juicy cheeseburger on it and poured myself another glass and sat down on the other end of the couch and dug in. He got up and got his plate and a bottle of water and sat next to me, eating in silence while we watched the mindless movie. I almost forgot about all the drama of the day as the wine and grease effectively soaked into my brain, until he muted the movie and asked simply, "Want to talk about it?"

I raised my eyebrow at him with attitude, "About my bi-curious boyfriend asking me to move in with him this morning, and then retracting that when his ex-wife and kid showed up on his doorstep eight hours later?" I quipped and then shrugged my shoulders. "No, not really."

"He didn't retract it," Reid said firmly. "If you're going to tell the story, tell it right."

"Whatever man." I brushed him off, taking another drink of wine.

"Can you honestly sit there and tell me if you were in his spot that you'd be able to just kick them out without a second thought for someone else?"

"I don't want to talk about it, Reid." I laid my head back on the couch and closed my eyes.

"Because you know, deep down under all that pain and fear, that I'm right."

"Fuck you."

"You're not my type."

"Get out." I tried sounding assertive and dominant and almost chuckled, knowing I was trying to dominate a Dom.

"Nah, I got tomorrow off to take care of you because you ran away." He sucked his teeth. "So you're stuck with me."

I groaned. "I'm fine, I had to come out here for work, anyway. I didn't run away."

"Say whatever you want to say, Kyson, but I have strict orders from Cora not to leave your side until you're back in New York." He looked over at me with wide eyes. "And we all know she's far scarier than any of us all wrapped together. So I don't plan on disobeying her."

"I thought you were the one to give the orders to women, not the other way around." I shot out, deflecting my shit to call out his. "Or are you actually the sub?"

His eyes narrowed and darkened through my alcohol haze, and I swallowed at the change in his intensity as he stared at me.

"Dexter shouldn't have told you that." He said with a bite to his tone.

"Why?" I asked, happy to talk about anything other than me.

"Because that part of me doesn't exist anymore." He stood up from the couch and took our plates over to the table.

"How can you just... turn that off?" I inquired.

"Easy." He said as he poured the rest of my wine down the drain.

"Hey!" I yelled in outrage as he ignored me.

"I fucked up and someone got hurt and I decided never to go down that path again." He admitted, like my outburst never happened.

I paused, frozen still, as his words processed through my sluggish brain. "What do you mean, someone got hurt?"

He shrugged his shoulders, leaning against the counter with his hands in his pockets, and the stance reminded me so much of Dexter.

Fucking Dexter was everywhere.

"That's a story for another day, my friend. But back to you." He pointed to me, and I rolled my eyes and fell back against the couch.

"I'd rather not."

"He's distraught, you should know." He said evenly, but I could hear the anger in his voice. We may have bonded over the auction and the crazy traumatic birth of Annabelle, but his friendship with Dexter went far deeper than that, and his loyalty to him was obvious. "He never got to say goodbye to Sammy when she took him." He added, making me look his way. "Just one day... poof. He was gone." I could see the pain in his eyes as he tried to make me understand Dexter's hang-ups. "Can you imagine having a child and then they're gone, with no closure or explanation that you could wrap your head around? Because I fucking can't. And I think we both know Dexter is a hell of a better man than me, so I know it destroyed the very center of his soul."

"Why are you telling me this?" I asked, I already knew that Hope took Sammy away one day with only a dear John letter left for Dex to find.

"Because I know you love Dex, and I know he fucking loves you deeper than almost anything else in this entire world, and I think you're fucking perfect for each other and I don't even believe in love anymore, so that says something." He said it like it was plain as day written across the sky. "But the one thing he doesn't love you more than, and never should love you more than, is his child." He leaned forward and stared right at me. "And Sammy is his child, regardless of what his DNA is."

"I know," I said, sinking further into the couch. "I know I messed up Reid. Hence all the wine."

"Then call him." He instructed.

"It's late there." I looked at my watch. "Fuck, it's late here."

"If you think for one second he's sleeping, knowing you're upset and here all alone with the likes of me—" He glared like he was the worst company in the world. "Just call him."

"Will you leave if I do?"

"Yes, but only because I have the suite across the hall." He said, standing up off the counter. "I'll be back tomorrow at seven am sharp to..." He paused with a wicked glint in his eye, "bug the ever-loving shit out of you all day."

"Ugh, Reid." I groaned. "I have to work tomorrow; you can't tag along. I work with very private people."

"Then tell them I'm your assistant or something for the day."

"You're going to let me boss you around?" I scoffed, and he grinned.

"Maybe. Maybe not. It will be fun either way."

"For you!" I hollered after him as he walked out my door, flipping me off.

He stopped the door from closing and looked back at me, "Just letting you know I have my jet on the tarmac at LAX, fueled with a team of staff to fly me home when I say so, should you decide you want to go home early and end this little break." He didn't give me time to reply before letting the door finally shut behind him with a deafening thud.

I laid my head back against the couch and felt myself smiling a little at having a genuine friend in Reid. He had his issues, didn't we all? But he was a good friend to both me and Dexter.

I grabbed my phone from the bed and laid down in the center, hating that I was across the country from the man I loved, even angry or not. I just missed him.

I clicked on his name and hit send, putting the phone to my ear and praying for some sort of guidance from some higher power to be an adult and come out of this conversation with Dexter still in my life.

Chapter 20 – Dexter

I laid down in Kyson's bed, which smelled like us, and took a deep breath, letting it calm me after a chaotic day. I left Hope and Sammy in my apartment to sleep for the night, offering the guest room to them, knowing it had once been Sammy's room, and went to Kyson's for the night.

It felt invasive to come into his space after how he left things with me earlier in the day, but I hoped that if I kept my fingers dug into our life together, he wouldn't be able to dislodge me so easily.

And something deep inside of my heart told me not to trust Hope to be completely alone with Sammy right now. There was something in how she had looked at him when she talked about her own self-care these last few years that left me... on edge.

So staying down the hall, able to watch across the courtyard, helped ease that nagging feeling in my gut.

I pulled the red envelope from my pocket, now that I was finally alone in the silence, and ran my thumb under the edge of the intricate seal. I didn't know when Ky wrote this note, but something told me it wasn't after Hope showed up. He seemed like he was still in shock when I got home, not like he was calm enough to write a letter at that time.

I pulled out the cream-colored paper and ran my fingertips over the writing, like a gentle caress through the ink, and took a deep breath as I started reading his words.

Dexter,

My love.

This morning, you caught me off guard when you asked me to move in with you, and you perceived that hesitation as reluctance instead of what it truly was.

Shock.

Disbelief.

Unworthiness.

And so many more emotions I know you recognize because they live inside of you as well.

I've been blessed to have you come into my life, but the part of me that has been hurt and used in the past continuously waits for you to decide I'm not worthy of you, or that you're better suited for a heterosexual relationship after all.

And I spend every single day waiting for the other shoe to drop and my happy, healthy, and loving bubble to burst.

So this morning, I was trying to convince myself that you weren't being cruel and joking with me when you told me you wanted to live together.

There is nothing in this world I would like more than to continue building our lives together as one Dexter Chase. Not a single thing.

I know you have reservations about titles and big moves because of the pain that you've experienced in the past during your marriage, but I'd marry you today if you agreed. So please do not think for one moment that I don't want to live with you, waking up, side by side with you for the rest of our lives until we're both old and wrinkly and unable to see our asses or our elbows. Because I want that and so much more with you, baby.

Since Annabelle came into our lives, I'm overwhelmed with a desire to see you get the family you so desperately deserve, Dex. And I know it won't look the same as the last time you did it, but you can have that again.

With me.

We will never replace Sammy, and I'd never try to because he is your son through and through. And someday when he is older, I want to help you reach out to him and tell him about yourself and how much you still to this very day love him because I love you. And I want you to be complete.

I love you more and more with every single breath I take, baby.

Please never doubt that love again, because it kills me to know you think you're unworthy of it. And believe me, I know that single thought has run through your head on repeat today in our time apart. So many times I wanted to pick up my phone and call you to reassure you and confess these feelings to you. But I wanted something more impactful than a phone call.

So I wrote this letter, confessing my undying love for you in ink, so similar to the art I wear every day, shamelessly on display.

Written words are a dying form of love, one I never want to cease between us. Because I want to cover my body with words and symbols of my love for you.

For you and you alone, Dexter Chase.

I'll never love another the way I love you.

I'll never be whole enough to ever even try, because you'll own my heart and soul for the rest of my life.

Marry me, Dexter.

I know this is still new, but we have the rest of our lives to do things the 'right' way.

So marry me anyway.

Marry me and let me love you how you deserve to be loved, from now until forever.

I love you until my very last breath and beyond Dexter Chase.

Always yours,

Ky.

The letter fell from my fingertips as tears welled in my eyes.

I'd confirmed his greatest fears today when I hesitated to outright choose him.

"My God," I whispered as pain ripped through my heart, knowing how deeply I'd hurt the man I loved.

The man I was going to marry and raise children with.

I grabbed my phone for the hundredth time since he left, pulling up his name. But this time, instead of me pressing send, it started ringing in my hand.

Kyson Hart.

His name flashed on the screen, and I slammed my thumb down on the accept button before rushing to get it to my ear.

"Baby?" I gasped, hearing nothing on the other end. "Ky? Talk to me." I whispered in anguish. "Please."

"I'm sorry." He said, and his voice broke.

"No." I rushed on, standing up and pacing his bedroom. "No, you have nothing to be sorry about. It's me that owes you an apology that will take the rest of forever for me to make right. I'm so sorry. I panicked, and I was in shock, and I didn't know how to process everything."

"I never should have told you to make her leave." He admitted and I could hear the tears in his voice as I wiped my own off my face. "Ultimatums aren't how healthy adults form relationships, Dex, I know that. I fucking know that." He sighed.

"You were scared and hurt, and you reacted appropriately to the situation."

"He's your son." He said. "My God Dexter, I don't care what the DNA tests said, that boy is yours. In just a few minutes I got to spend in his presence, I could see so much of you in him. Whether it's that age-old argument of nature versus nurture or something else completely, that boy is yours. And for me to tell you to make her leave, knowing she would take him with her... fuck Dex. If you had any idea how I truly felt about him, what I'd written just hours before that moment in time. You'd know I never meant it. I'm not that person. I'm not a bad person, I promise."

"I know Ky, I know you're not. I know your heart because I live inside of it. Every single day, baby. I only exist nowadays to love you."

"No," He cried again, and it broke my heart to hear his pain through the phone while being unable to comfort him physically. "You exist for him. Reid said today that the only person you love more than me is Sam, and he was right. That's exactly how it should be. That's exactly how I want it to be, because that shows the loyalty in your heart."

"Reid? You talked to Reid?" I asked, confused, as I tried to keep up with what he was saying in my exhausted brain.

He snorted a laugh through his tears and took a deep breath, "He's here. In L.A. In my hotel, actually."

"How? Why?"

"I don't know." He sighed again with a smile in his voice. "Something about Cora threatening him with bodily harm if he didn't bring me back to New York to you."

"Jesus." I cursed, falling back onto his bed, feeling lighter than I had a few minutes ago. "Are you coming back to me?"

"Tomorrow." He said without hesitation. "I canceled my meetings and I'm flying back with Reid on the Jones Jet." He laughed softly before pausing. "That's if you'll still have me."

"I'll do you one better than that, Kyson Hart," I said, sitting up and planting my feet on the floor for grounding as I said the words I never thought I'd ever say again in my life. "Marry me."

I heard his quick breath in through the phone, "What?"

"I read your letter," I replied.

"Oh, my God." He groaned. "I wrote that before everything happened today."

"Does that mean you take it back? Do you not mean all of it now? Now that Hope has crashed into our life for the moment. Because I'm committed to you Kyson, I let her stay in my guest room only because of Sam, but I'm not there. Does that change things for you?"

"No!" He cried. "God, no Dex. I meant it. Every word, I still do. I want to marry you. I want kids with you."

"Then say yes," I growled in that deep voice that made him weak. "Because my toxic masculinity won't allow me to believe it unless you answer my proposal with affirmation."

"Yes!" He yelled through the phone. "Yes! Yes! Yes!"

I laughed and felt my heart completely thaw for the first time in years, knowing things were falling in place. "I love you Ky. So fucking much. I want to be with you so badly right now."

"I love you too. I know, I ache being this far away from you."

"I know." Sighing, I looked around his bedroom. "I'm at your apartment, by the way. In your bed right now."

He groaned through the phone. "Don't tease me like that right now, Dex. You know I love the way you look on my black sheets."

I chuckled and shook my head. "I needed to be close to you and Sam tonight, and this was the best way I could come up with."

"How is he? Is he as fantastic as I imagine he is?" He asked with genuine curiosity.

I smiled with an overflowing heart as I thought about the boy next door. "He's perfect, Kyson," I whispered. "He's so fucking perfect and it breaks my heart to know I'm going to lose him again for a second time."

"Maybe you don't have to, Dex." He rushed on, "Maybe you guys can work something out. Maybe this is your chance."

"Maybe," I said gently, hating the desire that swelled in my chest at the thought. "And you'd support that? You'd stand by my side if I co-parented a child with a woman I was married to?"

"For you, I'd walk through hell and back."

I groaned. "It will be hell and back, dealing with Hope. I just want to warn you, because I'm not always the best version of myself when she rattles my cage."

"Then I'll stand by your side and keep your cage calm and settled."

"I love you. You're incredible."

"I love you more."

We talked for hours, as I told him about Sammy and all the things we had talked about and everything that Hope had confessed to. I told him how I didn't trust her, that something was gnawing at my gut about her, and he confirmed the best place for them was next door, so we could keep a close eye on her until we figured it all out. When we ended the call, it was nearly two am my time and he would be back home by early afternoon.

I would have the man of my dreams and the love of my life back in my arms in a few hours. And with any luck, I could introduce him to Sam and build some sort of relationship with him and Hope that would be beneficial to her and our son.

Because Ky was right, he was a fucking spitting image of me, and I felt it in my soul that the boy was mine.

And I was going to do whatever I needed to, to prove it to myself and the world.

And I was going to do it with Ky at my side.

Sunlight shone through the open blinds in Ky's apartment, and I groaned momentarily before remembering that my son was next door and that Ky would be home soon. I jumped out of bed with renewed purpose and looked across the courtyard to see Sammy sitting on the couch with his papers and crayons, watching some kid's show on the tv and my soul relaxed knowing he was so close again. I quickly got dressed and dialed the one person I knew could help me today with this.

"Morning." Mav's baritone voice rang through the phone. "I'm told that Reid and Kyson are boarding the jet back from L.A. in an hour."

"That's right. We talked last night, and I want to thank you and Cora for meddling in the situation. Though, I'm not exactly sure how you two even knew about it, to begin with."

He chuckled, "Reid had to get approval to keep his jet at LAX for longer than the original flight plan called for and Cora has that freaky mother's intuition, and the rest is history."

"Well, I'm surely not going to complain about any bit of it. But that's not why I called."

"So, why did you call?"

I sighed, trying to figure out how to explain my father's intuition when I didn't even feel like a father. "Sam is mine." I rushed out, sighing at the lack of tact.

"She told you that?" He asked surprised.

"No. She didn't, she wants us to get back together, which isn't going to happen. And I'm not sure she'll ever admit that she stole my son from me without proof first. But I know it, Mav. Deep in my bones. He's a replica of me and his mannerisms and personality are me, a perfect match. I don't know how to explain it other than..." I paused, unable to put it into words.

"A father's intuition." He finished for me. "Don't worry about explaining it to me, Dex, I get it now. What do you need from me to make sure she doesn't take him away again?"

I sighed, "I don't know, proof I guess. She's at my place right now, and I'm at Ky's. I'm literally sitting here staring at my son sitting on my couch right now and it's so fucking surreal. But I'm going to address it with her today and go from there. So I guess I could use some eyes in case she bolts."

"Say no more." He said easily. "I'll put men on your place, and you let me know if she moves. We won't let her slip away again until you get the proof you need that you're Sam's biological father. And fuck, even if you can't, we'll get him back. One way or another."

"What do you mean?" I asked, as my ruthless friend showed his teeth.

"Everyone has a number, Dex, you know that. And I'll stop at nothing to make sure my nephew is safe at home with my brother."

"I appreciate it, man." I confirmed, watching as Sammy laughed at something on the T.V. "I'm going to go over and see what progress I can make before Ky gets here and she realizes there's not a hope or prayer of us getting back together and becomes vindictive."

"Understood. I'll text you with the details of the tail when they get there."

"Thanks, Mav."

"Anytime Dex. Say hi to Ky for us when he gets home. Cora's chomping at the bit to get over there and meet Sam too, by the way, so I'll hold her off as long as possible. But you know how she is..."

I laughed good-heartedly as I headed for the front door. "I'll see her in an hour, then."

"See ya then." He agreed, laughing.

I hung up the phone, slid it into the pocket of my jeans, and walked down the hall to my apartment. I didn't knock; it was my home after all and walked in.

Sam still sat on the couch watching tv and looked up at me when I walked in with bright eyes. "Hi!" He said excitedly.

My heart soared that he was happy to see me, and I smiled brightly at him. "Morning. How are you?"

"Hungry. But good." He said, looking out of the corner of his eye at the cartoon and snickering again.

"Where's your mom?" I asked, looking around the space. "I told her to help herself to the food."

"She left." He said, shrugging his shoulders, not even pretending to pay attention to me anymore, too captivated by the blue dog with an Australian accent jumping around the television pretending to be a unicorn or something.

"What do you mean, she left?" I asked, walking over and standing in the way to get his attention back. "When did she leave?" The hair on the back of my neck stood up as I looked around the apartment and didn't see any trace of her things anywhere.

"Uh—" He paused, looking around, "When Chip and Dale was on."

"When was—" I stopped, shaking my head. "Okay, buddy." I walked over and ruffled his hair again. "Let's get you some food and then we'll find your mom."

"Okay, thanks!" He said, hopping up and down on his knees on the couch. "Do you have the cereal that turns the milk into chocolate milk? That's my favorite."

"I think I'm fresh out," I said distractedly, as I walked to the kitchen. "I'll see what I can find." As I opened the fridge and pulled out yogurt and a banana, I called over my shoulder. "Does your mom leave you alone like this a lot?"

"Sometimes." He answered, turning around to look over the back of the couch now that his show was on commercial. "One time, she was gone for four bedtimes. In a row." He elaborated with wide eyes. "Our neighbor, Mrs. Penelope, let me come to her house and stay until she got back."

"Four—" I stopped, cursing under my breath and looking away. "Four fucking nights." I shook my head and fought the rage that was boiling in my body. "Do you like bananas? And yogurt? It's all I have right now, but we can go to the store after breakfast and get whatever you want."

"I love yogurt!" He jumped over the back of the couch like a dare-devil and bounded up to the counter. "Mom doesn't buy it because she said it's only for rich people." He looked down at the cup of creamy goodness in front of him and then looked up at me. "Are you rich?"

"Kind of," I answered truthfully. "I can make sure you have yogurt at least."

"Cool." He said, and I was quickly learning that was a favorite word of his. He dug into the yogurt, and I walked around my apartment to make sure Hope didn't just get in the shower or something while he got distracted by T.V.

But sure enough, the place was empty. When I walked into my bedroom, I found Sam's backpack laying on the end of the bed with a large manilla envelope laying on top. Dread and excitement lit my nerves on fire as I reached for it and opened it up.

There was a handwritten letter on top in Hope's writing and I started there.

Dex,

You were wrong when you said you were the best off out of the men I had affairs with. There was one other that was even more elite than you were at the time, but he was also the cruelest.

When I found out I was pregnant, I tried to end my relationships with others, and for the most part, I was successful. I wanted to be a good wife and mom; I swear I did.

But this man, this elite and powerful man, had other things to say about it.

I didn't know until later on that he had a personal vendetta against you, and that was why he had approached me to begin with. Showering me with attention and gifts that you never bothered with until I was hooked on the high of being wanted. And then I found out I was preg-nant, and I wanted to give my baby the best chance possible at a happy home, so I walked away from the materialistic things he offered me.

Six months into Sam's life, he approached me in a boutique one day and threatened to tell you everything. Every sordid tale and memory of my affair with him to humiliate you and destroy our happy home. But I think deep down, he knew you'd forgive me for the affairs for the chance at keeping Sam happy and at home, so he went one step further.

He threatened Sam's life.

He told me that if I didn't do exactly as he said, he'd take Sam from us both, and then he would ensure that our sweet baby had a terribly rough life.

And he had the power to do all of that because his name is Judge Keith Cross.

My chest seized as I recognized the name of a man that had risen through the circuit courts using blatant forms of bribery and blackmail to do so.

He was also the judge that oversaw my petition for custody of Sam.

Her letter continued as I fought with the rage boiling through my body.

He planned the whole thing, the story of how I'd fallen in love with a man that was Sam's real father, and he even produced the forged paternity tests to make you lose your petition for Sam in his own courtroom.

I went along with it all because if I didn't; he had documents already drafted to steal Sam from us and place him in the worst foster care homes in the city. He would have destroyed our precious son to get back at both of us.

Sam is yours Dex, I have the real reports that I stole from Keith before I left for Texas with Trey. Plus, you can redo the tests now and the proof will speak for itself, the DNA will be a perfect match. As if you needed that to know in your gut that our boy is yours. I saw how you watched him last night, and I'm so sorry I stole these years from you both. I thought I was doing what was right for Sam in the long run. But I was wrong.

Keith wanted you to lose everything, and he succeeded because I was too weak and scared to fight him.

But you're not.

I've done my research on you since then, I know you're powerful and connected and can protect our son in ways I couldn't. And I want you to do that, Dex, you deserve that.

You and the man that opened the door yesterday to your apartment.

I can tell you love him, and I can tell that he loves you and I'm sorry for coming in the middle of that. I had a plan when I showed up to come clean and beg you to help, but seeing that you'd moved on hurt. And I let it get the best of me at the moment.

But the bottom line is… I'm not fit to raise Sam. I'm weak and selfish and I just simply cannot do it anymore.

He's a great boy. He's so much like you it is painful sometimes, and I want him to know his father and live happily in comfort with security, knowing he's safe and doesn't have to struggle through life anymore.

In this envelope, you'll find the original paternity test, proving you're his father. I've also attached the written correspondences from Keith over the years, speaking in mostly veiled threats and coded phrases to make sure I stayed where I was in Texas, maintaining the charade, but it's better than nothing. The form from Trey signed relinquishing his 'rights', though that won't be needed once you prove the paternity. And also, the form I signed, relinquishing my rights to Sam as well.

Please don't think that I've made this decision lightly, or that it came easily for me. Because I will miss my son, but I won't show up and try to take him from you either. Though I may one day reach out and ask you for permission to meet him again if I ever get myself on track and become worthy of him.

Please, all I ask of you is that you tell him how much I loved him. How much he meant to me and how I thought I was doing what was best.

The thought of him thinking of me with some sort of respect or understanding someday when he's older is the only thing keeping me sane right now.

So I guess that's it.

Just love him and raise him to be a good man and you'll be fine.

And for what it's worth, I don't think I'm capable of loving a man, but if I could, I came closest with you.

Thank you, Dexter.

Go give our boy the world.

"Hey, can we go to the store now? I finished my yogurt and banana." Sam asked from the doorway, and I looked up quickly, transfixed by the sight of him.

My son.

"Yeah," I said, swallowing down the emotion of all of it. "Give me just a few minutes and we can go, okay?"

"Cool." He said, turning and running off at lightning speed back to the living room as I tried to wrap my head around it all. But everything else could wait for now, because right now, I had a trip to the grocery store with my son to make.

I quickly snapped a picture of all the documents and sent them off to Maverick with the mind-blown emoji, quickly explaining how Hope was gone, leaving Sam with me, and then sent him a text asking how the fuck to get a kid to the grocery store with no car seat.

Turns out, that Sam used a booster seat at home. Luckily Saint came in and saved the day, letting me borrow one that his son used in his car to get to the grocery store and back.

It was such a surreal fucking moment watching my son run around the grocery store, throwing all sorts of junk food in the cart, each time looking at me for approval as he moved on to the next sugary goodness calling his name. He surprised me when he grabbed fruits and vegetables as well, tossing them in amongst all the sugar.

By the time we got back to my apartment, I felt drunk on life, trying hard to grasp it all while battling the spins and nausea at figuring this all out on the fly. My heart ached for the pain my little boy would feel when he realized his mom wasn't coming back for him, but I hoped he found peace in my presence like I did with him.

And I couldn't wait to tell Kyson.

He was due to be home any minute now, and I was nervously pacing the kitchen as Sam lay in the center of the guest bed, napping off his sugar high.

What if Ky backed out now that Sam was mine, full-time? It was a giant step in our relationship, but I didn't want to bring Ky into Sam's life as just my boyfriend. This was our chance at a fresh start with my son and how we handled this was going to pave the way for the rest of his life.

I just didn't know what the right answer was until I got to see and speak to Ky.

The front door opened behind me, and I whipped around as the beautiful man himself popped his head in. "Hi." He said shyly, setting his bags down on the floor by the door.

"Hi," I said as I slammed into him, wrapping my arms around his body and clinging to him like my life depended on him.

Which it fucking did.

"I missed you." He said into my neck, tightening his hold on me before quickly pulling back. "Where's Hope and Sam?"

"Sam's napping in the bedroom," I said, pulling him back to me and kissing his lips long and leisurely, tasting him like it was for the first time all over again. He groaned into my mouth and opened for me, letting me deepen it even further as my tongue swirled with his. "I love you. And I'm so, so sorry." I pulled back and laid my forehead against his.

"We're both sorry, and we're both forgiven, Dex. And we're en-gaged." He said in an excited whisper with a giddy smile on his face before I crashed my lips back down on his.

"Yes, we really fucking are." I smiled and then stilled. "But there's something I need to tell you first. In case you change your mind."

"Change my mind?" He asked, stepping backward with a scowl on his perfect face. "Why would I change my mind?"

I grabbed the stack of paperwork off the counter and laid it out for him. "Hope is gone." His eyes rounded as he shook his head back and forth in confusion. "She left this morning and left all of this for me." He picked up the paternity test and his eyes rounded as he read the actual results and he turned to me with shock burning bright in his eyes.

"He's yours?" He whispered. "We knew he was, but this... this proves it?"

I nodded silently, still in shock myself. "It's a long story, one you can read about in the letter she left, but the judge in the case was blackmailing her and he forged the results. She left Sam with me because she doesn't feel fit to parent him anymore."

"What if she changes her mind?" He questioned, with fear clear in his voice. "What if she just shows up one day and tries to take him?"

"She signed over her rights." I showed him the next form. "She said that someday she might ask us for permission to meet him again, but not until she's got herself on track, and even then, I can decide what's best for Sam when that time comes."

"Oh my god Dex, you have your son." He smiled brightly at me.

"We have our son," I affirmed, turning him to face me as I slid my hands into his hair and stared deeply into his eyes. "We have to teach Sam that I'm his dad, and it's going to be a shock at first for him, I think. But when we do that, I want him to know that you're his dad, too. Because you're going to be just as big a part of his life as I am and I want him to know he has us both, rooting for him and supporting him in everything. I don't want him to feel like he lost his mom today, but instead, I want him to of gained us both."

"You're so fucking perfect," Kyson said, leaning forward and kissing me deeply again. "Are you sure, though?" He whispered, "I don't want to make this harder on him. Two dads are hard to wrap your head around when you're not even used to having one dad."

"I'm sure. We're going to take it slow and answer any questions he has about it, but something tells me he's just going to roll with it. He's so fucking perfect, Ky. He's so smart and so inquisitive and you'll see how great this is going to be."

"Okay." He smiled and nodded his head. "Let's give that little boy the world. Together."

I slid my fingers through his and led him towards the guest room to silently watch our son sleep in the center of the king-sized bed. Sam was curled up on his side with his baby blanket clutched tightly in his hands as he slept peacefully. I leaned against the door frame and Ky leaned against my chest as we watched him from across the room.

"You're right, he's perfect," Ky whispered after a while, and I smiled into his hair and kissed his temple.

"You're perfect, and for once we're both going to have the perfect life we both always have dreamed about but never imagined could happen to us."

He laid his head back down on my chest and sighed contently. "I love you, fiancé."

I chuckled and kissed his forehead again, "I'm going to make you my husband sooner rather than later."

"Hmm." He hummed in approval and tightened his arms around my stomach as we watched over Sam.

Chapter 21 – Kyson

I sat on the couch in Dexter's place, looking at Sam as he looked at me. Dex was in the shower when Sam woke up from his nap and he had walked out into the living room, rubbing the sleep from his eyes, and found me instead of his dad.

To his credit, he didn't freak out or anything, just walked over and sat down on the couch next to me. "Hi." He said in his sweet little voice.

"Hi, Sam." I replied with a soft smile.

He watched me intently for a minute before turning on the couch to face me. "You were here yesterday, when my mom and I got here. And then you left. And you looked sad."

I nodded my head slowly, "Yeah, I was here."

"And you were sad." He reiterated sternly, and I smiled at him.

"Yes, I was sad when I left."

"Because I was here?" He asked and started chewing his lip.

"Not at all." I answered quickly. "I was sad because I had to leave for work. And I wanted to get to spend time with you instead."

He processed that and then nodded his head slowly, looking around the space. "Do you know where my mom is?"

"I don't." I answered truthfully. "But I know that she left a letter, asking us to take care of you and love you as much as she does for a while."

He cocked his head to the side a bit and chewed on his lip again. "I get to stay here?"

I nodded again, "If you want to." I looked around the apartment, trying to see if through a kid's point of view. "It's a pretty great apartment. And there are lots of fun things to do all around the city."

"Like the statue of Liberty?" He asked quickly. "And the big apple?"

I chuckled at him a bit and nodded my head again. "Yeah, and parks, and food trucks, and stores. There's something new to do every day if you want."

"And I get to do them?" He asked, "With you?"

"If you want to."

"I want to." He said enthusiastically, hopping up and down in his seat, scooting closer to me. "You have drawings on your arms." He declared a second later.

"I do." I rolled up my sleeves further to show him more of them as he scooted even closer. "I have birds," I pointed out a sparrow and a raven. "And flowers." He rushed to point out a rose and then a daisy. "That's right." I chuckled. "And there are animals." He jumped up on his knees and pointed out a lion and an elephant on each arm excitedly.

"Lions are my favorite animal." He said excitedly. "I was a lion for Halloween last year, and mom said I could be one again this year!"

"Lions are great." I said, "They have long manes, and long sharp teeth."

"And claws!" He held up his fingers and roared like a lion and I laughed, falling back on the cushion like I was afraid of him. I caught Dex as he came out of his bedroom, watching us with a mesmerized look on his face.

"Hey." I said to him, pulling him out of his trance.

"Dad!" Sam jumped up on his feet and called out to him. "He has a lion on his arm! I love lions!" He jumped around roaring, but I was too sucked into watching Dexter try to process the feeling of hearing his son call him Dad for the first time in his life.

"Hey Sam." I said, as he plopped down on the couch next to me. "How did you know he was your dad?"

Sam looked at me like I had three heads and then looked over at Dex as he walked over and sat down on the coffee table to be near. "I have a picture of us. And mom always said you were my dad. Hang on, I'll get it."

The little boy jumped off the couch and ran for the guest room as I laid my hand on Dex's knee in support. He lifted it to his face and took a deep breath. "He called me dad." He whispered against my wrist, and I brushed my fingers through his damp hair in silent support of the life-changing moment.

"Here!" Sam yelled breathlessly as he rushed back out with a faded picture in his hands, handing it to Dex and me to look at.

It was from when Sam was a baby. Dex was standing with him in his arms and a megawatt smile on his face as Sam laughed with chubby baby cheeks and two front teeth.

"See." Sam said, pointing to the baby. "That's me. And that's you." He said, looking up at Dex.

"That's right." Dex said, clearing his throat from the emotions trying to choke his voice off. "You were only about seven months old in that picture."

"Yeah, I was just a little baby, but I'm a big kid now." He paused and turned to look at me. "Where were you?"

I froze as uncertainty filled my heart. Dex tightened his hand around mine in my lap and answered for me. "He doesn't have any pictures with you yet, Sammy. But he's your dad, too. Just like me."

Sam was silent for a minute while he looked back and forth between us. "Two dads?" He asked confused and then his face broke into a bright smile as he jumped off the couch, trying to click his heels together. "Two dads!" He shrieked, "That's so cool!" Dex laughed and I sagged into the cushions of the couch in relief at his excitement and then he froze and turned back towards us. "Can we take a picture and print it out, so I have one with you, too?"

I nodded, trying to clear the tears from my eyes at his request as he jumped up on the couch next to me and tucked in against my side. I wrapped my arm around his back and pulled him close as Dex took his phone out. "Smile big now, you two."

"Cheese!" Sam cheered, and I smiled brightly through the tears, knowing my first picture with Sam was going to preserve me with teary red-rimmed eyes, but I was going to treasure it, anyway.

"Cheese." I joined in and Dex took a million pictures and then joined us on the couch for a selfie of the three of us, with Sam sandwiched in the middle with both his little arms around our necks and a giant smile on his face.

We were going to be alright. The three of us were going to figure it all out one day at a time.

Epilogue – Dexter

"Shh," I whispered into Ky's ear before leaning down and biting his neck as he moaned again.

"I can't." He panted. "You feel so good." He ran his fingers over my scalp, and I shuddered as I slammed into him again. "Just like that, baby. Hard and deep." He begged, and I pulled back and did it again.

He brought his legs up even further, opening himself more to me as I took what I needed from his body. "You're such a good little toy." I hissed into his ear and then covered his mouth as I slammed deep, sucking the air out of his lungs. "Take it Kyson. Take my cock like a good little cock slut."

"Yes!" He cried through my fingers, and I sat up, wrapping my hand around his neck to silence him as I started thrusting faster, chasing my pleasure as he took his. I wrapped my free hand around his cock and stroked him as he groaned. His face and chest were red from the blush the two orgasms I'd already given him this morning left on his skin, but I wanted one more. I needed it.

"Give it to me baby, come on my cock and milk me. Take every drop." I demanded, and he exploded in my hand, spurting come over his chest as his ass tightened around my cock and the spasms dragged out my orgasm. Tilting my head back, I roared as I filled him up, emptying myself until my lungs ached for air and my body went limp above him. I fell forward, and he opened his arms, welcoming my weight on top of him as we both caught our breaths.

"How do you still have the power to amaze me?" He asked as he lazily ran his fingers up my spine.

"Fuck if I know, but I never want to find out what the alternative looks like because this feels too damn good to give up."

He chuckled and then patted my ass. "Okay, get up. Sam's going to wake up any minute now and we need to shower."

"Hmm." I hummed and pulled out of him and then crawled out of bed and walked into the primary bathroom. I got the shower going and stepped in as he joined me and we quickly washed up, knowing without a doubt that Sam would be up soon. Our son was a clock when it came to sleep, which was a blessing and a curse.

Eight am on the dot he would wake up and get out of bed, but today he'd be even more excited and hyper when he woke up because his favorite person in the entire world was coming to visit him today.

"Dad!" His little voice rang out into the bathroom only seconds after the thought left my brain. "Get ready! They're going to be here soon!"

Ky chuckled as he rinsed his hair out and I popped my head out at the end of the walk-in stone shower. "We're coming, little man. Go get yourself a banana and we'll be right out."

"Okay! But hurry, I need to get dressed and do my hair. I have to look good." He complained and then tore back out of the bathroom towards the kitchen for his breakfast.

"That boy and his looks." Ky joked as he soaped up a loofah and started washing my chest.

I snorted at him. "He gets it from you, Fabio." I joked, and he rolled his eyes.

"Okay, Adonis."

I leaned forward and slid my fingers through his hair, holding him captive and kissing him senseless. "I love you."

He smiled against my lips and shook his head. "Not nearly as much as I love you. Thank you for giving me this life, Dexter."

"Thank you for loving our son as much as I do." I leaned to the side and sucked his ear lobe into my mouth and growled, "And thanks for being a good boy and letting me fuck your ass three times on a Sunday morning."

"Daddy!" Sam groaned from the doorway to the bathroom. "Hurry up! You're as slow as Dad is!"

"Hey!" Kyson groaned, "I am not!"

"Then hurry!"

"Okay, okay," I said, turning off the water. "We're coming."

"Good!" Sam yelled, running back out of the bedroom and giving us privacy. We hurried up to get dressed, and I cleaned up the kitchen as Ky got Sam dressed and did his hair. He came running back out of his bedroom, all spiffy and ready as a knock sounded on the door. "She's here!" He screamed at the top of his lungs. "I'll get it!" I followed him to the door as he pulled it open and jumped up excitedly. "Anna!"

Maverick rolled his eyes as his daughter tried to throw herself out of his arms to get to Sammy as he held his hands up for her, jumping from foot to foot. "At least let us get in the door first Sam." Mav chided, ruffling Sam's styled hair as he walked by and set Annabelle down on the floor safe away from the door.

"Sorry!" Sam said and then threw himself down on the floor next to Anna, smothering her in affection and getting a face full of baby drool and screeching back for it.

Mav and Cora took their coats and boots off and smiled at the two of them on the floor, rolling around. It was Sunday morning and our turn to host family brunch for the Jones family and Reid.

It was Sam's favorite day of the week, hands down.

Even though he went with Ky over to Mav and Cora's place a couple of times a week, it was different when everyone got together for Sunday brunch.

"Could they be any more perfect?" Cora asked as she hugged me and turned to watch our kids playing.

"Not a chance," I said honestly and winked at Ky across the room where he and Mav were sitting watching the kiddos. "Come on, you can help with the mimosas."

"Yum, my favorite." She clapped and followed me to the counter and helped chop up the fruit for the breakfast beverage of choice.

"The fun is here," Reid called as he walked in, taking off his scarf and jacket.

"Uncle Reid!" Sam cheered, running up and wrapping himself around his legs for a hug. Reid picked him up and tossed him over his shoulder as he kicked off his boots and carried him over to where Anna was pulling herself up on the couch, angrily screaming for Reid's attention.

"Oh come here, Angel." Reid cooed, swooping down to pick her up, and she grabbed two big handfuls of his cheeks and gave him a wet, sloppy kiss with a giggle. "Ooh, baby drool." He laughed as he turned to me at the counter and nodded. "Morning man."

"Morning Reid, you're bright-eyed and bushy-tailed this morning," I noted as I poured a cup of coffee for him.

"This breakfast lunch combo thing is quickly becoming my favorite meal of the week." He admitted, twirling the kids around on his shoulders.

"Easy Reid, she just drank a ton of milk. You're liable to get some back—" Cora warned seconds too late as Anna spit up breast milk all over his hand.

"Oh gross, it's warm." He sputtered, handing Anna off to a laughing Mav and dumping Sammy off onto the couch in a fit of giggles before walking to the bathroom to wash up.

Ky walked over and wrapped his hands around my waist and laid his cheek against my back, watching our happy and dysfunctional chosen family with genuine happiness. "We're some of the lucky ones, Dex." He whispered and kissed the back of my neck. "Thank you for peeping into my window all that time ago and choosing me to become obsessed with. I would have missed out on all of this if you hadn't been such a stalker."

Cora snorted champagne next to us and walked away shaking her head and I grunted, poking his side. "You'll pay for that comment," I warned him,

He leaned up and whispered into my ear, "Spank me for it?"

"My palm is twitching already with the promise of it."

"I can't wait."

We were some of the lucky ones. Because we had found the family that we weren't born into but chose every single day, anyway. And I wouldn't trade any of them for the world.

The End

Earning His Eden

R eady for the next King of Hawthorn's story?

Have a nibble to hold you over for now.

Get it on Amazon Right Here! https://a.co/d/4LORIkB

Yes Sir.

I've taken care of everything Sir.

Do you need anything else from me, Sir?

My new assistant had no idea what her words were doing to me. Every time she demurely spoke, looked down at the floor when I gave her instructions or chewed on her plump bottom lip with uncertainty, I lost another piece of my sanity.

I ached to bite that lip with my own teeth until she whimpered into my mouth.

I lived in a constant state of pain every single day with her at my side.

Pain radiated through my body from my need to own her.

To worship her.

To please her.

To dominate her.

The problem was, it had been years since I let my Dom out of his cage.

And I had vowed never to open that door again after how it ended last time.

And Eden wasn't some sub in the lifestyle who knew what she was getting into with a man like me.

No, she was pure, and untouched by the darkness that the world of kink brought out in me. I didn't deserve her trust or innocence. I was unworthy of that incredible gift. My hands would stain her perfect snowy skin with the first inappropriate touch.

Her curves made my mouth water.

My fist longed to wrap her long copper hair around it and force her to her knees.

My soul ached to help her find her confidence with praise and punishments suited for pleasure.

Hers and mine.

But I knew I couldn't give in to my desires. It was impossible.

Yet, with each minute that she spent in my personal space, the need to possess her grew inside of me until I broke, giving into the monster that called to me from the shadows of my soul.

But once I had her, I'd never let her go. I was going to own her forever.

Reid Haskins' story is in Book 3 of the Kings of Hawthorn Series, Earning His Eden. Get it today! https://a.co/d/4LORIkB

Stalk Me!

Want to stay up to date with all of my shenanigans and upcoming news? Pretty Please?

Check out my website: www.ammccoybooks.com

How about TikTok, are you there? https://www.tiktok.com/@ammccoy_author?is_from_webapp=1&sender_device=pc

Facebook? I've got a readers group there! Twisted After Dark: A .M. McCoy's Reader Group is mostly unhinged and full of exclusive news! https://www.facebook.com/share/g/b41rkBMkSurWz43i/

IG? https://www.instagram.com/ammccoy_author/

Amazon? https://www.amazon.com/stores/A.-M.-McCoy/author/B07QNRJMLB?ref=ap_rdr&isDramIntegrated=true&shoppingPortalEnabled=true

I think that's all for now!